◁ P9-CET-882

MURDER MOST WHOLESOME

I was hanging up the dish towel on the oven door handle when the kitchen phone rang. "O'Connell Organic Farm and Spa, Dana speaking. How can I help you?"

"Dana, it's Zennia."

Her normally low and relaxed voice sounded so high and strained that it took me a moment to realize it was really her.

"Zennia, are you sick? Did something happen?"

"That's why I'm calling. I'll have to miss work today."

"What's wrong?"

"Do you remember Birch, the man I introduced you to at the farmers market?" Zennia asked, a tremor in her voice.

"Of course I remember. Did you guys end up getting together?"

No response.

"Zennia? Are you still there?"

"Dana, Birch is dead. Someone killed him in my flower garden . . ."

Books by Staci McLaughlin

GOING ORGANIC CAN KILL YOU

ALL NATURAL MURDER

GREEN LIVING CAN BE DEADLY

A HEALTHY HOMICIDE

MURDER MOST WHOLESOME

Published by Kensington Publishing Corporation

Murder
Most
Wholesome

Staci McLaughlin

KENSINGTON PUBLISHING CORP.
http://www.kensingtonbooks.com

To the extent that the image or images on the cover of this book depict a person or persons, such person or persons are merely models, and are not intended to portray any character or characters featured in the book.

KENSINGTON BOOKS are published by

Kensington Publishing Corp.
119 West 40th Street
New York, NY 10018

Copyright © 2016 by Staci McLaughlin

All rights reserved. No part of this book may be reproduced in any form or by any means without the prior written consent of the Publisher, excepting brief quotes used in reviews.

If you purchased this book without a cover, you should be aware that this book is stolen property. It was reported as "unsold and destroyed" to the Publisher and neither the Author nor the Publisher has received any payment for this "stripped book."

All Kensington Titles, Imprints, and Distributed Lines are available at special quantity discounts for bulk purchases for sales promotions, premiums, fund-raising, and educational or institutional use. Special book excerpts or customized printings can also be created to fit specific needs. For details, write or phone the office of the Kensington special sales manager: Kensington Publishing Corp., 119 West 40th Street, New York, NY 10018, attn: Special Sales Department, Phone: 1-800-221-2647.

Kensington and the K logo Reg. U.S. Pat & TM Off.

ISBN-13: 978-0-7582-9490-6
ISBN-10: 0-7582-9490-5
First Kensington Mass Market Edition: March 2016

eISBN-13: 978-0-7582-9491-3
eISBN-10: 0-7582-9491-3
First Kensington Electronic Edition: March 2016

10 9 8 7 6 5 4 3 2 1

Printed in the United States of America

Chapter 1

I pointed to a round, bumpy vegetable I'd spied on a folding table at the Blossom Valley farmers market. "What on earth is that thing?" I asked Zennia.

She gave me a patient smile. "It's cauliflower, Dana."

"But it's orange," I said.

"Some varieties are."

None that I'd ever seen. Then again, Zennia, the health-minded and Zen-like cook at the O'Connell Organic Farm and Spa, the bed-and-breakfast where I worked, could identify more vegetables than anyone I knew. I surveyed the rest of the produce that was laid out on the table. "You must be in heaven when you shop here."

She picked up a clump of pea pods. "Based on the way you keep wrinkling your nose, I'm guessing you're not as enthralled as I am."

I reached up and touched my nose. "It's an automatic reflex. I don't think all vegetables are bad.

Those peas you're holding would taste downright scrumptious if you drowned them in melted cheese."

"Good grief," Zennia muttered. "And spoil the sweet peas?"

It was a warm evening in early June, and I'd agreed to accompany Zennia to this week's farmers market. The event was held at Blossom Valley's largest park, an expansive square of lush, green lawn outlined by a wide sidewalk. Two dozen vendors had set up a collection of tables and displays, each overflowing with ripe vegetables, sweet-scented fruits, or brightly colored flowers, in hopes of attracting customers. One innovative farmer had chosen to back up his pickup truck to the sidewalk and lower his tailgate to reveal several types of lettuce, saving himself the time and trouble of unloading his crop.

On the grass, children played tag while a handful of people sunbathed on beach towels and others tossed Frisbees or balls to their dogs. In the summer months, the park would host outdoor concerts, eating competitions, and the Fourth of July fireworks show, but for now, fruits and vegetables were the main focus.

Even though my primary responsibility at the O'Connell farm was to provide marketing services, my official duties rarely took up the entire workday. I often helped Zennia prepare and serve meals for the guests. It couldn't hurt to stop by the market and expand my food knowledge. Considering I didn't recognize several types of produce for sale, I clearly needed to brush up.

"Next time I make my spring barley risotto, I'll be sure to have you help me," Zennia said, sorting through a pile of string beans. "One bite and you'll realize why I love vegetables as much as I do."

I gestured to a nearby stall, where a variety of cheeses and several bottles of local olive oil weighed down a folding table. My mouth watered at the sight. "Right now, I'm going to check out what kind of Monterey Jack that guy is selling."

"Suit yourself." Zennia moved on to a booth where a woman was peddling asparagus while I homed in on the cheese guy, a tall, thin man with a pronounced Adam's apple that bobbed up and down as he told me about each and every cheese on his table.

"If you're looking for a good Jack cheese, try the dill. What you want to do is toast slices of ciabatta bread and spread on a little mayonnaise. Add the dill Jack, a layer of tomato slices, and a sprinkle of salt, and you're all set." He kissed his fingertips. "Perfection. Put it under the broiler for a minute, and it's even better, if that's possible."

I selected a wedge and studied the other offerings. "What about the garlic Jack?"

The man rubbed his stomach, as if the mere mention made him ravenous. "All you need is a hunk of plain, old bread to go with that."

I picked up a wrapped piece of garlic Jack and paid the man for both cheeses before storing my purchases in the reusable tote Zennia had given me a few months back. With a nod of thanks, I walked over to the booth where I'd seen Zennia before we'd separated, only to find she was no longer there.

The crowd had picked up considerably while I'd been shopping, but I spotted her bright yellow blouse across the lawn. A few feet away from the table where she stood, an older man was giving her the once-over. He sported a short, gray beard and wore a long-sleeved thermal shirt and cargo shorts. I'd have to let Zennia know she had an admirer. With her long dark hair and tall, athletic figure, she probably had several more.

As I headed in her direction, I stopped to buy a container of ripe, red strawberries. I'd noticed pre-made sponge cake shells at the Meat and Potatoes grocery store when I'd shopped there last week. With a little whipped cream, I could make an easy strawberry shortcake.

I gingerly placed my strawberries in my tote and looked across the grass toward Zennia again. My gaze drifted to the left, and I shivered. The man I'd noticed admiring her stood in the same spot, seemingly transfixed. He watched as Zennia browsed among the tables and talked to the sellers. When she moved to the next table, he advanced a few steps in her direction, his stare never wavering.

I started across the lawn to warn Zennia. Maybe that guy had a perfectly innocent reason to be fixated on her, or maybe not. Either way, I didn't like the way he was acting. I picked up my pace.

Out of the corner of my eye, I saw something moving through the air and jerked my head around in time to see a Frisbee streak straight toward my face. I raised my arm to deflect it. The plastic disc hit my forearm with a sharp sting before falling to the grass.

A boy of about ten ran over and picked it up. "Sorry about that," he mumbled to his feet.

"No problem," I said. "Those Frisbees have minds of their own."

He ran back to his friends. I scanned the people before me and frowned. Zennia was still there, but the man in the cargo shorts had vanished. I checked the nearby tables and spotted him standing behind a trio of women who were huddled in a semicircle, comparing the contents of their bags as if the items were never-before-seen vegetables. Maybe they'd all bought the orange cauliflower. The man cast one last look at Zennia before moving farther back into the crowd and out of sight.

I chuckled to myself. I really needed to stop watching so many scary movies. Seeing masked men with machetes stalking young co-eds was making me paranoid.

Shaking my head at my own foolishness, I reached Zennia as she was paying the vendor.

"There you are," she said. "Find anything good?"

I hefted my bag. "Cheese and strawberries."

"That's a lovely combination. I found baby artichokes. I keep meaning to plant artichokes at the farm, although I'm not sure we have space for any more crops."

I tried to spot the mystery man, but couldn't find him. "I don't think you noticed, but a guy was totally checking you out while you were shopping."

Zennia's cheeks instantly turned pink. "I'm not some young girl. No one checks me out anymore."

"Give yourself more credit. Mid-forties is prime dating age."

"Says the girl who's not even thirty," Zennia said.

"I'm awfully close. Besides, I saw this guy for

myself. He was staring at you so long, I almost considered calling the cops."

Zennia waved her hand, like she was swiping the compliment away, but I could tell she was pleased. "Shall we keep shopping? I think I saw sunflower bouquets when we first came in. Those will certainly brighten the farm's dining room."

We wandered around the square, stopping at the occasional table. By the time we were halfway through the stands, my bag was becoming uncomfortably heavy, though it paled in comparison to Zennia's two teeming totes.

"I believe I have enough for the week," Zennia said. "Do you need anything else, Dana?"

"No, I'm good." We stepped to the edge of the park and away from the vendors. "Can you carry both bags by yourself?" I asked.

"I'll manage." We carried our purchases to the parking lot and stopped at Zennia's Prius.

I bent down and gently set my own bag on the pavement so I could help Zennia load her bags into the trunk. As I straightened up, I glanced across the lot and froze.

He was back. The man who'd been watching Zennia.

This time, he stood next to the open passenger door of a nondescript white van, the kind that always made me think of stories I'd heard about Ted Bundy. Once more, he was staring at Zennia.

"Zennia," I said sharply.

She was in the middle of lifting one of the bags to place in the trunk. When I said her name, she turned toward me. "What?" The movement sent her off balance, and the bag slipped from her grasp and hit the pavement. Two heads of cabbage and several small onions fell out the top and rolled under a nearby car.

"The cabbage is making a run for it," she joked as she bent down to retrieve the wayward vegetables.

I knelt down with her and helped gather the onions as quickly as I could. "Forget about the cabbage. I saw that guy again." From my crouched position, I couldn't see over the car, but I jerked my head in his direction. "Do you know him?"

Zennia stood and scanned the lot. "What guy?"

I tossed the last onion in the bag and rose. I looked toward the van where I'd seen him standing only moments ago.

For the second time that day, the man had disappeared.

Chapter 2

"I'm telling you, the guy was there a minute ago." I pointed across the parking lot. "Right by that white van."

"Are you sure?" Zennia said. "Maybe you're hallucinating from all that saturated fat you eat." But as she spoke, the man appeared from the other side of the van. When Zennia saw him, her face turned ashen. "I don't believe it," she whispered.

The guy started moving in our direction. I felt in my back pocket for my phone, ready to call for help, not that there was any chance help would arrive in time. "Who is he?"

Zennia placed a visibly trembling hand to her mouth. "It's Birch. But it can't be."

"Who's Birch?"

I wasn't sure she'd heard me until she whirled around, a silly grin on her face, like a teenage girl who'd caught sight of her favorite movie star. "Birch was my one true love. I can't believe he's back."

At that, she practically ran to the man, with her

Birkenstocks slapping against the asphalt. When she reached him, he swept her up in a bone-crushing hug. In all my time working at the farm, Zennia had never mentioned a man she was romantically involved with. Who was this guy?

I realized my mouth was hanging open and closed it with a snap as Birch and Zennia pulled apart. They immediately huddled together and started talking, but from this distance, I couldn't hear what they were saying.

I considered driving home without interrupting their reunion, but my car was parked only two spaces from Birch's van. I couldn't possibly sneak by without being seen, and it seemed rude not to say anything. I gave them another moment to reconnect before I walked over.

As I got closer, I noticed the man's shorts were frayed along the bottom, and his shirt had a few stains. He wore a string of colorful beads around his neck.

I stuck out my hand. "Hi, I'm Dana Lewis."

Zennia laid a hand on her cheek. "Dana, I forgot all about you. Where are my manners?" She gestured toward Birch. "Dana, this is . . ."

Before she could answer, Birch grabbed my hand and clasped it in both of his, pumping it up and down with a vigor that made my brain vibrate. The area around his eyes collapsed into wrinkles as he beamed at me. "Birch. My parents named me after the tree. Trees are one of nature's greatest gifts, and I've spent my life embracing the outdoors because of this."

"Nice to meet you. I gather you're a friend of Zennia's?"

"*Friend* is not a strong enough word for our deep-rooted link." He wrapped an arm around Zennia and pulled her toward him until their hips were touching. He tilted his tan face toward her and said, "She is my soul mate."

Zennia shifted her weight and eased away at this declaration, but she smiled at him nonetheless. "I can't believe you're here after all these years. You haven't changed a bit."

He reached up and touched his hair. "Kind of you to say, but the gray says otherwise." He gazed at Zennia. "But you've only gotten more beautiful. Remember how inseparable we once were? I thought we'd be together forever, but we must follow fate wherever it takes us."

"And where did fate take you?" I asked, picturing Birch trekking through far-off lands, with only a backpack and a walking stick to help him along.

"To Oregon. I've been running a T-shirt shop on the beach up until a few months ago when I moved back to the commune."

Not quite the exotic traveling life I'd envisioned.

Zennia took a step back. "You were living in Oregon? And now you're back at Evergreen? Why didn't you try to get in touch with me?"

"My God, how I wanted to," Birch said. "When you left the commune all those years ago, I was forced to reflect on my own life. If you could brave the world, what was I missing by staying put? Once I went to Oregon, I thought about finding you time and again, but I didn't want to interrupt your own journey with fate." Birch took Zennia's hands in his and gazed at her face. His own hazel-green eyes were filled with sadness. "Seeing you again, and feeling all this love swell into my heart, I know I made the wrong decision."

"Hey, Birch, you ready to hit the road?" a voice called from behind us, breaking the spell. A large, broad-shouldered man in his late sixties headed in our direction, carrying a stack of empty wooden crates.

Birch whipped his head around. "Frank, I've had the most glorious surprise. I can't believe my good fortune."

He gestured toward Zennia, but Frank didn't even glance in her direction as he dropped the crates on the ground behind the van, swung open the back doors, and started to load them in.

"That's great," he said, "but we have to get back. Ryan's expecting us."

"Of course. I'd forgotten," Birch said. "While Ryan might be expecting us, I'm the one who needs to do the talking. I sense he's not going to be happy."

Frank grunted. "Not my problem." He placed the last crate in the van.

"It could be your problem, now that my confidence has wavered. And after Ryan's meeting, you and I need to sit down alone and talk. There's another issue that must be addressed."

"Then let's go. It'll be dark soon."

Without acknowledging Zennia and me, Frank slammed the back doors shut and went around the side of the van toward the driver's door.

Birch went through the contents of his pockets, coming up with a wadded-up piece of paper and a pencil stub. He tried his best to unwrinkle the paper. "I must have your number. We can't let this opportunity escape us."

Zennia recited her phone number while Birch used the side of the van as a writing board. As he was putting the paper back in his pocket, the van's engine roared to life.

Birch hastily hugged Zennia. "How I wish I could stay longer, but work awaits."

He swung his lanky body into the passenger seat with a grace that belied his years and pulled the door closed. He stuck his head out the window. "This is such a magnificent day to find you once more." The van lurched forward, and Birch pulled his head back inside as it sped away.

"Wow, Zennia, how cool that you and Birch have reunited after all this time," I said, as we watched the van drive out of the lot. "It's like something out of a Hallmark movie."

Zennia blinked rapidly, as if trying to bring her mind back to the present. "I returned to the commune after a brief time away, and the members told me Birch had also left. I figured he'd moved to India to study further enlightenment. I can't believe he's been living one state away this whole time."

I laid a hand on her arm. "You've got plenty of time to make up for those lost years. No reason you two can't pick up where you left off." I could practically hear the violin music swelling in the soundtrack of my imaginary movie as the two lovers became inseparable once more.

"I'm not sure I want to," Zennia said softly.

The music in my head screeched to a halt. "What? But I thought he was your one true love."

"Sure, that's what we called each other at the time, but that was twenty-five years ago. I was young and in love, wooed by an older man. When I went back to the commune, only to find out he was no longer there, I was heartbroken, of course, but I moved on. I imagine he has too, even if he is back at the commune."

Twenty-five years? I was barely out of diapers when all this happened. "I didn't realize communes even existed these days," I said. "Where is it?"

"There are dozens of communes around the country. This one is about an hour from here, deep in the redwoods. The location is a former logging camp."

I raised my eyebrows. "Only an hour away? Why haven't I heard of it?"

A mysterious smile appeared on Zennia's face, reminding me of the Mona Lisa. "Those searching for the sanctuary of the commune are able to find it. As for the others, the commune prefers not to advertise its existence."

Zennia made it sound like a modern-day Shangri-la. I felt the urge to get in my car and drive around searching for the place to see what was so special about it.

"You never went back later, even to visit?" I asked.

"No. I occasionally see one or two of the women at the farmers market here, although lately the newer residents have taken over running the booth. As for the commune itself, once I learned Birch left after I did, I saw no reason to return. While I still keep the ideals of the commune close to my heart, my home is in Blossom Valley."

"And I, for one, am glad we have you," I said. "Esther's place wouldn't be the same without all your healthy dishes." While I didn't always love Zennia's meals, with her emphasis on vegetables, tofu, and limited fats, I knew the guests appreciated her efforts. And she loved having an impact on other people's health.

"Thank you, Dana." She pulled her car keys from her pocket. "Now I'd better get home and get these vegetables out of the hot car, or all that spinach will wilt."

"Good idea," I said. "I'll see you in the morning."

"I have an early breakfast scheduled with a friend, but I should be at the farm by the time you start work. Have a good night."

I headed to my aging red Civic, unlocked the door, and placed my bag of fruit and cheese in the passenger seat. Before I started the car, I checked my phone and saw that Jason had texted to see if we were still having dinner at my apartment tonight.

I'd met Jason when he'd reported on a murder at Esther's farm for the *Blossom Valley Herald,* where he worked. At first, he'd been a little too pushy for my taste, but after spending time with him, I'd come to realize that he was simply a dedicated newsman. I'd also realized he was an even more dedicated boyfriend.

I confirmed our dinner plans, put the phone away, and drove home, thinking about Zennia and Birch, the story of two star-crossed lovers. If only Zennia had never left the commune, or if Birch had stayed put and awaited Zennia's potential return, they might still be together. Instead of feeding guests at Esther's farm, Zennia might be spending her days feeding a bevy of children with food she and Birch grew themselves.

Ten minutes later, I pulled into my parking spot at the Orchard Village apartments and carried my bag up the outside stairs to my apartment. I tried the knob and found the door unlocked.

I started mumbling under my breath about my younger sister Ashlee's naïve attitude. Sure, Blossom Valley's crime rate was ridiculously low, but still, people were occasionally robbed or murdered around here. It wasn't all date nights and makeup parties, like Ashlee seemed to think.

Inside the apartment, Ashlee sat on the couch, wearing pink pajama shorts and a white T-shirt. She had one bare foot propped up on the coffee table as she applied a coat of bright pink polish to her toenails. Chunks of her long blond hair, three shades lighter than mine, threatened to slip out of her ponytail and onto her handiwork.

Near the table, a dozen shoe boxes littered the floor. Some were missing their lids, while others lay on their sides, with shoes spilling out.

"What's all this?" I asked as I headed into the kitchen area to put away my groceries.

"You know that store, It's a Shoe In? It's going out of business. Everything's on sale."

I finished putting my food away and stowed my folded shopping bag next to the fridge before joining Ashlee in the living room. "Did you decide to buy the whole store?"

She fanned her toenails with her hand. "As if.

But I needed sandals, and I couldn't decide what color I wanted. And then I saw the cutest pair of wedge heels, which led me to the boots, and before I knew it, I bought all these."

I surveyed the wreckage that was strewn across the carpet. "I bet you'll never wear half of these."

"Yes, I will. In fact, I'm wearing one pair of sandals tonight, which is why I'm painting my toe-nails. Jasper won't know what hit him." She propped her other foot on the table and dipped the brush in the nail polish.

"Jasper? Is this a new guy?"

"Yep. Met him at the movie theater."

I sat down on the other end of the couch, earn-ing a sharp look from Ashlee as I jostled her. "What happened to Zack?"

"We're done. He started talking about commit-ment and not seeing other people, and I had to bail."

All this talk about Ashlee's many boyfriends reminded me that I was supposed to be getting dinner ready. "Jason will be over in a little while."

"See, that's what I'm talking about. Where's the thrill? Don't you get tired of seeing the same guy all the time?" She waved her hand around as she talked, and the polish brush came dangerously close to my nose.

I pulled my head back. "Actually, I like it. A lot. Wouldn't kill you to settle down yourself. For longer than a month anyway."

Ashlee scrunched up her nose like last week's half-eaten bologna sandwich was still sitting in the trash. "Talk about boring."

"But what about true love?" I asked. "Zennia ran

into a guy she hasn't seen in twenty-five years at the farmers market today. You should have seen the look on that guy's face. He was thrilled."

Ashlee bent over another nail. "What about Zennia? Was she as happy to see him?"

I thought of the way Zennia shifted away from Birch. "She was definitely surprised, but pleased."

"I bet she was just being nice to the guy."

I stood. "We'll see. She and Birch might fall in love all over again."

Ashlee snorted. "What kind of name is Birch?"

"One his mother was apparently fond of." I headed toward my room. "I need to clean up and get dinner ready."

I took a quick shower and dried my hair before donning a pair of jeans and a long-sleeved, light blue top that matched my eyes. When I came out, Ashlee was no longer on the couch, and her bedroom door was closed. I went into the kitchen and searched the cupboards for the box of Hamburger Helper I'd bought earlier in the week, then grabbed the ground beef out of the fridge. Nothing like a home-cooked meal.

While the meat was browning, I washed and tore up lettuce for a salad and preheated the oven to bake a frozen loaf of garlic bread. For a second, I almost felt like Julia Child, if Julia Child had used a lot of prepackaged processed foods in her cooking.

A few minutes later, Ashlee came out of her bedroom in a pair of sandals, a denim skirt, and a blouse cut so low that I half expected to see her belly button. She entered the kitchen and spun around. "How do I look?"

"I don't think Jasper is going to notice your nail polish."

Ashlee studied her feet. "Because my new sandals are so awesome?"

"Yeah, that's it," I lied. If Ashlee wanted to parade around town with her ta-tas hanging out, who was I to stop her?

Someone knocked on the door. Ashlee beat me across the room and swung the door open like she was expecting a representative from the Publishers Clearing House Sweepstakes to be standing there with an oversized cardboard check. Instead, Jason waited on the doorstep in jeans and a dark gray Henley shirt.

"Well, if it isn't Mr. Forrester, the famous newsman," Ashlee said with a wink. She stepped aside to let him in.

He moved past her with a quick "Hi, Ashlee." I had to give him credit—his eyes never once strayed below her chin.

"Hey, gorgeous," he said to me. He enveloped me in a hug. The short hairs of his reddish-brown goatee tickled my forehead as I inhaled the spicy scent of his cologne. I was tempted to stand in his embrace all night, but my stomach suddenly growled.

Jason laughed and let me go. His warm green eyes sparkled. "Did you swallow a monster?"

I clapped a hand over my belly. "Guess I'd better feed that thing before it attacks." I remembered the hamburger was still cooking on the stove and dashed into the kitchen. I grabbed the spatula and rapidly stirred the meat. "I hope you like your

Hamburger Helper well done," I called over my shoulder.

"Better than raw. Need any help?"

I scanned the directions on the back of the box and started adding the rest of the ingredients. "Nope, but thanks." I placed the garlic bread in the oven, set the timer, and grabbed two beers from the fridge. As I made my way to the couch, Ashlee plopped in a chair at the kitchen table and started texting. Jason settled down next to me, and I handed him a beer. "How was work?"

"Slow. The gas station outside of town got robbed last night, but that's the only big news. And Mrs. Garrenson was cited for disturbing the peace when she ran through her neighborhood screaming about her lost poodle. She swears it was an alien abduction this time."

"Didn't she blame aliens last time her dog ran away?" I asked.

"No, that was a cosmetics company conducting experiments."

"Right. How could I forget?"

Ashlee exhaled loudly from her spot at the table. "What good is being a newsman if nothing exciting ever happens around here?"

"People love the news, no matter how small," Jason said.

The timer dinged. I set my beer down and went to the kitchen area to pull the garlic bread from the oven. Jason came over and sliced the bread while I dressed the salad and loaded our plates.

As we carried our food to the kitchen table, Ashlee jumped up and went into her room. I'd seen her prep for enough dates to know she was touching up her makeup and making sure every last blond hair was in the correct place. Maybe she'd find the rest of her blouse while she was in there.

"Alone at last," I said to Jason as I draped my napkin in my lap. I picked up my fork and speared a noodle.

Jason took a swig of beer. "Anything exciting happen at the farm today?"

"Updated the Web site, tweeted about Esther's latest composting class, and cleaned out the pigsty. You know, the usual."

"And how is Wilbur?" Jason gave me a devilish smile that brought out his dimples. "Is that pig ready to be someone's ham hocks and bacon?"

I dropped my fork and covered my ears in mock horror. "No, don't even say that! You know how much Esther loves that pig." I put my hands down. "But that reminds me. Something interesting did happen at the farmers market. Zennia and I went there after work today, and guess what?"

"You ate a vegetable and liked it?"

I grimaced. "Don't be ridiculous. An old boyfriend of Zennia's showed up. They haven't seen each other in over twenty-five years. The guy couldn't stop staring at Zennia, claimed he'd found his long-lost love."

"What are the odds?" Jason asked. "Sounds like a movie."

"That's what I thought. Turns out Zennia used to live on a commune in the redwoods years ago. When she left, this guy moved to Oregon, but now he's back."

"No kidding." Jason snapped his fingers. "Is this the Evergreen commune?"

I picked up my fork. "You've heard of it?"

"I did a story a few years back, not too long after I started working at the paper. Drove out there to interview the residents and then wrote an article about their work and living conditions."

Ashlee came out of her room right then, straightening out the cord to her ear buds. I was relieved to see that she'd thrown a sweater over her blouse. Of course, the sweater was unbuttoned and did nothing to hide her cleavage, but at least she'd given herself the option to cover up.

I turned back to Jason. "What was the place like? Did the women have daisy chains in their hair? Did everyone sit in a circle, singing and smoking pot?"

Jason choked down a laugh. "What do you think this is? A Cheech and Chong movie? No daisy chains, and no one was smoking pot that I saw. Or smelled."

"And no one sang 'Kumbaya' either?"

"Not in the last forty years, I'm willing to bet."

I heard the jangle of keys as Ashlee pulled them from her bag. She slung the bag over her shoulder. "Later," she said and headed out the door.

I leaned back in my chair. "Maybe my impression of communes is out-of-date. I'll have to search the *Herald*'s archives online and find your article. The whole idea fascinates me. Imagine living as one big happy family, sharing the land and all your possessions, having a community to support you."

Jason put down his fork and stared at me. "Sounds like you're ready to move there yourself."

I shook my head and tucked a chunk of hair

behind my ear. "I'm not quitting my job at the farm just yet. In fact, I bet I'm romanticizing the entire concept. Still, a commune's probably not the worst place to live, now or all those years ago."

Jason cleared his throat and leaned across the table. "Now that Ashlee's gone, how about we forget about the past?" He reached for one of my hands and gazed at me with a look that made my insides light up. "Let's focus on the present and what the two of us could be doing now that we have the apartment to ourselves."

I winked at him. It was the best idea I'd heard all day.

Chapter 3

At six the next morning, the blare of the alarm dragged me out of a dreamless sleep. I slapped at the black plastic clock until the noise stopped, then pushed myself to a sitting position so I wouldn't be tempted to close my eyes and fall back asleep.

Jason had left by ten the previous evening, but I'd gotten caught up in a *Law & Order* marathon. It wasn't until Ashlee slinked in well past midnight, with her hair mussed and her lipstick smeared, that I'd ambled off to bed.

I threw off the covers and staggered to my feet, succumbing to a huge yawn as I stumbled to the bathroom. After taking a quick shower, I made my way to the kitchen for my usual Pop-Tarts breakfast. While I nibbled the frosted pastry, I clicked on the TV and watched the morning news.

Since Blossom Valley and its neighboring towns were small, the closest news reports came from the Bay Area. There was an overnight shooting in Oakland, a house fire in San Francisco, and plenty of commuter traffic for the newscasters to talk about.

Ashlee had complained last night that there wasn't anything worth reporting in Blossom Valley, but I'd take no news over bad news any day.

I swallowed the last of my breakfast, washed it down with milk just this side of spoiled, and finished getting ready. Ashlee still wasn't up, and I made sure to relock the front door on my way out. The sky was cloud free, and the air was warm. In the distance, I heard the siren of an emergency vehicle and said a silent prayer that firemen were merely on their way to rescue a cat from a tree.

With little traffic on the drive to work, I reached the farm in minutes. Only three cars occupied parking spaces, but I knew it wouldn't stay this quiet for long. The county fair was rolling into town soon, which always brought overnight guests. Jason and I would be going, and I could practically smell the cotton candy already.

I parked in my usual corner spot and followed the walking path past the flower and vegetable gardens. Once at the cabins, I hung a left and crossed the patio to enter the farmhouse through the kitchen door.

Esther, owner of the farm and spa, stood at the counter in brown Capri pants and a denim shirt. A tub of Zennia's homemade yogurt with the lid off sat before her. Clumps of yogurt hugged the outside of the tub where it had run down the sides, while green strawberry tops and random blueberries littered the workspace.

As I stepped toward the counter, I felt something crunch under my shoe and lifted it up to find bits of granola stuck to the side. In all my months working at the farm, I'd never seen the kitchen this messy.

"Esther, where's Zennia?"

Esther whirled around with a jerk. Several blueberries flew from her spoon and onto the floor. Behind her, I could see two tall glasses full of berries and yogurt. "Dana, thank goodness you're here. Zennia hasn't shown up this morning, and I'm trying to get breakfast ready for the guests."

"Is she sick?" I grabbed a broom from the nearby closet and started sweeping up the granola dust and blueberries. "Wait, she mentioned an early breakfast with a friend this morning. Maybe she lost track of time."

"But she hasn't called, and she's not answering her phone. That's not like Zennia." Esther swiped her forehead with the back of her hand and patted her gray curls. "Thank goodness we have the ingredients for these parfaits, or I'd be like a maiden without a milking stool. As it is, these parfaits aren't enough to feed the guests."

I swept the pile of spilled food into the dustpan and emptied it into the trash. I spoke to Esther over my shoulder as I stowed the broom and dustpan back in the closet. "I saw scones in the freezer a couple of days ago, and I know Zennia was making a fresh batch of her honey butter yesterday. We can thaw out the scones to serve with the parfaits."

Esther blew out her breath. "That should be enough. I knew you'd think of something."

She pulled down two more glasses from the cupboard while I rummaged in the freezer for the bag of scones. I placed them in the oven to defrost, grabbed the two finished parfaits, and carried them to the dining room to see if any guests were waiting.

A couple in their early thirties sat at a table near the window, holding hands and talking. When they saw me approach, the woman eased her hands away to make room for the glasses.

"Scones with honey butter will be coming up in a moment," I told them.

As I stepped away, an older man entered the dining room through the French doors off the patio and headed straight to the sideboard to pour himself a cup of coffee. I hurried to the kitchen to see if Esther had finished another parfait.

Instead, she was talking to Gordon, the farm's manager. He was dressed in his customary suit and tie, with his black hair slicked back like a waterfall of oil.

"She must be on her way by now," Esther was saying. "She never misses work."

"Are you and Dana covering breakfast for today?" Gordon scowled at the food-strewn table. "Zennia had better be here to take care of lunch."

"Is Gretchen here yet?" I asked of our twenty-four-year-old, ultratalented spa specialist. An extra pair of hands in the kitchen couldn't hurt.

"Yes," Gordon said, "but she's with an early client. You two are on your own until Zennia arrives."

"I only hope she's okay," Esther added.

As usual, Esther was worried about the employees, and Gordon was concerned with the business. Although Esther was the boss, Gordon handled the day-to-day operations. His focus on the bottom line never wavered.

"Esther's right," I said. "She's probably driving over here this very minute."

Gordon sighed, straightened his tie, and picked up the clipboard he always carried. "Just make sure the guests are kept happy until then," he told me before he strode out of the kitchen, already concentrating on the next task on his to-do list.

While Esther prepared more parfaits, I lined two small baskets with linen napkins and placed scones in each one. That done, I retrieved the crock of honey butter from the fridge and spooned portions into individual ramekins. "It really isn't like Zennia to be this late without calling," I said.

"Don't I know it." Esther dropped a blob of yogurt in a glass. "I'm beside myself with worry, picturing all sorts of terrible accidents from car wrecks to killer bee stings."

I stopped on my way to returning the butter crock to the fridge and looked at Esther. "Killer bees?"

She blushed. "I was watching the nature channel last night. And you know how many flowers Zennia has in that garden of hers."

"I think we can rule out bee stings, but I'll definitely give her a call as soon as breakfast is over. Maybe she just overslept."

"Maybe," Esther agreed, but she didn't sound convinced. Neither was I.

I placed the butter ramekins in each basket, carried them out to the waiting diners, and dashed back to the kitchen for the other parfait. Another couple arrived, and Esther confirmed they were the last of the guests. Once they were served,

Esther wiped down the countertop and table while I washed and dried the handful of dishes.

I was hanging up the dish towel on the oven door handle when the kitchen phone rang. Esther was trying to squeeze the lid on the top of the yogurt bowl, so I snatched up the receiver from its place on the counter.

"O'Connell Organic Farm and Spa. Dana speaking. How can I help you?"

"Dana, it's Zennia."

Her normally low and relaxed voice sounded so high and strained that it took me a moment to realize it was really her.

"Zennia, are you sick? Did something happen?"

"That's why I'm calling. I'll have to miss work today."

Across the room, Esther stopped fighting the yogurt lid and started mouthing things to me that I couldn't figure out. I held up a finger for her to wait a moment. "What's wrong?" I said into the phone.

"Do you remember Birch, the man I introduced you to at the farmers market?" Zennia asked, a tremor in her voice.

Realization dawned. Zennia must have hooked up with Birch last night. That's why she wasn't at work, and now she was embarrassed. I couldn't help but smile. "Of course I remember. Did you guys end up getting together?"

No response.

"Zennia? Are you still there?"

"Dana, Birch is dead. Someone killed him in my flower garden."

Chapter 4

I placed one hand on the table to steady myself and sank into the closest chair. "Zennia, what are you talking about? What do you mean someone killed Birch?"

From behind me, I heard Esther gasp. A moment later, she sat down next to me and repeatedly tapped my knee until I looked at her. She mouthed, "Who?" and lifted her hands up in a pantomime that would have made me laugh if the topic hadn't been so serious.

Before I could answer her, Zennia started talking again. "I met a friend for breakfast early this morning. When I came back home, Birch was dead in my front yard."

"Maybe he had a heart attack. Or a swarm of killer bees attacked him." As I said the last, I squeezed my eyes shut. Esther and her crazy ideas. Good grief.

"A swarm of bees?" Zennia asked.

"Never mind. Forget the bees," I said. "Why would you think he was killed?"

"From what the police said. As soon as I found Birch, I called nine-one-one. You wouldn't believe how many people showed up. Not to mention the sirens. They must have woken up the whole neighborhood."

I remembered the sirens I'd heard as I was leaving the apartment this morning and wondered if they had come from the emergency vehicles en route to Zennia's house or if they were on another call.

"I overheard one of the officers mention ligature marks. That means he was strangled, right?"

I gulped. "That sounds right." Esther touched my knee again, and I covered the mouthpiece on the phone to talk to her. "Zennia isn't here yet because a friend died in her front yard this morning."

Esther stopped patting my knee and started patting her chest. "Mercy me. Someone she knows?"

"Yes, but from a long time ago. She ran into him last night at the farmers market." Zennia was talking again, and I tuned back in.

"What should we do about lunch service?" she asked. "The police said they'd let me go as soon as they're finished with their questions." Her voice rose in pitch. "How long are they going to be here?"

"I don't know, but you shouldn't be alone at a time like this. I'll be right there." I hung up and turned to Esther. "I'd like to go help Zennia. I have a light workload today, and I could be back before lunch service. Would that be okay?"

Esther was nodding before I'd even asked the question. "Of course, the poor dear. Zennia needs someone with her."

Gordon strode into the kitchen, muttering into his cell phone. He ended his call and looked from Esther to me. "What's wrong?" he demanded. "Have you heard from Zennia?"

"There's trouble at her house. I'm on my way to see her," I said.

"What about your marketing projects?"

I knew that would be Gordon's first question, and I was ready for it. "As I told Esther, I have nothing pressing today, and I'll be back before lunch prep."

His gaze turned sharp. "Does this mean Zennia won't be in at all? What kind of trouble are we talking about?"

"Someone died in her yard," Esther said. "Can you believe it?"

Gordon took a step back. "My God, is Zennia all right?"

"Yes," I said, "but the sooner I can get to her, the sooner I'll find out what's going on."

Gordon looked at his watch. "Good idea, but I need you back by eleven at the latest. Tell Zennia to get here when she can, providing she's up to it."

I checked the rooster clock on the wall. That gave me well over two hours, plenty of time to offer Zennia support and spring her from the cops. At least I hoped that's what would happen.

I hurried to the office for my keys. Once in my car, I sped down the freeway and took the off-ramp for Zennia's place on the outskirts of town. I'd only been there once before, and I soon got lost in the maze of small streets.

I cruised through the neighborhood, trying to

find a familiar landmark. At last, I saw a cluster of police cruisers at the end of a cul-de-sac and knew I'd found Zennia's house. All the curb parking inside the cul-de-sac was taken. I parked my car in the first available space at the corner and walked back.

As I got closer, I recognized the massive branches of the ancient oak and the dark green hedge that ran all the way around Zennia's yard. I knew from my previous visit that, on the other side of the hedge, a wrought-iron bench sat underneath the oak tree. One could sit there and enjoy the view of her green lawn with dozens of thriving bushes all along the border. At the time, I'd thought it was the perfect spot for reading a good book on a warm summer day.

But now, yellow crime scene tape ran atop the hedge on the side closest to the sidewalk. Several official-looking people clustered together just inside the hedge, and I felt a shiver run up my back. That must be the spot where Zennia discovered Birch's body.

I reached the corner of the hedge and turned to walk up the driveway. A uniformed officer who probably wasn't old enough to drink yet held up one hand. "Ma'am, this is a crime scene."

I read the officer's nameplate. "I'm here to see Zennia, Officer Sanguinetti. She's expecting me."

The officer spoke into the radio at his shoulder. A moment later, the front door opened, and Zennia rushed out of the house. She raced down the driveway and grasped me by the arms. "I'm so glad you're here."

I gave her a hug and studied the worry lines around her eyes. "Are you all right?"

She pulled me toward the street and away from the officer. "Not really. The police have been perfectly polite, but still, they're intimidating. I wanted to call you as soon as they arrived this morning, but they kept asking me questions and telling me to wait. I didn't know what to do."

"I'm sure they'll be out of here soon. Any idea what Birch was doing here? Did you talk to him again after we ran into him yesterday?"

"No. You can imagine my surprise when I found him this morning. I went to fill the bird feeders along the edges of the lawn before I left for work, and there he was."

"You didn't notice him when you came back from breakfast?"

"His body was right up next to the hedge." She shivered but kept talking. "Almost like someone was trying to hide it."

I noticed the cop was inching incrementally closer, so I led Zennia a few feet down the sidewalk. "Did you realize the body was Birch right away?"

"Only when I got near him." Zennia paled at the memory. "For some ridiculous reason, I thought he might be taking a nap. How absurd is that? As soon as I saw his face, frozen like that, I knew."

I recognized the hysteria in her voice and rubbed her back until she regained her calm. "It must have been such a shock."

"I think I may have screamed. Then I ran in the house to call the police."

The sound of an engine reached me, and a familiar-looking white van rumbled into the cul-de-sac. The brakes emitted a squeaking noise as the van slowed to a stop behind the patrol cars. The driver's door opened, and I recognized Frank as he climbed out.

"Hey," I said to Zennia. "Isn't that the guy who was with Birch last night at the farmers market? What's he doing here?"

Officer Sanguinetti marched over to Frank before Frank could reach the sidewalk. I could practically see the officer gathering his courage as he sized up Frank's bulky frame. "Excuse me, sir, you can't block those cars."

Frank glared at him. "I ain't staying. I'm picking up my friend."

"What's the name of your friend?" Officer Sanguinetti asked.

Frank caught sight of Zennia and me. "Where's Birch? I'm supposed to pick him up," he said, ignoring the officer's question.

Zennia and I exchanged uneasy glances. Which one of us was going to break the news of Birch's death? Was it even our place?

Officer Sanguinetti spoke into his radio, and I automatically looked back at the door of Zennia's house to see who would emerge this time.

After a pause, Detective Palmer, one of Blossom Valley's few police detectives, came out of the house. Even if I hadn't known he was a cop, I would have pegged him as one, thanks to his buzz cut and neutral, navy blue suit.

He stared at me as he walked down the driveway. This wasn't the first time I'd been peripherally involved in a murder investigation, and I steeled myself for a lecture about how I was always around whenever someone stumbled over a dead body.

Instead, he bypassed me and spoke to Officer Sanguinetti in a low voice. I was straining to catch a word or two when Frank loomed into view.

"What's this all about?" he demanded. "Why won't anyone tell me where Birch is?"

Detective Palmer broke away from the officer. "Sir, I need to ask you to come inside with me to answer a few questions."

Frank took a step back. "No way. I know my rights, and you pigs can't hassle me."

I flinched at the word *pigs,* but Detective Palmer showed no reaction. "Sir, I'm asking for your cooperation in this matter."

Frank threw his shoulders back and looked between the two cops, as if deciding which one to swing at first. I noticed Officer Sanguinetti's hand creeping toward his utility belt, whether to grab his gun or his Taser, I wasn't sure.

After a tense moment, Frank's shoulders slumped. "Aw, hell, let's get your damn questions over with. Otherwise, you'll slap some trumped-up charge, like obstructing justice, on me. That's how you guys work." He was still grumbling as he headed toward the house, with Detective Palmer stepping into line behind him.

At the door, the detective turned back and pointed at me. "Don't go anywhere. I want to talk to you next."

I gulped. "You bet," I called to him.

He shut the door, and I pulled out my phone to check the time. Eleven o'clock was approaching fast, but no way would I leave before Detective Palmer had a chance to question me.

"Any idea how long Detective Palmer will be?" I asked Officer Sanguinetti. "I have to get back to work."

He shrugged. "Whenever he's done with his questions."

I bit my lip to keep from making a sarcastic comment. I didn't want one of those obstructing justice charges either.

Beside me, Zennia grabbed my arm. "I can't seem to organize my thoughts this morning. Maybe I'll brew myself a cup of ashwagandha tea once the police stop using my kitchen table as a place to fill out paperwork."

Officer Sanguinetti cleared his throat.

"Not that I mind," she added hastily. "Of course I want to do anything I can to help, but I'm not used to such chaos in my house. It's usually my sanctuary."

I laid my hand on Zennia's, which still gripped my arm. If I ever needed a tourniquet, her hands could make a suitable replacement. As if reading my mind, she loosened her grip.

"Don't worry about lunch, Zennia. We only have four or five guests right now, and not all of them will eat at the farm. I'd be surprised if I need to serve more than one or two tables."

"No, I want to help. I know I left everyone in the lurch this morning when I didn't even call. And frankly, being in Esther's kitchen is exactly what I need right now."

"Whatever you're comfortable with," I said.

We watched the police move around the yard,

but with the hedge dividing the lawn from the driveway, I couldn't see much. After a few minutes, voices drew my attention back to the house. Detective Palmer came out with Frank, who was visibly more relaxed. He managed a gruff "Bye now" as he passed Zennia and me.

The two men stopped at the bottom of the driveway, where Frank slapped Detective Palmer on the shoulder. "Sorry I gave you such a hard time before," he said. "I'd better get my van out of the way of your guys."

"You still have the card I gave you inside?" Detective Palmer asked.

Frank felt the front pocket of his checkered shirt. "Right here. I'll give you a holler if I think of anything that might help. I want you to catch who-ever did this to Birch." He climbed into the van, started it up on the third try, and backed out of the cul-de-sac.

"He sure changed his attitude," I said to Detective Palmer. "What did you say to him? He was practically eating out of your hand."

"Trade secret," he said without a hint of a smile. He moved toward the house. "You're up," he said over his shoulder. He went inside, leaving the door open behind him.

"If you don't hear from me in an hour," I told Zennia, "send in a rescue party." Too bad I was only partly kidding.

She gave me a reassuring pat, while I took a deep breath to calm my nerves. A few seconds later, I squared my shoulders and marched toward the house. I was ready to face the detective and his questions, whatever they might be.

Chapter 5

Entering Zennia's home was like walking into the garden center of a home improvement store. Potted plants lined the windowsills and spider plants fell over the sides of several hanging pots. Two wicker chairs with thick cushions occupied the center of the room, and what looked to be a recycled wood crate with a sheet of glass on top served as a coffee table. A rocking chair sat in the corner next to a short palm tree, and a bookcase against the nearest wall held books about meditation, natural medicine, and organic gardening. I didn't spot a television anywhere, but that didn't surprise me, considering Zennia's aversion to what she considered time wasters.

Detective Palmer sat down in one of the wicker chairs and motioned for me to sit next to him. As I did, I glanced into the nearby breakfast nook and saw a uniformed officer filling out paperwork at a small, round table.

"Care to tell me what you're doing here?" Detective

Palmer asked as he took a notebook and ballpoint pen out of his inside jacket pocket. He clicked open the pen and scribbled at the top of the page.

I crossed my legs, then crossed them the other way, trying to get comfortable in the chair. I gave up and put both feet flat on the floor. "Zennia called the farm to tell us that she'd found Birch dead this morning."

"What time was this?"

"Fairly early. Shortly after eight?" I shifted my feet. Though Detective Palmer was only asking me routine questions, I felt like a giant laser beam was shining straight down on my head, burning my skull.

"Are you asking me or telling me?"

I straightened up in the chair, annoyed. "Telling you. I remember checking the clock to see if I had enough time to drive over here and still get back to the farm to help Esther with lunch service. If Zennia isn't back at work by that time, of course." I suddenly felt too constricted in the chair and stood up to move around.

Detective Palmer looked up from his notebook to see what I was doing and then resumed writing. "Did you know the deceased?"

I walked over to the fireplace to study the pictures on the mantel. I recognized younger versions of Zennia in several of them. "I met him for the first time last night. I saw him staring at Zennia at the farmers market and thought he was a stalker creep, but it turned out he's Zennia's long-lost boyfriend from their days at a commune."

He raised his eyebrows at that. "Commune?"

"Can you believe it? There's a commune not more than an hour from here. I guess the two of them lived out there for a while."

"You must be talking about Evergreen." He consulted his notes. "How did he seem? Happy to see her? Upset?"

"He was thrilled. Acted like their reunion was written in the stars, that fate had brought them together again."

"What else do you remember about the conversation?"

"Not much. Zennia and Birch talked briefly before I joined them, and then we didn't have a chance to say hardly anything before that guy, Frank, showed up. He and Birch got in the van and left right after that."

"That all you can remember?"

I straightened a photo on the mantel. "That's all that happened."

Detective Palmer checked over his notes and then tucked his notepad and pen back in his jacket pocket. He rose from the chair. "That's all for now. Call me if you think of anything important."

"Of course."

He started past me, but stopped. "Otherwise, don't call me."

Ouch. "What do you mean?"

Detective Palmer glowered at me. "You know exactly what I mean. Somehow you manage to put yourself in the middle of every single murder investigation in this town. I want you out of this one. Understand?"

"I wouldn't say I've been involved in *every* case," I said. His glower deepened, which I would have thought was physically impossible if I wasn't actually seeing it. "But no worries. The thought of looking into Birch's death never even crossed my mind."

"Right," he said.

He walked over and sat down at the table across from the uniformed officer. I took that as my cue to leave and slipped out of the house.

Outside, Zennia was pacing in her driveway. When she saw me, she rushed over.

"How was it? He wasn't too hard on you, was he?"

"Detective Palmer is always perfectly polite."

"But it's the way he studies you, like he knows all your inner secrets. Any minute, I thought he was going to ask me about the time I stole all the coins from my grandfather's wishing well when I was six."

I chuckled. "He's a good detective, but he's not that good." I pulled my phone from my pocket and cringed. "I need to get to the farm."

"Did the detective say I was free to go with you?"

"Shoot, I forgot to ask."

"That's all right. I'll run in and find out."

She dashed into the house, leaving me alone. Officer Sanguinetti still stood at the end of the driveway, but he was watching the street. The people I'd seen working in the yard earlier were gone. I edged closer to the hedge that separated the driveway from the lawn area and peered over, holding my breath in anticipation.

There was little to see. Little yellow plastic triangles with black numbers littered the grass next to the hedge. Birch's body was nowhere in sight.

I noticed a gap in the hedge a little farther along the driveway and moved over to the opening. As long as the police were finished searching for evidence, it couldn't hurt if I took a closer look, right?

I'd just turned my body sideways to slip through the space when I heard someone clear their throat right next to me. Officer Sanguinetti had snuck up the driveway while I'd been snooping.

"This is still a crime scene, ma'am."

I felt my face heat up. "Right. I forgot. Sorry about that."

Zennia came out of the house, saving me from further embarrassment. She was followed by Detective Palmer and the other officer. Zennia had donned a light sweater and carried her purse, definitely a promising sign that the police were done with her.

Remembering Detective Palmer's warning to me, I stepped away from the hedge before he could notice how close I was to the lawn and get the wrong idea, even if it was the right idea. "Are you able to leave now?" I asked Zennia.

"Detective Palmer told me the police are finished for now. They might come back to search the yard more, but if I'm not home, that's fine." She pulled out her car keys. "I can't wait to get to work. I need a break from all this."

"Great. I'll see you at the farm in a few minutes."

I went down the driveway and walked to the corner. As I unlocked my car door, I looked up at the house I'd parked in front of and saw the blinds drop back into position in an upstairs window.

Someone had been watching me. If they made a habit of looking out that window, they might have seen who entered and exited the cul-de-sac this morning when Birch was murdered. Detective Palmer might hit pay dirt with a witness.

As I slid into the driver's seat, I heard a horn toot and saw Zennia drive past. I started my car and followed her, glad I wouldn't have to re-navigate the small streets on my own to find my way out.

When we reached the freeway, she settled on a steady fifty-five miles-per-hour, while I pulled into the passing lane and zipped ahead with a little wave.

At the farm, I entered through the lobby and found Gordon standing at the check-in counter, typing on the reservation computer's keyboard. "Zennia's not with you?"

"She's right behind me. You know how slow she drives."

"Can't fault her for being fuel-efficient. Think of the money she saves."

"Think how long it takes her to get anywhere."

Gordon shrugged. "So long as she gets here before the guests are ready to eat."

"Good point." I walked past Gordon and said, "I have a little work to finish in the office. When Zennia gets here, could you let her know I'll help her in the kitchen in a few minutes?"

He nodded, his attention back on the screen. I went down the hall, dropped my purse in the desk drawer, and moved the mouse to activate the computer. I felt too fidgety to be working on the computer, but I always posted my blog first thing and today's post was several hours late already, thanks to everything that had happened this morning.

I opened the word processing program and forced

myself to concentrate as I edited my discussion on naturally flavored water. After a few more changes, I uploaded the blog to the farm's Web site and made sure the photos were formatted correctly. While I was on the site, I also answered a handful of comments from the previous day.

That finished, I pushed back my chair, stretched, and went into the kitchen to see if Zennia needed any help. She was sitting at the kitchen table with a butcher's knife clutched in her hand. Several piles of freshly cut vegetables lay before her, so I knew she'd been working on them, but now she looked at a mound of diced zucchini as if she'd never seen the vegetable before.

"Zennia, are you all right?" I asked, an uneasy feeling settling into my stomach.

She slowly looked up at me. "I don't think I can do it."

"Do what? Make lunch? I can finish for you, if you'll tell me what to do."

"That's the problem. I can't remember what to do. My mind is a complete blank."

I studied the piles on the table. "Okay, let's try to figure this out. I see zucchini, and eggplant, and asparagus," I said in a singsong voice, like I was addressing a classroom of kindergarteners. Zennia showed no reaction, and I tried again. "Were you going to sauté everything? Put them over a bed of quinoa like you sometimes do?"

Zennia set down the knife and pushed herself up from the table. "I need to go home."

That uneasy feeling started to spread to my limbs. "Wouldn't you rather stay? I'm sure Esther would let you use her sitting room upstairs to rest."

"No, I made a mistake coming to work. I should go home."

"Will you be okay by yourself? Is there a friend you can call?" I didn't like letting Zennia leave in her current state, but someone needed to stay and feed the guests.

"I'm sure a bit of quiet time will fix everything." She looked at her hands. "I'm sorry I won't be able to help with lunch after all."

"Don't give it another thought. Worry about yourself."

"Thanks, Dana." Slightly dazed, she wandered through the doorway and into the hall. I watched her for a moment before turning my attention to the contents on the table. What on earth could I serve the vegetables with? I had no idea how to cook quinoa. Or any of the other grains Zennia kept stocked in the kitchen.

I opened the pantry door to see if I could find a box of rice with cooking directions on the back, but all I found were canisters of pastas and grains that Zennia filled from the bulk bin at the health food store.

I heard the back door open, and Gretchen came in. With the spa tent on the other side of the guest cabins, Gretchen and I rarely saw each other. Sometimes I felt like we worked at completely different places.

"Gretchen, please tell me you know how to cook quinoa."

She gave me a blank look. "I don't even know how to spell it."

"Too bad. I'm trying to come up with lunch for the guests, and I have no idea what I'm doing."

Gretchen ran her hand through her short black hair. "I wish I could help, but my next massage client will be here any minute. I came in to grab extra towels from the laundry room."

"That's all right. I'll figure something out."

Gretchen left the kitchen, and I went back to searching the pantry. My eyes settled on a jar of natural peanut butter. Hmm . . .

Zennia had baked a fresh loaf of seven-seed wheat bread yesterday afternoon, and she almost always kept a jar of strawberry preserves in the refrigerator. What guest wouldn't love a throwback to their childhood with a peanut butter and jelly sandwich for lunch?

With one eye on the rooster clock, I quickly assembled five sandwiches, based on the number of guests I'd seen at breakfast. Now what to do with the vegetables? I couldn't throw them away.

I stared at the diced eggplant, hoping for inspiration. When none came, I scooped everything into a large bowl, drizzled olive oil on top, and added a splash of balsamic vinegar and a dash of salt and pepper. After giving the vegetables a good toss, I plucked out a piece of zucchini to try.

Unsurprisingly, it tasted like zucchini. But wasn't that why people were staying here? For all the healthy living? I'd tell them we were experimenting with a raw food diet today.

Gordon came into the kitchen as I was spooning my vegetable salad onto each plate. "I saw a couple heading for the dining room. Zennia told me on her way out that you'd be taking over lunch, and I wanted to make sure we were on track." He saw the plate closest to him. "What the hell is that?"

"Peanut butter and jelly on homemade bread with a seasonal salad tossed in a light vinaigrette." Not a bad spin, if I did say so myself.

"We can't serve peanut butter and jelly sandwiches to the guests. People will demand their money back. They'll pack up and go home."

"Aren't you exaggerating a wee bit?" I said. "They might question it, but if we present the food with confidence, they'll think we planned this meal weeks ago."

"Somehow I doubt that, but we don't have any alternatives at the moment. You'll have to do your best."

I grabbed two plates and carried them into the dining room, where the couple who had arrived first for breakfast this morning now sat. I placed a plate in front of the woman. She eyed the food and then me. "Seriously?"

"We're following the raw food diet mentality," I said, crossing my fingers behind my back.

"Sure you're not cleaning out the fridge?"

"I think it will be delicious," her companion said as he poked an asparagus spear with his fork.

"You would. Coming here was your idea."

"And it's been perfectly charming," he said, looking up at me with a rapidly reddening face.

The woman continued to goad him, and I retreated to the kitchen. Perhaps her disappointment in her companion would take her mind off her sandwich.

I finished lunch service without garnering any more comments about the meal. After I'd cleaned up the kitchen, I called Zennia to see how she was feeling. When she didn't answer, I called Jason to talk about Birch's death, but I could tell he was only half listening. He was already hard at work on his story for the next morning's edition of the *Herald*.

We hung up, and I started researching costs for ad placements in a few of the national magazines. Soon, the afternoon was gone.

Esther came into the office as I was wrapping up work for the evening. She sank into the guest chair near the door and fanned her face. "The temperature sure has picked up today."

"Really? I haven't been outside since lunch." I closed the program I'd been using and shut down the computer.

"Gordon told me about Zennia leaving in the middle of lunch service. I'm sorry I wasn't here to help. They switched the day for my weekly Bunco game because Edna's getting a new hip tomorrow."

"Lunch was no problem. We only had a few guests." I didn't mention that I'd served them peanut butter and jelly sandwiches, although I didn't think Esther would care as much as Gordon had.

Esther fiddled with a button on her denim shirt. "But what if she's not back by this weekend? We're expecting a full house."

"I don't think Zennia will miss any more work. The shock from this morning probably caught up to her, but after a good night's sleep, she'll be fine." Wouldn't she?

"I hope you're right. I don't like thinking about Zennia being alone at a time like this."

Her comments echoed my own thoughts, and I tried to quell the worry I could feel building up. "You know, I tried calling her a couple of times this afternoon, but she didn't answer. I think I'll try again." I lifted the receiver on the desk phone and punched in Zennia's number. Esther watched me as I listened to the ringing. When Zennia's voice mail kicked on, I hung up.

"Still no answer?" Esther asked.

"She's probably sleeping," I assured her, but I caught myself staring at the phone all the same. Why wasn't Zennia answering? Had she turned off the ringer so she wouldn't be disturbed?

Or had something else happened?

Chapter 6

"I bet Zennia's busy meditating," I told Esther. "Still, I'll swing by her place on my way home."

"That's a wonderful idea," Esther said. "Maybe I'll follow you out there." She chewed on her lower lip. "Do you think we'll stay long? It's getting on to dinnertime."

I knew Esther's eyesight wasn't the best at night, and she wouldn't visit Zennia if it meant driving after dark. Ever since she'd almost swerved into a minivan full of kids when she couldn't see the lane stripes, she'd restricted herself to daytime driving. "I'm not sure, but you can ride with me."

"I couldn't ask you to drive me back out here later," she said, although I could tell she was torn.

"I don't mind."

She stood and patted my arm. "If you're sure, I'll run upstairs and freshen up."

Once she was gone, I pulled out my phone and called Jason. He answered on the second ring. "Hey, beautiful. Dinner tonight? I'm finally caught up at work."

"Afraid I need a rain check. Esther and I want to stop by Zennia's place and see how she's doing. I'm surprised you're not over there interviewing her right now."

"I've spent most of the day trying to gather information from the police and doing background research. I might contact Zennia tomorrow."

"She heard one of the cops say Birch was strangled. Is that true?"

"It's too soon to release the cause of death, but that's the rumor. Unfortunately, I don't know much more than that, but I've put together a story with less."

Esther came back into the office wearing the same clothes she'd left in, but she'd combed her hair and applied a coat of pink lipstick.

"Time to go," I said, "but I'll try to call you later."

"I'd like that," Jason said.

I gathered my belongings, and Esther and I walked out the door. During the drive, Esther prattled on about her Bunco game and how one of her friends was trying to convince her to take up quilting again. I offered comments here and there, but I knew little about Bunco and even less about quilting.

Once I'd exited the highway, I maneuvered through the streets of Zennia's neighborhood, only making one wrong turn before I located her yellow house again. This time, I parked in the driveway, and Esther followed me up to the front door.

I rang the doorbell but got no response. After a minute, I rang the bell again.

"Where could she be?" Esther asked.

As I put my finger on the buzzer a third time,

the door opened a crack, and Zennia peered out. The look of relief on her face was evident. "Oh, it's you two. I thought you were more ghouls trying to get details about poor Birch's death."

"We wanted to make sure you were all right," I said. "I tried calling, but you didn't answer."

"I turned the ringer off. Everyone in town has been calling and asking completely inappropriate questions. These people are despicable!"

The venom in her voice made me wince. Zennia was normally so unflappable. "Ignore them. They'll have moved on to another topic by tomorrow."

"I can't imagine anything will be as exciting as a murder, but let's forget about those gossipmongers." She stepped back from the door and beckoned us inside. "I'm glad you two are here to keep me company. Stewing in one's own thoughts isn't healthy."

Esther stepped up and gave Zennia a hug. "I'm awful sorry about what happened to that man. You let us know how we can help."

Zennia hugged her in return. "Thank you." She gestured us into the house, and we all stepped inside.

The interior of her home had a decidedly more relaxed feel now that Detective Palmer and the other officer were gone. I bypassed the wicker chairs and took a seat in the rocker in the corner, brushing aside a large plant frond that hung over the back. While Esther chose a wicker chair and tried to get settled, my gaze fell on an open bottle of whiskey on the coffee table. Uh-oh.

Zennia caught me looking. "It's for medicinal purposes," she said.

I'd never known Zennia to drink, not even a little wine with dinner, but if ever she was going to start, the day she found the body of her former lover might be a good time. She sank into the other wicker chair and put a hand to her head. "I still can't believe someone killed Birch in my front yard."

"What was he even doing here that early?" I asked. "And how did he know where you lived?"

"I have no idea."

No doubt the police were searching for answers to those very questions.

We fell silent. Esther fingered the hem of her blouse while her eyes flitted around the room. Zennia rubbed her temple and stared at her lap.

Trying to think of a topic that didn't involve Birch or the police, I looked around for inspiration and noticed a plastic tub of beads next to the bottle of whiskey. I leaned forward and picked up a large cobalt blue bead. "This is lovely."

Zennia raised her head, her face brightening. "I wanted to honor Birch in some way. I'm making a necklace. That way, when I sense my memory of him slipping away, I can wear the necklace and feel closer to him."

"I should remember that for my Arnold," Esther said. "Sometimes I miss him terribly. It's hard to believe he's been gone for two years already."

Zennia capped the whiskey bottle and set it on the fireplace mantel. Then she knelt down on the floor next to the table. "Would you like to make one with me now?"

"I'd love to." Esther pulled the wicker chair closer to the coffee table.

"What a nice idea," I said. I fingered the St. Christopher necklace given to me by my dad years ago and that I still wore almost every day. "Maybe I could make a bracelet in honor of my dad." Plus, creating the jewelry was a good way to distract Zennia from the morning's events.

"Whatever brings you peace," Zennia said.

I knelt on the other side of the coffee table as she handed out elastic cords to each of us.

"Use any beads you like," she said.

She opened a zippered pouch on the table and pulled out several large needles and little metal coils. She passed around the needles, and I copied her as she threaded the cord on the needle. Across from me, Esther did the same. Zennia then clamped a metal coil on the other end of her cord, and Esther and I followed suit.

"Okay, we're all set," Zennia said. She selected a speckled bead from the bin and slid it over the needle. "This reminds me of my time at the commune. Seems like we were always making jewelry or other crafts."

I picked up the cobalt blue bead that had first drawn my attention and held it up to the light, turning my hand to watch the bead sparkle. Blue had been my father's favorite color, and the choice seemed fitting.

"How did you and Birch meet?" I asked Zennia. "Was it at the commune, or did you two move there together?"

"We met at a coffee shop where I was waitressing in San Francisco. I'd moved there from a little town in Iowa a few weeks before, and I didn't know another living soul. I was feeling lost."

"Didn't you say you met Birch when you were only nineteen or twenty?" I asked. "And you moved to San Francisco by yourself?" I tried to remember my mindset back when I was twenty. I was a sophomore in college and still trying to figure out my life at that age. Though I was technically living on my own, my parents were a short drive away if I needed anything. I wasn't sure I could have moved halfway across the U.S. by myself.

"With all the stories I'd heard about San Francisco, it seemed like the perfect place for me, a city where everyone loves taking care of their bodies both physically and spiritually." She dropped an orange glass bead onto her cord. "Birch came into the café one day. He was twenty years my senior, but otherwise, we were like two peas in a pod. I'd start a sentence and he'd finish it. Everything I told him, he agreed with."

I had to question Birch's motivation. Zennia was an attractive woman, and when she was younger, she must have been downright hot, as Ashlee would say. Birch probably took one look at Zennia and agreed to whatever she said in hopes that she'd fall for him. I kept that thought to myself. "Had you ever considered living on a commune?" I asked instead.

"Not at all, but Birch had recently returned from living there for the summer and was absolutely smitten. Once we became inseparable, he insisted that we go back together. I was young and inexperienced in life, and his description made it sound absolutely heavenly."

"And it wasn't?" I picked through the container of beads and selected a white-and-blue striped one. I added it to my growing row.

"Not quite as heavenly as I'd pictured. But I was in love, and I thought that was all I needed."

"Puppy love makes us do foolish things," Esther said. She'd managed to find several animal-shaped beads and seemed to be fashioning a farm-style necklace. "Before I met my Arnold, I almost ran off with my first steady boyfriend. It was prom night, and he wanted to take his daddy's truck over the county line where he'd heard a pastor would marry us even though we were too young. If we hadn't run out of gas, who knows what would have happened."

"I've never gone quite that far," I said, "but it's easy to get swept up in the moment, especially when the guy promises to love you forever."

"Isn't that the truth?" Zennia dug through the pile of beads. "And don't get me wrong about the commune. Evergreen is a wonderful place to live, but rather limiting. I saw the same people day after day. We had the same conversations over and over. I felt like I wasn't growing as a person. The commune was so insular that I decided I needed to leave. Unfortunately, I couldn't convince Birch to go with me, so I left without him."

"That was a bold move," I said.

"It certainly took a fair amount of courage. After all, I thought Birch was the smartest man I'd ever met. When he told me I was making a mistake, I second-guessed myself every step of the way."

"Was it the second-guessing that brought you back to the commune to look for Birch?" I added a final bead to my bracelet and held up both ends to make sure the pattern was consistent.

"I wanted to see him again so I could decide once and for all if living in the great wide world alone was better than living at the commune with Birch. Life contains many choices, and you have to be willing to give up one thing to keep another."

I knew exactly what Zennia meant. I'd left the Bay Area a while back to move home and help my mom after my dad died of a heart attack. At the time, I'd felt like I'd given up my independence in order to be loyal to my mom, but in the end, the trade-off had been worth it. I couldn't imagine leaving Blossom Valley and my life here for anything.

Zennia laid her almost-finished necklace on the table and took mine. "Let me finish that off for you." She removed the metal coil and needle and tied the ends together. She handed mine back, added two more beads to her necklace, and started to tie it off.

As she added one last knot and pulled on both ends, the cord snapped. The beads slid off in one smooth motion and clattered onto the coffee table. Esther and I scrambled to stop the rolling beads, but several fell to the floor.

Zennia watched them go. "That's quite an omen, isn't it?"

"Don't be silly, sweetie," Esther said. "Could have just as easily been me."

"No, as I was making this necklace, I felt like it didn't represent Birch. Perhaps the years apart have taken their toll and I've lost the essence of his spirit. Maybe I should visit the commune, get an idea of how Birch spent his last few months." She dropped her cord on the table. "Dana, I know tomorrow is your day off. Any chance you could go with me? I'd rather not make the trip alone."

My mind buzzed at the suggestion. Here was my chance to see an honest-to-goodness commune, and maybe even find out more about Birch and why he was murdered.

I slipped the bracelet on my wrist, stood up from the table, and looked at Zennia. "What time do we leave?"

Chapter 7

At nine the next morning, I pulled up to Zennia's house. Esther and I had kept Zennia company until eleven the previous night, cooking scrambled eggs for dinner and talking about her days before and after her stint at the commune. Even when I could barely keep my eyes open, Zennia still seemed eager for us to stay. She only agreed to let us leave after I reminded her that I'd see her again this morning. By the time I'd run Esther back out to the farm and gotten myself home, I'd gone straight to bed.

I rang Zennia's doorbell, bouncing on the balls of my feet in anticipation of our trip to the commune. After a minute, she opened the front door.

"Morning, Zennia. How did you sleep?"

She waved me inside. "I spent much of the night thinking about Birch, but I managed to nod off around three. Of course, I woke right up at five, but two hours of sleep is better than none, I guess."

"Maybe seeing the commune today will help you deal with Birch's death."

She locked the front door from the inside and led me through the kitchen. "I'm grateful to Esther for cooking the meals at the farm today so I can go out there. I can't remember the last time in my life I felt this unbalanced." She opened a door that led to the garage.

Inside, a gardening table sat against one wall, with trowels, seed packets, and small pots covering the surface. Four cardboard boxes were stacked in a nearby corner. Other than those items and Zennia's Prius, the garage was empty, a far cry from my mom's, which was overflowing with unused furniture, boxed-up mementos, and Christmas decorations.

Zennia pushed the button to open the garage door, and we got in her car. On the drive, she turned on a New Age music CD and concentrated on the road, seemingly deep in thought. I studied the passing landscape. The pear trees in the nearby orchards were laden with white blossoms and fruit buds, and endless rows of grapevines covered the hills.

Several miles outside of town, we reached an interchange. Whenever I drove out this way, I followed the road west to the small coastal town of Mendocino and the Pacific Ocean, but Zennia aimed her car east, toward the redwood forest and the far-off mountains beyond.

As the road wound through the trees, stores and roadside attractions popped into view every now and again, beckoning with their signs that touted one-of-a-kind curios, homemade goods, and hand-picked vegetables. An occasional driveway or mailbox marked the existence of a residence hidden somewhere among the trees.

Zennia swung around a turn, and a small hill with a large structure loomed into view. I'd seen the signs for the Mighty Eagle Casino ever since we'd left the freeway, but the sight of the massive building and paved parking lot among the dense trees still caught me off guard.

"Wow. I've heard people talk about the casino, but it's bigger than I imagined," I said.

"A blight on the landscape," Zennia said.

After roughly fifteen more minutes, she turned onto an unmarked, narrow road surrounded on both sides by towering redwoods. My stomach started to protest as she maneuvered through a series of turns. I rolled down the window to let in fresh air.

"Feeling all right?" Zennia asked.

"A little carsick is all."

"Tell yourself it's mind over matter."

"Somebody needs to tell my stomach," I said, gulping in a lungful of air. "Are you sure this is the right way? All these side roads look the same to me."

"I remember the route. Plus, there are signs, if you're aware of them. At the turnoff back there, a daisy was painted on the post."

I checked the side mirror, though the post was long gone. "Guess I was too busy trying not to throw up to notice."

Zennia laughed. "Only a few more minutes and we'll be there."

Sure enough, just when I thought I was in danger of ruining Zennia's upholstery with the contents of my stomach, she flipped on her turn signal. She turned down a one-lane, unpaved road. Redwood trees lined both sides, and a few of the longer branches scratched against the sides of the car, making screeching noises that set my teeth on edge.

As we approached a rickety bridge, a wood sign declared we were at the Evergreen commune. We crossed the bridge, and the lane opened up into a large dirt lot cleared of trees and bushes. Across the way, a long, single-story building beckoned. Past that, I could see a meadow, with a large red barn and several smaller wooden structures where the land rose up. To the right of the barn, an enormous area with rows of plants was surrounded by a wire fence. Several people worked among the rows, but from this distance, I couldn't tell what they were growing.

Zennia drove over to the long building and parked next to a battered, slightly rusty Datsun pickup. I got out and inhaled the cool crisp air, feeling my stomach start to settle down now that I was no longer inside a moving vehicle. A strong breeze blew through the trees, creating a hushed sound, almost like a whisper.

The other cars in the lot were mostly older models with dents, dings, and scratches in the bodies, and I wondered where the people who owned them were. I wasn't sure if I was expecting a group of giggling children to pour out of the building and shower us with daisies, or maybe a bearded man in a robe to wave his arm and declare us his guests, but I found the place spookily quiet. "Where's the welcome committee?"

Zennia shrugged. "Going about their regular business, I assume. I'm sure we'll find someone inside."

She shut her car door and took a moment to study the building.

"Does the place look the same as the last time you were here?" I asked.

"I see more outbuildings back near the tree line. Perhaps they added cabins. Back when I lived here, this building was the hub of the commune. Everyone ate their meals in the large gathering room, and we held our meetings here when the weather kept us from meeting outside."

We walked over, and Zennia pulled open the glass door. We stepped into a massive room with parquet floors and several round tables with folding chairs. On the other side of the room was a small stage with speakers and a microphone stand. The walls were covered with motivational posters and handmade blankets.

"This room is almost the same as when I left twenty-five years ago," Zennia said as she headed toward a hallway on our left. I followed along, noting a bulletin board on the wall as we passed. One flyer offered a free slightly used recliner, while another sought volunteers to help organize a group outing.

Partway down the hall, Zennia stopped at an open door. Birch's friend, Frank, sat inside at a desk covered in papers and binders. He was lifting up the corners of the papers and peering underneath, clearly searching for something.

Zennia knocked on the doorframe, and he quickly straightened the papers into a pile before standing and offering his hand. His gaze lingered on Zennia. "Oh, it's you, Zennia. I'm sorry we didn't get a chance to talk yesterday." His tone was one of curiosity with a hint of gruffness, definitely an improvement from the hostility I'd seen when he'd encountered Detective Palmer at Zennia's house yesterday morning.

Zennia smiled at him fondly. "How have you been, Frank?"

He ran a roughened hand through his short gray hair. "I have to be honest. Not great after what happened to Birch, poor guy. I still can't believe he's dead."

"Neither can I," Zennia said. "And killed in my own yard, no less."

"Any idea why Birch was at Zennia's house so early in the morning?" I asked.

Frank looked between Zennia and me and didn't answer.

"I'm Dana. I work with Zennia," I said. When he nodded, I went on. "About Birch?"

"I'm the one who drove him there."

I waited, but Frank didn't elaborate. "And why was he there?" I asked again.

"To see Zennia."

Well, duh. If Frank had initially been this un-helpful with Detective Palmer, I had to give the detective credit for not shooting him.

"I gathered as much," I said, keeping the frustra-tion from creeping into my voice.

Zennia chuckled. "You haven't changed a bit, Frank. You always were a man of few words."

Frank puffed up a bit. "I can't believe you still re-member me. I didn't know that was you at the farmers market until Birch told me later. Otherwise, I would have stopped to talk. But boy, you were a wisp of a girl when I saw you last, and now"—he moved his hands in the shape of an hourglass— "you're a full-fledged woman."

Zennia smoothed her skirt down over her hips. The trace of a smile appeared. "It was a long time ago. I'm not surprised you didn't recognize me."

"What happened after you and Birch left the farmers market the other night?" I asked.

"He spent most of the ride back here talking about everything he remembered about Zennia. Just went on and on. I didn't pay much attention, to be honest. Once we got back, I had work to do here in the office, so I didn't see him again until first thing yesterday morning."

"But what on earth was Birch doing at my house yesterday?" Zennia asked.

Frank turned and opened one of the desk drawers. He pawed through the contents while he spoke over his shoulder. "Said he wanted to catch up, find out what you'd been doing all these years."

"How did Birch know where Zennia lived?" I asked.

Frank closed the first drawer and opened another. "After the farmers market, Birch made me stop at the health food store to pick up flaxseed on the way out of town. He's friends with Jan, the lady who owns the place, and started gushing about how much he used to love Zennia and how their destiny was to meet again. I got no use for that mushy stuff, but Jan ate it up. She said Zennia was on her mailing list and gave Birch the address."

That seemed like a huge invasion of privacy on

Jan's part. Obviously she thought Birch was a decent enough guy to give out her customer information, but who's to say he wasn't a stalker? Or worse?

"Why did you drop him off that early? He couldn't have known if Zennia was even up yet."

Frank slammed the drawer shut, causing the desk to shake. "He gave up driving a few years back. If he wanted to see Zennia, he had to hitch a ride with me and that's what time I was driving through town. I told him he could ride with me on my errands and I'd stop on my way back here, but he was so damn excited about talking to her that he wasn't thinking straight."

On the one hand, the notion of showing up at someone's door at the crack of dawn was highly romantic. On the other, it was slightly pathetic.

"I live in a safe neighborhood." Zennia wrung her hands and paced the confines of the office. "There's rarely any trouble. Who could have killed him?"

"You got me." Frank opened yet another drawer and started to rummage through it. "I know I left that damn calculator in here. I bet someone stole it."

I glanced around at the corners of the room as if the calculator might magically appear. Zennia halfheartedly tipped up a binder to peek underneath, then let it drop back into place.

"Would it be all right if we walked around the commune, Frank?" she asked. "I was hoping to see where Birch has been living the last few months, maybe talk to his friends."

"You're welcome to do anything you want. We have the same open-door policy as we did back when you were staying here. Birch was a popular guy, so you won't have any trouble finding his friends."

"Thanks. I can't wait to see what's changed and what you've kept the same."

Frank didn't respond. He sat back down at the desk, still searching the drawers. Zennia and I returned to the main room. We exited out a door on the back side, where several picnic tables occupied a brick patio. Beyond the patio, the meadow I'd noticed from the parking lot stretched out for several hundred feet and stopped at the tree line, where a small herd of goats grazed in a fenced-off area near the barn.

The barn's enormous double doors were propped open in the warm spring air, and even from this distance, I could see a handful of people milling around inside. "Shall we start at the barn?" I asked Zennia.

She pressed her palms together in front of her chest and took a deep breath before she slowly exhaled. "Yes, I believe I'm ready now. It helps that Frank said everyone liked Birch. I expect to find lots of good memories here." She started across the field.

I paused as Zennia headed for the barn. I wasn't sure *everyone* had liked Birch. In fact, someone from this commune may have very well killed him.

Chapter 8

I caught up to Zennia as she entered the building. Though the outside gave the impression of an old-fashioned barn, the inside reminded me of a warehouse. The smooth cement floor was swept clean. Rows of shelves laden with such items as folded-up quilts, jars of honey, and preserves filled the majority of the vast space. A long table with two computers sat against the wall to my right, while a table in front of me held several open boxes.

As I took in my surroundings, a petite, elderly woman with a rather pronounced nose carried two jars to the table and carefully wrapped them in newspaper before placing the jars in one of the boxes. She offered a high-wattage smile. "Can I help you?"

Zennia seemed at a loss for words, so I jumped in. "I'm Dana, and this is Zennia. We're friends of Birch, and we were hoping to talk to people here to find out more about his life at Evergreen."

The woman's smile dimmed. "Yes, poor Birch. His passing is such a tragedy." She rested her hands on the edges of the box. "But we always welcome visitors, especially friends of the dearly departed." She sniffled and pressed her lips together as if reining in her emotions.

Another woman, this one in her late fifties or early sixties, stepped over and put an arm around the woman. She wore her hair in a long braid that was more gray than brown. With her long tank dress and leather sandals, she could have easily passed for Zennia's older sister. Or at least her stylist. She said to the woman, "Pearl, you must stay strong in these troubled times."

Pearl bobbed her head. "I need to make tea for the sewing circle," she said. "Excuse me." She scampered past me and headed toward the main building.

The woman with the braid came up and embraced Zennia. "Zennia, you're always looking as lovely as a flower. When Birch returned from town two nights ago, chattering on about running into you again, I thought his heart would explode from pure emotion."

"Millie," Zennia said, hugging her back, "how long has it been since we've seen one another? Two, three years?"

"Yes, at one of the harvest festivals, as I recall." She turned toward me. Pale blue eyes, set in a tan, lined face that had seen years of sun, stared into mine. "And who is this young doe who looks as if she's spent her days frolicking through a field of flowers?"

I assumed Millie was talking about me, though I couldn't recall the last time I'd frolicked in a field, one full of flowers or otherwise. "I'm Dana."

Millie leaned in close enough that I could smell the floral scent of her breath. "You're a lucky girl. Heed Zennia's advice in life, and you'll never be steered wrong."

"Millie, there you are," a guy in his late twenties said as he walked into the barn.

He was dressed in a black T-shirt, tan chinos, and a baseball cap. He wore wire-rimmed glasses and carried a laptop in one hand, reminding me of the computer engineers who populated Silicon Valley. I'd expect to see him typing out computer code at the Daily Grind coffee shop, rather than being here at the commune.

"I wanted to show you this new ordering system," he said. "I think you'll like it."

Millie stiffened. "You know how I feel about you and your programs, Ryan. I have no interest in seeing anything of the kind."

He held up his laptop. "But I've updated the interface to make information easier to find. It'll make your job faster."

"A rushed job is a sloppy job," she said. "The method we've been using all these years has never failed us, thank you."

"You can't fight progress," Ryan said with a tired sigh. Clearly they'd had this argument before. "As soon as I finish my beta testing, I'd like to implement the program here at Evergreen."

Millie crossed her arms and stepped toward him. "We were doing fine before you got here, and we'll be fine when you leave, if you catch my drift."

I raised my eyebrows at Zennia. It sounded like life at the commune wasn't quite as peaceful as those whispering redwoods and cups of tea might suggest.

"Millie, I know you'll come around," he said.

"Don't count on it." She turned her back on Ryan. "Zennia, may the sun keep you warm in all your travels. As well as you, Dana." She patted Zennia's arm and left the barn.

Ryan shrugged at Millie's departing figure, then popped open his laptop and set it on the table next to one of the computers. "Old biddy," he muttered. "What a fool."

I motioned Zennia toward the exit, and she followed. Once we were outside, I said, "Sounds like those two have an ongoing feud. Do you know Ryan?"

"No, but Millie's been here a long time." Zennia gazed across the meadow. "In fact, she was living here before Birch and I came, and she was always one to follow the old ways. Over the years, I've run into her at various events, like that harvest festival, and she's never once shown an ounce of interest in technology."

"I bet she could have told you a lot about Birch, though. Too bad she took off before you could ask her anything."

"Perhaps we'll run into her again before we leave."

We trekked across the bumpy ground, following the tree line. The meadow was littered with gopher holes, and I tried not to think about the number of snakes that were probably lurking in the tall grass or inside those holes. Did rattlers come out this early in the season?

To take my mind of the possibility of snakes, I

said, "The commune seems to produce quite a few goods, if those shelves in the barn are any indication."

"Yes," Zennia said. "They jar tomatoes, blackberries, strawberries, and anything else, plus they make their own lemon curd, fudge, and granola. Not to mention all the blankets and quilts the ladies sew. It's a lot of work, but it's what keeps this place going."

We reached the other corner of the meadow and followed a well-trodden path up a slight incline to an A-frame building with a newer deck running along one side.

I glanced in the large picture window near the door and saw five or six women sitting in rocking chairs in a circle. Some were knitting, while others were quilting.

I followed Zennia inside. The women silently rocked while they worked at breakneck speed. The only sound was the rapid clacking of needles.

When no one looked up or acknowledged our presence, I cleared my throat. As one, all of the women stopped what they were doing and set their projects in their laps.

"Yes, dear?" a plump woman with short, curly hair asked.

"Hi, we're old friends of Birch, and we were hoping to learn more about his time here," I said, basically repeating what I'd told the woman in the barn.

As if by an invisible signal, all the women began knitting and sewing again. I shivered at their synchronized motions. Were these commune residents or alien robots? Were they discouraged from talking to strangers?

"Birch was a gentle soul," one woman finally said, not pausing in her knitting.

"He used to play the guitar for us while we worked in here," another said.

Zennia settled into an empty rocking chair. "Tell me more."

I looked at the circle of women, and then at the beautiful day outside. Could these women offer any insight into who would want Birch dead, or would they simply entertain Zennia with tales of how wonderful the man was? I suspected the latter.

I leaned down by Zennia's ear. "I'm going for a walk."

She nodded as one of the women launched into a story about Birch's guitar playing at the last picnic. I opened the door to leave, only to encounter the woman I'd seen in the barn earlier. She carried a silver tray upon which a teapot and half a dozen cups sat. Her eyes grew wide when she saw me. "I didn't expect any extras today," she said. "I don't know if I have enough cups."

"That's all right. I'm off to take a walk." She looked relieved as I held the door open for her. She slipped inside the room, and I headed down the porch steps, picking up the trail where it ran by the building.

I followed the path as it meandered through the trees and eventually came upon a small pond. Across the water, two houses stood silent. A clothesline was set up next to one of the houses, and several shirts hung from the line. A dog came out of a dog house and barked at me. From where

I stood, I could see that the trail dead-ended at the houses, so I turned and retraced my steps to the quilting house, as I'd come to think of it.

I watched Zennia through the window for a moment as she laughed at something one of the other women said. She was clearly enjoying herself. I decided to investigate the commune a little more. I followed another path that branched off from the first one, wondering where it would take me.

After winding around shrubs and stepping over a fallen log, I came upon a decent-sized stream bordered on both sides by thick, thorny blackberry bushes. My mouth watered at the sight of the berries. I used to pick them every summer at my grandmother's house when I was a kid. I was tempted to try one now, but they all looked too green.

Instead, I followed the path as it ran alongside the stream. When I came to a tiny footbridge, I stepped onto it and looked down at the water.

The stream wasn't deep, and I could see several tiny fish swimming near the edge, flitting back and forth as if playing a game of tag. Shouldn't those fish be in school? I almost slapped my forehead at my own stupid joke.

A twig snapped from somewhere behind me, and I turned to scan the trees. Most likely a squirrel was romping around. I was fairly certain bears didn't roam these woods. Did they?

I focused on the fish again until I heard another crunch. The little hairs on the back of my neck stood up. Maybe it was time I was leaving. I'd seen enough horror movies about girls lost in the woods to know what would happen if I stayed.

Fighting the urge to run, I stepped off the bridge and marched back down the path. As I reached the end of the blackberry bushes, I practically bumped into Frank.

I gasped at his unexpected appearance and took a step back. He, on the other hand, didn't seem at all surprised to see me. Had he followed me out here?

"What do you think you're doing?" he growled. "This place isn't safe for people like you."

I swallowed hard at Frank's angry tone. "People like me? What's that supposed to mean?"

He only glowered in return as I looked up at his large form. From this angle, he appeared almost as tall as a redwood.

I needed to get the hell out of here.

Chapter 9

"I'm taking a walk in the woods." I heard a tremor in my voice and took a quick breath in hopes of steadying it. "You said Zennia and I were welcome to go anywhere on the commune."

He crossed his arms. "That's when I thought you had the good sense to keep out of the poison oak."

I looked down to see my feet firmly planted among a cluster of bright, shiny leaves. I stepped back onto the trail.

Frank frowned at my shoes. "That's not proper footwear if you're going to be tramping around the woods." He shook his head. "City folk."

"I wasn't tramping. And I was sticking to the trail until you came out of nowhere and scared me."

"Huh," Frank grunted.

I noticed that Frank hadn't offered an explanation as to what he was doing out here. Was he taking a walk, too? Or following me?

Either way, I was ready to head back. "Well, if you'll excuse me, Zennia's probably wondering where I am."

I stepped forward, and Frank moved aside to let me pass. At the first bend in the trail, I looked back. Frank still stood where I'd left him, watching me. I quickened my pace.

At last, the quilting house came into view. Zennia stood outside, talking to a woman with an afghan draped over one arm.

"There you are," Zennia said when I joined them. "I was about to send the Forest Service to find you."

"Sorry, I lost track of time. It feels like the woods go on forever." I didn't mention my run-in with Frank. I wasn't entirely sure whether I should have felt threatened or not.

The woman with the afghan touched Zennia's elbow. "Now that your friend is here, I need to get to lunch. That cornbread goes fast." She followed the path down the slope and into the meadow, heading toward the main building. As fast as she was walking, she must really like that cornbread.

"Does everyone eat their meals together?" I asked Zennia as we picked our way more slowly down the slope.

"The commune provides three meals a day, and anyone is welcome to eat in the main dining room, but residents can also eat in their homes. Eating together provides a sense of community for those who want it."

We reached the meadow. The other woman was already out of sight inside the building. "How many people live here?"

"It fluctuates. I'd say around fifty-five or sixty. Some people pass through only for a season while others stay for years. Frank and Millie have been here the longest, although I vaguely remember one of the other women from back when I lived here."

"Are there enough houses for all these people, or do they share?" I asked, thinking of the cabins by the pond.

"Both. There are quite a few cabins scattered around the property, plus a dorm-style structure that sleeps thirty. Bear in mind that the farther out from the main building you get, the more the amenities drop off. When I lived here, the cabins way out in the woods didn't have indoor plumbing or electricity, but not everyone is bothered by those things as long as they can live in solitude."

"Who gets to pick the cabins?" I asked, caught up in what Zennia was saying.

"They used to try and give the cabins to families, especially those with children. As for the rest, the policy used to be that the longer you've lived here, the more permanent your housing."

The policy made sense, but I wondered if the newer arrivals resented having to wait their turn for one of the private cabins. Obviously, no one would have killed Birch strictly for a shot at his house, but the living arrangements might have created tension.

When we reached the end of the meadow, I expected Zennia to go in the back door, but she started around the side of the building instead.

"Don't you want to join everyone for lunch?" I asked.

She slowed her steps but didn't stop. "I'm sure we'll find something to eat on the drive home, unless you're absolutely starving."

"No, I can wait. I just thought you'd want to talk to people about Birch. Having everyone gathered at lunch seems like a good way to accomplish that."

"The women who were knitting and quilting told me all sorts of stories about him, and I'm starting to get a good sense of Birch's time here the last few months. He was clearly loved."

Zennia unlocked her car, and I got in the passenger side. Once we were both buckled up, she started the engine and backed out of the lot. The drive back to civilization seemed to take half the time as the trip out here, and she soon reached the turnoff for the highway.

As we neared the Mighty Eagle Casino, Zennia said, "Why don't we stop for lunch?"

I glanced at her in surprise. She'd described the casino as a blight, and now she wanted to eat here? "Are you sure?"

"I've heard the restaurant serves organic salads. I'm curious to see what they're offering."

Without waiting for an answer, she turned into the casino's driveway. Even at lunchtime on a weekday, the parking lot was two-thirds full, with several shiny Cadillacs taking up two spaces each. A shuttle bus was parked to one side.

Zennia parked in a vacant spot. As we walked toward the casino entrance, I marveled at the size of the large, stone structure. I pulled open the door, and a blast of arctic air greeted us in the dimly lit, smoky room. I grabbed my upper arms at the chill and started coughing from the smoke. A neon sign on the back wall promised a café if I'd only follow the flashing arrow. I headed in that direction.

On my way by, I watched as one elderly woman

sitting at the penny slots took a roll of bills out of her bra, peeled off a five, and shoved the roll back in her bra. She saw me looking, scowled, and snatched the front of her blouse closed like I was a peeping pervert. As if.

The air in the café was considerably fresher, and the light was much brighter. A young woman with a dragon tattoo on her neck extracted two menus from a holder on the side of the hostess stand and led us to a table by the window.

Through the glass, I saw mostly trees, with only a small shed interrupting the view. It gave the intended illusion of being close to nature for anyone who didn't want to actually go outside.

We sat down, and the hostess handed each of us a menu. "Your server will be right with you," she said. "I believe Olive is assigned to your table."

At that, Zennia sat up straighter and jerked her head around, checking each corner of the room.

I eyed her. "You seem awfully excited all of a sudden." I flipped open the menu and scanned the contents. Burgers, wraps, and sandwiches fought for space among offerings of fish and chips, ribs, and fried chicken. I smacked my lips. "After seeing this menu, I'm pretty excited myself. The only question is whether I can eat the bacon cheeseburger and fries and still drink an entire chocolate milkshake."

When Zennia didn't comment on my lunch choice, I peeked over the top of the menu. She was still scanning the restaurant.

I lowered my menu. "You always give me a hard time when I pick an unhealthy dish for lunch. What's going on?"

Zennia stopped looking around and placed her hands in her lap, like a child caught misbehaving. "Nothing. I'm deciding on what to order."

"It helps if you open the menu."

Zennia blushed and reached for hers, but I put my hand on top before she could pick it up.

"You told me you wanted to try this restaurant for its organic salads," I said, "but you obviously aren't interested in the food, and you've been acting strangely ever since the hostess mentioned Olive. Do you know Olive?"

"No, I don't," Zennia said firmly. She pulled the menu out from under my hand and popped it open, hiding her face. I continued to stare at the back of her menu, trying not to get distracted by the giant picture of a hot fudge sundae while I waited for her to look at me. Eventually, she did. "I have a confession to make."

I put my elbows on the table and rested my chin in my hands. "I'm all ears."

Zennia studied the tablecloth like I might quiz her on it later. "I didn't come here for the organic salad."

"Good thing, because I checked the menu, and they don't have one."

That earned me a small smile. "I wanted to stop because one of the quilters mentioned Birch's sister, Olive, works here as a waitress."

"I didn't realize Birch had a sister, but you didn't need to get me here under false pretenses."

"But I have no real reason to see her," Zennia said. "It's pure curiosity that made me want to pull in, and I'm ashamed of showing such weakness."

I leaned back in my chair and smoothed down

the tablecloth that I'd managed to wrinkle with my elbows. "Maybe she can fill in what Birch has been up to the last few years."

Zennia shook her head. "I doubt if she's spent much time with him. One quilter said the relationship between Olive and Birch was . . . how did she put it? Complicated. That's the word she used. She said Olive had every reason to hate Birch."

Zennia's declaration brought one question to mind. Did Olive hate Birch enough to kill him?

Chapter 10

A waitress stepped up to our table. "Hi, I'm Olive. I'll be your server today. Can I start you off with anything to drink?"

I took a good look at her. I wasn't sure of her age, but I guessed she was close to Birch's sixty-plus years, based on the murder's worth of crow's feet at the corners of her eyes and the deep wrinkles around her mouth. She appeared to be a couple of inches shorter than me, which put her at five foot three, and she carried an extra thirty pounds on her frame.

"Iced tea, please," I said.

"Hot tea for me," Zennia said. "Anything herbal is fine."

"Be right back with that," Olive said.

She left, and I leaned toward Zennia. "Okay, tell me what you know."

Zennia slid her napkin from under her silverware and spread it in her lap. "You know I don't like to gossip."

"But you're the one who told me about Birch and his sister. And insisted we stop here for lunch so you could see her. Why?"

"Shame on me. I don't know what I was thinking."

She started gnawing on her bottom lip, and I couldn't help but wonder at her state of mind. Zennia was generally more self-assured than this. Birch's death must still be weighing heavily on her, even after our trip to the commune.

"Okay, you don't have to tell me." I picked up my menu again, wondering if I could eat all the food I was planning to order, or if my intentions were bigger than my stomach.

I heard a sigh from across the table and put the menu down.

"I don't know what's wrong with me," Zennia said. "You're not the type to spread gossip around either. I'm most likely hesitating because the story doesn't cast Birch in a particularly good light."

Zennia paused. I waited, not wanting to push her.

After a moment, she started up again. "All the women were telling me about how happy they were that Birch was living at Evergreen. Even though he'd only been back a few months, a lot of the residents sought his guidance over issues that cropped up at the commune. Then one lady commented on how no one ever had a problem with Birch, and another lady started hemming and hawing and said not to forget about his sister's husband."

"Olive's husband didn't like Birch, not Olive herself?"

Before she could answer, Olive returned with our drinks. Zennia shut her mouth faster than an early morning robin that's snagged a worm.

"Ready to order?" She set down the drinks and put her hands behind her back, waiting for us to speak. She was one of those waitresses who memorized orders instead of writing them down. I wasn't sure when that method had become trendy, but I was always partly awed and partly alarmed, like I was a participant in a magic show that could go horribly wrong when I ended up with tofu and celery sticks instead of a burger and fries.

With slight misgiving, I ordered the bacon cheeseburger but decided against the shake, while Zennia opted for a garden salad with grilled chicken and oil-and-vinegar dressing.

"I'll put your orders in right away." Olive collected our menus and headed to the computer station in the corner.

"What happened with Olive's husband?" I asked as soon as she'd stepped away.

"Well, it's like this," Zennia said. She stopped talking, and her eyes grew wide.

Olive was standing at our table again. I tried to hide my surprise at her return, but I felt my face get warm as I wondered if she'd overheard my question.

If she had, she didn't show it. "I'm sorry. Did you say you wanted a side of fries or coleslaw with your burger?"

"Fries, please."

"Right, sorry." She went back to the computer.

I watched her for a moment to make sure she wouldn't be darting back to our table. When she stayed put, I turned to Zennia. "Well?"

"Olive's husband was killed in a car crash a few years back. Birch was the one driving."

"That's terrible," I said.

She nodded. "The police ruled it an accident. No charges were ever filed, but Birch blamed himself anyway. He refused to drive from that day forward."

"How about Olive? Did she blame Birch?"

"I have no idea, but the woman who was telling me all this said Olive never came to the commune to visit Birch when he moved back a few months ago, even though she lives in the area. They couldn't have been on the best of terms."

Olive returned to our table, carrying two large plates, which she set before us. "Can I get you anything else?"

I surveyed the food. "I think we're good, thanks." I took a bite of my burger while I thought about how I would feel if Ashlee were the driver of a car in which Jason was killed. Sure, my younger sister was one of the worst drivers I'd ever ridden with, but would I hold her responsible for an accident? I didn't think so. It would be like losing both a boyfriend and a sister at the same time.

"How come you never met Olive before now?" I asked. "I mean, back when you were living at the commune?"

Zennia picked up her fork and poked at a piece of chicken. "I don't know. We rarely left the commune, and the place doesn't get a lot of visitors. We were just living our own lives back then."

We finished our meal, each lost in our own thoughts. When Olive brought us the check, I realized we hadn't asked her a thing about her brother, but now, I didn't have the heart. Maybe those deep wrinkles and weathered skin weren't from long hours waiting on people in a smoke-filled casino. Maybe it was the grief of losing a husband first, and now, a brother as well. I almost reached over and offered her my condolences but remembered at the last second that I wasn't supposed to know her.

Instead, I left a hefty tip with the bill, though I knew it wouldn't dent her grief. Still, maybe it would give her a reason to smile, if only for a moment.

On the way out, I fed a dollar bill into a slot machine. The money vanished after a single pull.

The woman at the next machine crushed out her cigarette in an ashtray full of butts. "A guy won twenty thousand dollars on that machine yesterday."

"Too bad I wasn't here yesterday." I thought about sticking another dollar in, but then thought better of it. I joined Zennia where she waited by the exit, and together, we walked to the car.

Traffic on the drive back to Zennia's house was almost nonexistent, and Zennia pulled into her garage in short order. She shut off the engine but made no move to get out of the car.

As she fiddled with the clasp of her purse, a sense of unease settled in my gut along with the remains of my cheeseburger. "So, uh, I guess I'll see you at work tomorrow," I said brightly.

Zennia stared out the windshield toward her gardening table and remained silent.

"You are coming back, aren't you?" I couldn't serve peanut butter and jelly sandwiches to the guests every day. They'd start chucking the whole wheat rolls at me.

"I thought this trip today would help me find closure," she said, "but I still feel lost. If everyone loved Birch, who could have possibly killed him?"

"I'm sure the police will figure it out," I said, a trace of desperation in my voice. "You know how good Detective Palmer is."

Zennia held up her hand and pointed to a Band-Aid on her thumb that I hadn't noticed before. "I was slicing a tomato to add to my scrambled egg whites this morning, and all I could think about was how much Birch loved the first tomatoes of the season. He used to savor them like they were the most delicious food on earth. I teared up so badly that I cut myself. If I can't make my own breakfast, how can I possibly cook for all those guests?"

"You can handle it," I said. "As soon as you stand in front of the stove, you'll start cooking on autopilot."

She shook her head. "Not likely."

I wanted to argue more, but I knew I was arguing for Esther's and my sake, not for Zennia's. How could I pressure Zennia to return to her job when she was clearly struggling?

"Are you quitting?" I asked, almost afraid to hear her answer. The farm would be crippled without Zennia to cook for everyone. Gordon might keel over from heart failure the moment he heard.

"No," she said, "but I believe I need a vacation. Do you realize I haven't taken more than a couple of days off since the farm opened?"

"You certainly deserve a break," I said. "No one's questioning that."

"Good," Zennia said. "I believe I'll call Esther right now and let her know my decision."

I could only sit there, dumbfounded, as she got out of the car. The farm had lost its cook, even if only temporarily. Where did that leave the rest of us?

I suspected I'd find out soon enough. And I wouldn't like the answer.

Back at my apartment, I tossed my keys on the table and removed my shoes, placing them by the door. I settled onto the couch and clicked on the TV, trying not to think about anything: not dead bodies, not absentee cooks, not scary guys in the woods. I flipped through the channels until I recognized an old comedy show. My eyes fixed on the screen, and I felt my mind relax as I listened to the canned laughter.

Halfway through the episode, my cell phone rang, snapping me out of my vegetative state. I checked the caller ID and wasn't surprised to see Gordon's name. As soon as Zennia called Esther, Esther probably panicked and turned to Gordon for advice.

With a sense of dread, I answered. "Hi, Gordon."

"Dana," he said gruffly, "this is Gordon." Either he'd failed to notice I'd already addressed him by name, or that's how he always announced his presence on the phone. "I just spoke to Esther, and she says Zennia has decided to take a leave of absence."

My blood ran a little colder at his words. A leave of absence sounded a lot longer than a brief vacation. "For how long?"

"She didn't specify. She wants to keep the situation fluid."

More prerecorded laughter drew my attention to the TV, and I picked up the remote to turn it off. "What are we going to do about a cook?"

"That's why I'm calling you. Those peanut butter and jelly sandwiches aren't going to land you a feature in *Food & Wine* magazine, but they did get us out of a tight spot."

"Can you hire someone?"

"That takes time, which we don't have. We need a cook in that kitchen first thing in the morning. That's why I thought you could fill in."

"Gordon, I'm probably the least qualified person to cook for the guests."

"No, I am," he said. "I can't even cook toast."

"What about Gretchen?" I asked.

"Her schedule is full at the spa. Her massages and facials have been a steady source of income for this place, and I don't want to disrupt that."

Good to know my marketing job was so easily dispensed with. "And Esther?"

"She offered to cook on your days off, but she can't handle two meals every day, plus she's helping that friend of hers in the hospital."

"I don't know . . ." I let the sentence dangle while I tried to think of another solution. The thought of being responsible for feeding the guests was enough to give me heartburn.

I heard a strange noise coming over the phone. If I wasn't mistaken, Gordon was grinding his teeth.

"I'll pay you time and a half for the extra hours," Gordon growled.

That caught my attention. Ashlee and I paid our bills on time every month, but sometimes it was close. I couldn't afford to turn down extra cash that I could sock away in the bank, especially since I wasn't sure how much longer my car was going to start up in the mornings.

"Time and a half, you say?" I wanted to hear him repeat the offer so he couldn't deny it later.

"Yes," he choked out. "I'll pay you overtime."

"Deal, but I have to warn you, my cooking skills are limited. Really limited." Sure I helped Zennia chop vegetables and assemble side salads, but that was a far cry from planning and cooking a full meal.

"They can't possibly be worse than mine. Having you cook is the best we can do, given the circumstances," Gordon said. "Let's hope Zennia gets her act together and hurries back to work."

"Amen to that. I'll see you first thing tomorrow."

I ended the call and punched the number for Jason.

"Hey, gorgeous," he said when he answered.

"You have to help me. I'm in way over my head," I said.

"What's wrong? Is everyone okay?"

"Yes, mostly because I haven't cooked for anyone yet, other than those sandwiches, and that wasn't cooking but rather assembling, so I didn't technically make anything." I paused for breath.

"Slow down," Jason said. "Are you trying to tell me that you're going to be cooking at the farm?"

"For now. Zennia's taking time off, and Gordon asked me to fill in."

"And you said yes?" Even over the phone, I could hear the amazement in his voice.

"He's paying me overtime."

"He must be desperate. I hate to remind you, but Zennia is a healthy cook, as in vegetables, whole grains, lean protein, the whole gambit."

I groaned. "Man, I'm in big trouble."

"Okay, let's think. Breakfast is easy. Toast and jam, oatmeal, fruit. Doesn't Zennia usually cook omelets?"

A feeling of panic surged through me. "I can't make an omelet. I can barely scramble an egg. They always dry out and stick to the pan."

"Eggs are easy."

"Says who?" I asked.

"Tell you what, I'm wrapping up a few things here. I'll stop by when I'm done and show you how to make an omelet. We can even perfect your scrambled egg technique while I'm there."

The tightness in my stomach eased. "You mean it? That would be fantastic. Give me an hour. I need to go to the store."

"Are you sure? All you need are eggs, butter, milk if you don't have any cream—"

"Wait, slow down. Let me make a list."

"Don't you have that stuff in your fridge?"

"I have butter. And milk, although it tasted a little sour this morning. I used my last egg when I made those boxed brownies a few days ago."

Jason laughed. "You really are in trouble. On second thought, why don't you come over to my house around six? I have everything you need."

And then some, I thought to myself. "I'll be there."

I set down the phone and put my head in my hands. Starting tomorrow, I was the new cook in the kitchen. I just hoped I didn't poison anyone.

Chapter 11

With time to kill, so to speak, before dinner with Jason, I decided to visit Mom. When I was growing up, dinner often involved fried chicken and mashed potatoes with gravy, but after my father passed away, Mom had revamped her cooking style and purchased a slew of healthy cookbooks to go with the change. Surely one of those books would have simple recipes I could prepare at the farm. If not, I could always search the Internet, but it might take me longer to cull through the thousands and thousands of choices than to flip through a handful of books.

I called first to make sure she wasn't working this afternoon, and then drove the ten minutes to her house. The light blue, single-story home with the small lawn and dogwood tree out front hadn't changed since my last visit a couple of weeks ago, and I hoped it never did.

As I came up the walk, Mom opened the front door. Even on this warm day, she wore a sweater set and slacks. "I thought I heard your car. Come in, come in." She motioned me inside and closed the door before leading me into the living room. A partially assembled jigsaw puzzle waited on a card table.

The picture on the box showed a Victorian village at Christmas. I scanned the pieces on the table, picked one up, and pressed it into place, completing a tiny chimney. "Ta-da." I glanced back at the box. "Now you only have around five hundred pieces to go."

"Keep your hands off my puzzle," Mom said, but I could hear the smile in her voice. I sat down on the beige floral couch while Mom settled into the battered recliner that had been my dad's favorite seat. "What have you been up to lately?" she asked.

I realized with a start that I hadn't told Mom about Birch's death. "Life was nice and quiet up until a man from Zennia's past was murdered in her front yard."

Mom blanched. "Good heavens, is that where he was found? I read Jason's article, of course, but I didn't recognize the address. How is Zennia holding up?"

"Not well. That's why I'm here. She's decided to take time off from work, and I agreed to fill in as the farm's cook. I wanted to borrow a few of your cookbooks for ideas."

"How come every time you need to cook a new dish, you raid my cookbooks?" Mom teased.

"Because you have the largest collection of anyone I know."

She stood. "In that case, follow me. We'll find you the perfect book."

We went out to the kitchen, and Mom bent down

in front of her waist-high bookcase. She scanned the titles, mumbling to herself, "Too complicated, too many ingredients, too much technique . . ." She pulled a book off the shelf and handed it to me. "This one has basic but good recipes."

I squatted down next to her to get a better look. The cover showed a basket full of vegetables. That would definitely fit the bill. I took the book and set it on the nearby table.

Mom continued to sort through the rest. "You said the murder victim was from Zennia's past. Where did she know him from?"

"Turns out she and Birch met over twenty-five years ago in San Francisco where she was waitressing. They fell in love and moved to the commune out here. Do you know about the commune?"

"Evergreen?" Mom said. "Sure. Everyone knows about that place."

Everyone but me, apparently.

"Has Birch been living there all these years?" Mom asked.

"No, he moved away right after Zennia left and only came back a few months ago."

"How fascinating." She ran her fingers along the spines of the books. "Aha, here's another good one." She removed it from the shelf and held it out to me. "You know, I should give Millie a call. She lives out there, and I should make sure she's all right."

I was so absorbed in what Mom said that the book slipped through my fingers and fell to the floor. I barely noticed. Millie? The same woman who refused to use the new computer program at the commune?

"Um, Dana?" Mom asked, her eyebrows raised.

I scrambled to pick up the book I'd dropped. "Where do you know Millie from?"

Mom took the book from me and carefully brushed off the cover. "I've known Millie for years. I used to make quilts for a children's charity way back when, and Millie and a few other women at the commune used to donate their own work. The charity folded several years ago, but I run into Millie at the farmers market every now and again." After she'd inspected the corners to make sure they weren't bent, she handed the cookbook back to me.

I delicately set it on the table with the other one as if it were a Fabergé egg without its case. "How does Millie like life out there? Zennia said she's lived there since before even Zennia herself arrived."

"Clearly the commune suits her. Although the last time we talked, she was quite upset with a new gentleman who recently moved there."

"Do you remember his name? I saw her arguing with a guy named Ryan when Zennia and I were there earlier today."

She handed me another book. "I'm not sure if she ever mentioned his name. What were they arguing about?"

"He's created a new computer program that he wanted Millie to try out, but she refused."

Mom nodded. "Sounds like Millie. Her ancestors are Pomo Indians, and she's always embraced the idea of living off the land as simply and with as little waste as possible. Now that you mention it, I remember Millie saying that this new man wants to modernize the entire commune by selling their knitting projects and jarred food over the Internet, even using social networking sites to pull in business."

I blinked at Mom. I didn't realize she even knew about social networking. Maybe she was hipper than I gave her credit for. "How do the other members feel about that? Can someone new make such big changes?"

"Not by himself." Mom stood and dusted off her knees, abandoning her cookbook search as she warmed to the topic. "Decisions at the commune are made as a group, with the majority deciding what changes are allowed. If this Ryan fellow could convince enough members, especially the older ones who hold a lot of sway with the rest of the group, he could get the changes approved. Of course, with Millie fighting him, he's got an uphill battle."

I wondered how many members of the commune were involved in Ryan and Millie's dispute. How had Birch felt? Even though he'd only returned a few months ago, people might have listened to him because of his age and past experience at the commune. If he'd pushed for the changes, he could have made any number of enemies. Then again, if he'd squashed the idea, the other half of the commune would be unhappy. The women in the quilting cabin felt everyone loved Birch. Either they were wrong, or Birch had kept his opinions to himself.

"Earth to Dana," Mom said.

I rose from the floor and straightened out my pant leg. "I was thinking about this drama at the commune. I thought those places were one giant lovefest."

"Maybe when they first started," Mom said, "but nowadays, you have to make money to keep a commune running. They've got property taxes and groceries and upkeep to contend with."

The pressure of living at a commune was not unlike living in an apartment. "It's survived this long without problems," I said.

"I wouldn't say that. Millie hasn't specifically told me anything, but I've gotten the impression that money is always tight at Evergreen."

"Makes me wonder if all this is connected to Birch's death," I said.

"Hard to say. Someone could have killed him for any number of reasons." Mom placed a hand on the short stack of cookbooks. "Will these be enough?"

"To get me started." I picked up the books. "Can I come back if I need more?"

"Of course. Would you like to stay for dinner? It's fish night."

I smiled at that. Even though Ashlee and I had moved out of Mom's house a couple of months ago, Mom still stuck to her regularly scheduled dinners.

"Thanks, but Jason invited me over. He's going to show me how to make a proper omelet so I can wow the guests."

"A man who's good looking *and* cooks? I've told you before that he's a keeper. Don't let him get away."

"Get away? I'm not an ogre who's locked him in

a dungeon. In fact, Jason thinks I'm not half bad myself."

"You two are quite a pair."

I noticed she didn't say a pair of what, but I hugged her anyway. "Thanks for your help with my cooking adventure."

"Don't hesitate to call with any questions." Mom followed me to the door.

Once at my car, I placed the books on the passenger seat and started up the engine. I gave Mom a little wave before pulling away from the curb. There was just enough time to get ready before I was due at Jason's house. This ogre's hair could use a good brushing.

An hour later, I parked in front of the duplex where Jason rented one half. His side of the yard was well manicured and clutter-free. I couldn't say the same for his neighbor, who had a lawn full of weeds and a rusted heap of a car in the driveway. Jason had been ecstatic when his neighbor mentioned moving to Arizona, but so far, the move appeared to be all talk.

I walked up the path and knocked on the door. Jason opened it right away. His short reddish-brown hair looked damp, as though he'd just stepped out of the shower. He gave me such a teeth-rattling kiss that I worried a neighbor might see us and call the cops. "You're sure in a mood," I said as I stepped inside.

"Seeing you does that to me." He led the way into the kitchen area where butter, cream, and a carton of eggs waited on the counter. "Okay, first I teach, and then we eat."

For the next twenty minutes, Jason slowly went through each step involved in making an omelet, from heating the skillet to whisking the eggs to flipping the cooked egg layer over on itself. I nodded when it seemed appropriate and generally followed what he was saying, but I had a strong suspicion that I'd forget his instructions in the morning.

"Easy as pie, right?" Jason asked as he slid a perfectly formed omelet onto a plate. "Actually it's easier than making a pie."

Neither one seemed easy to me. I took a bite of the omelet. "This is so fluffy."

"Thanks to the cream."

"I hope mine turn out half this good," I said.

"Follow the steps I showed you, and you'll be fine."

We moved to the table and sat down to finish our omelets in companionable silence. Since Jason cooked, I did the dishes. Not a bad deal, considering how few I needed to wash.

When I'd dried my hands and folded the towel back up, I turned to him. "Ready to get whooped at a little Ping-Pong?"

"Don't get too confident. I've been practicing."

"Still won't help you," I said as I headed to the garage, with Jason close behind.

He hit the button to lift the automatic door. The evening light exposed a Ping-Pong table centered on the cement floor. One of Jason's buddies recently moved out of state and didn't want to bother taking the table with him. Jason offered to give the table a home, and the Ping-Pong games had become a regular activity for us. I had a two to one average in wins, much to Jason's chagrin.

He picked up a paddle and the ball. "Prepare to be beaten like that egg in your omelet."

"Give it your best shot." I grabbed the paddle on my side of the net and stood at the ready.

Jason served, and I smacked the ball back. We volleyed for several seconds before Jason missed a corner shot, and the ball bounced into a stack of crates lining the garage wall.

I watched as he hunted for the ball. "I drove Zennia out to the commune today. She wanted to meet Birch's friends."

"Was it everything you imagined? Did the women braid your hair and offer you flowers?"

"One woman offered me tea, but that was about it. The commune is definitely more modern than I expected."

Jason knelt down on all fours and peered between two stacks of crates. "I know the ball went over here somewhere."

I set down my own paddle to help in the search, but before I could start, Jason reached an arm in between the crates and pulled out the ball. "Got it." He jumped to his feet. "Now you're going down."

"Such hostility. It's only a game."

"Says the person who normally wins."

I raised my hands, palms up. "I can't help it if I have superior Ping-Pong skills."

"Whatever." He served again, and I lobbed the ball back to his side of the net. "Who did you meet out there?" Jason asked as he tried to concentrate on the game.

"Frank was there, the guy who drove Birch to Zennia's house the morning he was killed."

"Now *he's* a product of the sixties. Doesn't trust the cops, wants to live without the government interfering. From what I gathered off Detective Palmer, Frank would never leave the place if it weren't for needing groceries and trying to sell whatever the commune produces."

I missed Jason's shot, and the ball bounced off his bicycle. It dribbled back in my direction, and I scooped it up. "Sounds a lot like Millie. I didn't talk to her much, but it turns out my mom knows her."

Jason missed a hard hit, and the ball ricocheted off a crate and rolled down the driveway. He ran after it to stop it before it reached the street. "Nice one," he said when he got back. He tossed the ball to me.

I caught it and served. "My mom says Millie is super upset about plans to modernize the commune. Ryan, this new guy I saw when I was out there, wants to start up an online business."

"They need to do something," Jason said, never taking his eyes off the ball. "I've been digging around and found out the place is in serious financial jeopardy."

His words reminded me of what Mom had said earlier. "How bad is it?" I asked.

"The commune is close to losing its land. If that happens, the place will shut down."

It was my turn to miss the ball as it sailed by. If the commune closed, where would all the residents go? What would become of people like Millie? And what, if anything, did it have to do with Birch's murder?

Chapter 12

I fumbled around the garage floor, trying to trap the Ping-Pong ball under my hand before it could roll away. Just as it reached the corner of the garage, I slapped my hand down and stopped it. I stood up and caught Jason watching me, his green eyes full of amusement.

"Looks like I figured out a way to put you off your game," he said.

"Don't worry. It won't happen again." I stepped over to the table and put extra force behind my serve to prove my point. "Do you think the commune is bankrupt?" I asked as we hit the ball back and forth.

"I don't know, but according to the records I pulled, they missed the last two property tax payments. They're racking up late fees and penalties as a result."

"But the commune's been around for decades. It can't close." I had no idea why I found the idea unsettling, but I did. How would the residents survive out in the real world? Did they have any job skills? Family members to help them?

"The tax man won't be knocking on their door tomorrow, but they do need a long-term strategy to stay solvent."

Jason and I kept playing, but my mind was bouncing around more than the ball. Who at the commune was responsible for making sure the bills got paid? Would Millie have to accept Ryan's changes to keep the place open? How long until the government wielded its mighty hammer and seized their land?

I shook my head. I was starting to sound like Frank with that last one.

I suddenly noticed that Jason had stopped playing. He stood there with the ball clutched in one hand and a giant grin on his face.

"I'm ready," I said, holding up my paddle.

"I won."

"What?"

"I won the game," he said again.

I dropped my paddle on the table. "No fair. You distracted me with all this commune nonsense. I couldn't concentrate on the game."

"I figured your superior Ping-Pong skills would pull you through," he said.

"Ha, throw my words back in my face, why don't you?" But I was only kidding. I walked around the table to shake his hand. "Good game."

He took my hand in his and pulled me close. "You can do better than that."

We locked lips, and I felt a sizzle run through my body.

"I'd let you win more often, if I knew that would happen," I said.

"Who says we need a reason?" He kissed me again.

We headed into the house, and Jason hit the button to close the garage door on the way by.

"Care for a drink?" he asked.

I checked the time on the microwave. "Iced tea would be nice, if you have any. But I'll have to make it quick. I have to be at the farm early tomorrow to serve those omelets."

Jason grabbed a bottle of iced tea from the refrigerator and poured the contents into a glass. He got himself a soda, and we both sat on the leather sofa in his living room. He took a swig of his soda and settled back into the cushions with a contented sigh.

I laid a hand on his knee. "You seem pretty relaxed for someone who's been writing about murder," I said.

"You know how it goes. Lots of activity at the outset, then a lull if the police don't make an immediate arrest. My articles can only rehash the crime scene so many times before people lose interest."

"Do the police have a suspect in mind?" I knew Jason and Detective Palmer had a fairly cordial relationship for a newsman and a cop. The detective would occasionally share extra details under the agreement that the information wouldn't immediately show up in the *Herald*.

"Not that they've mentioned."

"Any idea how long Birch was dead?"

Jason leaned forward and set his can on a coaster.

"Less than an hour, since we know exactly what time Frank dropped him off and when Zennia found him."

"Detective Palmer must be happy that they can narrow down the time of death."

He rubbed his goatee. "Without a suspect to focus on, it doesn't help all that much."

"What about the cause of death? Have the police found the murder weapon?"

Jason nodded. "Strangled with his own necklace."

I shivered, remembering the beaded necklace Birch had been wearing at the farmers market. "The one with all the beads? I made a similar bracelet at Zennia's house, but I can't imagine that string is strong enough to strangle anybody with."

"Birch's was made from fishing line."

An image of fishing line cutting into soft flesh sprang to mind. That brought a bigger shiver. I wondered if the beads covering the line lessened the pain any, or if it even mattered since he ended up dead anyway. "Did Frank notice anything out of the ordinary when he dropped Birch off?"

"Nope. Being that early, the neighborhood was quiet. He vaguely remembers a woman walking her dog, but couldn't provide the police with a good description. The cops are canvassing the area to see if they can locate her."

"They don't think a lady with a dog killed Birch, do they?"

"No, but she might have seen something useful."

"Good point. Maybe a suspicious vehicle or even a person talking to Birch while he waited for Zennia," I said. "But I'd like to think if she possessed that kind of information, she would have called the police by now."

"People don't always like to get involved," Jason said.

I stood up from the couch. "I should get home. Five o'clock comes awfully early."

"No kidding," Jason said. "I try to sleep right through that part of the morning, unless there's a major story to cover." He rose from the couch, took my glass from me, and set it on another coaster. "If the omelet causes you problems, give me a call and maybe I can walk you through it. I'd go out there to help, but I have work."

"You've already been a huge help."

He put his hands on my shoulders and stepped forward for a good night kiss so intense that it would last me the entire drive home, maybe even part of the night. When we pulled apart, he swiped my bottom lip with his thumb. "Drive safe."

I let out my breath. "With that kiss, I'll be lucky if I can walk, let alone drive."

Jason gave me a wink and escorted me to my car. I got in and started the engine.

The sky had turned dark while we'd been sitting on his sofa, and I flipped on my headlights as I pulled away from the curb. My lips still tingled from Jason's kiss, but my mind mulled over everything from omelets to murder.

The next morning, my hands were coated with egg yolks, the farm's kitchen was a mess, and I was cursing my decision to help with the cooking during Zennia's absence. As planned, I'd arrived early and retrieved the freshly laid eggs from inside the nests of Berta and the other chickens. After collecting a basketful of eggs, I'd squeezed a pitcher of orange juice, then got cocky preparing the omelets and tried to crack the eggs with one hand like I'd seen on TV. Now there were eggshells on the floor, my fingers were covered in slime, and I wasn't sure there were enough eggs for breakfast.

Gordon walked in as I was wiping up yolk from the floor. He took one look at the goop and stepped back, checking the bottoms of his shiny wingtips to make sure he hadn't stepped in egg. "I wanted to see how breakfast preparations are going. Should I retrieve Esther to assist you?"

"No need. I've had a minor setback, but everything's under control." A total lie, but I didn't want Gordon second-guessing me on my first solo breakfast attempt.

"All right. Well, another guest checked in last night. You should have seven guests for breakfast."

I glanced at the remaining eggs in the bowl. "No problem." Maybe I could bulk up the omelets with extra vegetables. That thought reminded me that I needed to cut up the vegetables.

"I'll leave you to it." He cast another look at the state of the kitchen and left with a shake of his head.

Once he was gone, I kicked into high gear, grabbing anything produce-related from the refrigerator and stacking it all on the kitchen table for further inspection. After I'd sorted through the pile, I washed and chopped a bunch of baby spinach and cut up a carton of mushrooms and a bell pepper, although the pieces were all different sizes.

When I'd finished the prep work, I peeked around the corner into the dining room and gulped. Diners were sitting at two of the tables. I hastily filled a water pitcher and brought it out to the sideboard with the juice. "Help yourselves," I called out before rushing back to the kitchen to brew coffee. How had I forgotten to make coffee? Everyone drank coffee.

I ground the beans and added water to the machine. While the coffee percolated, I placed a skillet on the stove and turned on the burner, running through Jason's steps from last night in my head. After I'd slid the omelet from the skillet to the plate, I stepped back to mentally pat myself on the back. Julia Child couldn't have done better herself. Well, she probably could have, but the omelet looked pretty decent to me.

While I was on a streak, I decided to do another omelet. I poured more eggs into the skillet, grabbed the now-full coffeepot from the machine, and headed into the dining room. A lone man had taken a seat near the door, and I stopped at his table first.

"Coffee?"

"What kind?" he asked.

"Dark roast, fair trade, and organic," I said, repeating the words I'd seen on the package. "Fresh brewed."

"Don't mind if I do."

I filled his cup and moved to the next table, pouring coffee for whoever requested it. The moment

I'd filled the last cup, I carried the almost-empty carafe out of the dining room.

As I stepped into the hall, I caught an unpleasant whiff and sniffed the air. Uh-oh. I ran back to the kitchen to find that the eggs I'd left cooking in the skillet had dried up and were now a tiny, charred mess.

I plunked the carafe on the counter, switched off the burner, and dumped the eggs in the sink. I should have known better than to leave the kitchen while I was cooking eggs. I took a deep breath, tried to clear my mind, and started over. This time, I stayed right by the stove, but when I tried to fold the omelet, the eggs stuck to the skillet.

I felt panic well up as I stared grimly into the dwindling bowl of eggs. I couldn't afford to keep making mistakes. I tried to dislodge the omelet from all sides, but the eggs refused to budge. They were dangerously close to overcooking.

In desperation, I stirred the vegetables and eggs into a scrambled pile and dumped the contents on a plate. I looked between the messy heap and the pristine omelet on the other plate. I grabbed a fork and knife and cut up the perfect omelet until it matched the other one. Picking up both plates, I plastered a smile on my face and carried them out.

"Who was here first?" I said to the dining room in general.

A woman at one table raised her hand. "We were, but I don't eat eggs."

I swung around to the couple at the other table. "I only want coffee," the man said.

"Perfect." I dropped off one plate at one table

and the other at the second table. "I'll be right back with a bagel and fruit cup for you," I said to the woman.

"And I'll take more coffee," said the man.

"I'll take anything," the guy dining alone said, holding up his now-empty cup.

"Of course. I'll be right back." I rushed back to the kitchen, thankful so few guests were waiting. I had no idea how Zennia handled a full dining room.

After a flurry of activity and serious sweating on my part, I managed to serve food to everyone, including the final two guests who showed up as the earlier diners started to leave. Once the dining room emptied, I cleared the dishes, stripped the linens from the table, threw them in the wash, and sank into a dining room chair. I put my arms on the table, laid my head on top, and closed my eyes.

"Break time already?"

I jolted up in the chair, my heart hammering.

Gordon stood in the dining room doorway, his usual frown firmly in place.

"The diners are fed, the tablecloths are in the washer, and I'm resting for a minute."

"I suppose you've earned it," he conceded. "Besides, you'll need your strength for lunch service."

My insides plummeted. Holy crap, I'd forgotten about lunch.

I forced a chuckle. I didn't want Gordon to know how panicked I was. "Lunch . . . right, no problem. I'll have to remember to make enough for me, too."

"How you handle your own lunch is entirely up

to you. You can wait to eat until after the guests have finished dining, or you can take a lunch break before you start cooking."

"Before," I blurted out so fast that Gordon raised his eyebrows. "I ate breakfast early this morning, and I'm hungry," I said. In actuality, I'd be using my break to run into town and find something to serve the guests for lunch, even if I bought the food from another restaurant. But Gordon didn't need to know that.

"All right, but give yourself plenty of time. We don't want the diners waiting."

"I'll be back in time."

I went into the kitchen to clean up the mess from breakfast, keeping one eye on the clock while I washed the plates and mopped the floor. When that was finished, I drove into town to figure out what on earth I was going to serve the guests at noon.

Driving down Main Street, I passed Going Back for Seconds, which was the secondhand women's clothing store where Mom worked. I drove another two blocks, turned at the corner, and pulled into an empty parking space in front of The Health Nut, Blossom Valley's one and only health food store. I knew Zennia shopped here regularly, and though I'd never been inside the store myself, I thought it might be my best bet for figuring out lunch. Surely someone who worked here could guide me toward the items Zennia usually purchased.

I got out of the car and stepped onto the sidewalk. My head whipped up as a thought struck me.

The health food store.

Hadn't Frank said the owner was the one who'd given Zennia's address to Birch? Did she know that Birch had subsequently been murdered?

Or would I be the one to tell her?

Chapter 13

I pushed open the door to The Health Nut. A middle-aged woman with silver-blond hair stood behind the counter. Her cheerful countenance exuded such natural warmth that I felt like I'd known her for years, though I was positive I'd never met her.

"Can I help you?" she asked.

I glanced around the store, and my heart sank. The rows of shelves in the small space held bottles of vitamins and canisters of protein powders, with few jars and cans of actual food. I could also see a line of slightly tilted bins along the back wall filled with nuts, grains, and pasta and a rack of bread in the corner. What I didn't see was a plethora of fresh produce and meats with which to make lunch.

"I work with Zennia at the O'Connell Farm, and I'm filling in as the cook for a few days."

"Zennia," the woman said. Her eyes grew wide, and she closed the ledger she'd been writing in. She stepped out from behind the counter. "Zennia is one of my best customers." She studied me.

"You're far too young to be Esther, so you must be Gretchen or Dana."

"Dana," I said, offering my hand.

"Jan." We shook. "Is there anything specific you're looking for?"

"No, but I need to feed roughly half a dozen people at noon today, and I have no idea what to cook for them."

She tapped her bottom lip as she scanned the contents of the nearest shelves. "That's a tough one. We deal mostly in vitamins and supplements, with the idea that they'll enhance your regular diet to create a healthy body. Other than what we carry in the bulk bins, we're far too small to deal in the food selection you'd find at a supermarket, although we do have a bakery section."

My gaze was drawn back to the bread rack. I'd already ruled out serving peanut butter and jelly sandwiches two days in a row. What else did Zennia have in the fridge that I could use to make a sandwich? My mind remained stubbornly blank.

Jan snapped her fingers. "We do have a small variety of frozen meals in our freezer case."

"Where's that?" I asked, glancing around. I must have missed the freezer section when I came in.

She led me to the far corner of the store and around the display of bread loaves to a small nook that held a single freezer. I stared through the glass. She hadn't been exaggerating about the selection being small, but with time rapidly vanishing, I couldn't afford to be fussy.

I yanked open the door, grabbed an individual serving-size box of frozen vegetable lasagna, and flipped it over to read the back. The portion was meager, but I could always make a side salad with lettuce and green onions from the farm's garden, like I'd done for Zennia so many times. If I threw in a basket of rolls, the guests might not feel too deprived.

As I read the ingredient list, I could sense Jan watching me and looked over. She blinked rapidly and busied herself with a nearby display of wheat-grass powder.

I grabbed the other seven boxes of lasagna, effectively cleaning out her supply, and closed the freezer door. On my way to the front of the store, I grabbed a bag of dinner rolls, carried everything to the counter, and made a pile. Two boxes slid off the top and bumped into a collection of jars that were displayed on the counter. As I straightened them, I saw that the jars contained honey from the Evergreen commune.

I added a jar to my other purchases and saw Jan freeze. She glanced from the jar to me and back, like she wanted to say something. At this point, I wished she would.

"Any chance you've tried the lasagna?" I asked.

She picked up a box and scanned the bar code. A high-pitched beep sounded. "Sure. This brand is better than most."

"Good to know." Maybe lunch wouldn't be a total disaster.

Jan finished scanning the items and announced the total. I flinched at the giant cost for such tiny boxes. I felt through my pockets until I realized that in my haste to get into town, I'd forgotten to take any petty cash from the office.

Jan gave me another of her sidelong glances as I opened my wallet and pulled out my debit card.

I paused before swiping the card. "Is anything wrong?"

"What? No." She stepped away from the counter, as if the mere suggestion created enough force to propel her backward. "Well . . ." She moved up to the counter again. "Since you work with Zennia, I thought you might know if Birch died in her yard, like everyone is saying."

Aha, she had heard about his murder. "Yes, he did," I said.

Jan placed her hands on the counter like she was propping herself up. Her lips got smaller and smaller, and for a moment, I thought she was going to cry. "Dear Lord, and I'm the one who sent him to her house."

"What do you mean?" I asked, though I'd already heard the story from Frank.

This time, tears formed along her lower lids. "I can't help but feel responsible for what happened to Birch. He came in here the day before he was killed, and I'd never seen him so excited. He'd run into Zennia again after all these years and couldn't believe his good fortune. The absolute delight on that man's face . . ." She smiled at the memory. "I thought it was the sweetest story I'd ever heard, and I offered him Zennia's address with the idea that he could show up and surprise her. Now he's dead."

"You couldn't have known what would happen."

"A mugger must have been hanging around the neighborhood and killed Birch during a robbery. If I hadn't given him Zennia's address, Birch never would have been there in the first place, and he'd still be alive."

I set my wallet on the counter, forgetting all about the groceries. "How do you know Birch wasn't the intended target all along? Maybe the killer planned his death that day regardless of where Birch was and followed him to Zennia's house."

Jan looked at me like I'd told her deep-fried Twinkies could cure heart disease. "That's absurd. Birch was the nicest man I've ever known. He's been a regular at my shop since he moved back to the commune. I'd gotten the feeling that the last few weeks were rough on him. When I saw how happy he was that day, I wanted to help him."

"What's been going on the last few weeks?" I asked, wondering if it was related to the tax problems Jason told me about.

"He never said, which was unlike him. He was usually so open, but I know he's been taking on more responsibility at the commune. Maybe there's a problem there." She tapped one of the lasagna boxes. "Now that I remember, Ryan was in here that day as well, and those two wouldn't even acknowledge one another. Avoided each other like the plague, which is hard to do in a store this small."

Now that was interesting. Why would the men be ignoring each other? Like Millie, was Birch opposed to introducing technology to the commune? Or was Ryan to blame for the missing tax payments? Then again, there could be other problems in Birch's life I knew nothing about.

Another thought struck me. "Did Ryan overhear you two talking about Zennia?"

"Possibly. Like I said, this place isn't that big."

Which meant he could have overheard Jan giving out Zennia's address. Had Birch mentioned he'd be dropping by in the morning? "What about Frank? Did he come in with Birch?"

"Sure. He usually does."

"Did he talk to Ryan?" I was wondering how far the hostility toward Ryan extended.

Jan shook her head. "Well, no, but Frank's not much of a talker on his best day."

The boxes of lasagna were starting to sweat from being out of the freezer. I swiped my card and finished paying for the groceries, while Jan bagged everything. She handed me the bag.

"If you see Zennia before I do, please tell her she's in my thoughts."

"Absolutely. Thanks for your help with lunch."

I carried the grocery bag to my car. Once inside, I checked the clock and cursed. Where had the time gone? I backed out of the space and sped down the road, my foot never easing off the gas pedal.

After what felt like hours but was only minutes, I reached the farm, parked in the closest space, and trotted toward the lobby with my groceries. As I pulled open the front door, one of the couples from breakfast came out, and the man bumped into me, causing me to drop the bag.

"Oops, sorry about that," he said and picked it up.

I saw him look down at the contents, and my stomach seized as I imagined him discovering the frozen boxes. Thank goodness the dinner rolls lay on top and covered them.

"Excuse me." I grabbed the bag and hurried inside. Gordon frowned at me as I scuttled past the check-in counter, but I didn't slow down. When I reached the kitchen, I plunked the bag on the table, unpacked the contents, and grabbed an empty bowl. I rushed out the door to collect the makings of a salad.

By the time I'd plucked leaves from the lettuce plant, picked a few stalks of green onions, and managed to dredge up a couple of early season cucumbers that were probably too inedible to eat, I could see the guests drifting into the dining room through the French doors. Feeling like an organic salad inspector was breathing down my neck, I ran back into the house to throw together the salads, zap the lasagna in the microwave, and heat up the rolls.

It was déjà vu from breakfast as I carried the first salad plates into the dining room and saw the same diners waiting in hungry expectation. I shuttled back and forth until everyone was served and then cleaned up the kitchen while they ate. By the time I reentered the dining room, only one couple remained.

"Everything okay with lunch?" I asked.

"Great," the man said. "I'm stuffed."

"Yes," the woman agreed. "Delicious. Reminds me of my favorite frozen entrée that I buy."

I almost dropped the plate I was holding, but managed to recover before it could slip from my grip. "You don't say." I hurried from the room before she could ask for the recipe. God help me if she wandered into the kitchen and saw the empty boxes.

By the time I'd finished scrubbing the dishes and loaded the washing machine with the linens, the afternoon was half over. Exhausted, I sank into the office chair and booted up the computer so I could concentrate on my regular marketing duties. Fortunately, my workload had been light lately, and I only needed to deal with administrative tasks and the Web site's blog.

I soon became absorbed in work as I typed away at the keyboard. Esther entered the office while I was finishing the next day's blog post.

"Mercy me, are you still here?"

I checked the computer. Criminy, after six already? I'd been at the farm for almost twelve hours. No wonder my stomach was growling.

"I'm on my way out now," I said. I saved my work and shut down the computer.

"I can't tell you how much I appreciate you helping me like this while Zennia is out," Esther said. "Especially with me spending most of the day at the hospital."

"If anything, it's expanding my cooking skills." Or my microwaving skills, I thought.

After a quick good-bye to Esther and a nod to Gordon in the lobby, I made my way out to the car. Traffic on the highway was sparse, and I was soon pulling into the apartment complex parking lot. Ashlee's salsa red Camaro occupied the space next to mine, but I could hear the engine ticking when I walked past, which meant she hadn't been home long. I climbed the stairs to the apartment and let myself in.

I stopped inside the door and tried to figure out what was different from the usual state of our living room. Then it hit me. The floor was clean. Ashlee was home, but her usual trail of shoes, purse, jacket, and keys was nowhere to be found. Either aliens had invaded her body, or Ashlee was expecting company, most likely male company.

As I wondered who the lucky fellow was, Ashlee limped out of her room. She wore a bathrobe cinched at the waist, and a towel was wrapped around her head. In between each toe, she'd inserted a little piece of cardboard, a sure sign that she'd recently painted her nails and didn't want the polish to smear before it could dry. "Hey, sis, my date is going to be here any minute. Can you answer the door?"

"Is this the guy who made you dinner last week?"

"No, he liked his dog way too much. Let him sit at the dinner table and lap beer out of a bowl. Talk about gross. This new guy came into the vet office this afternoon with a cat he rescued from the side of the highway. We totally hit it off. We're going to double with Brittany and a guy I set her up with after he brought his turtle into the office."

Brittany was one of Ashlee's closest friends and an almost constant giggler. I hoped her date liked that character trait. "Are you sure your boss isn't running a dating service for his employees rather than tending to sick animals?"

Ashlee pulled the sash on her robe tighter. "You know, that gives me an idea. Instead of matching up our clients, we could totally play matchmaker for the animals we treat. A Lhasa apso came in today that would be perfect for this shih tzu we neutered the other day."

I shook my head. The nail polish fumes must be getting to her brain. "How about you get ready for your date?" I asked.

She shrugged. "Okay, but don't come whining to me when one of the networks makes a reality show out of that idea. I'll be the first to say, 'I told you so.'" She went back to her room and shut the door.

I went into the kitchen to scrounge up dinner. One glance in the fridge showed that Ashlee had finished the leftover Chinese food and the remainder of the pizza. I pulled out a pack of hot dogs and was searching the pantry for the buns when I heard a knock.

I left the hot dogs on the counter and went to answer the door. A twenty-something guy with a slight build stood before me. His short brown hair was stiff with gel, and his wire-rimmed glasses reflected the light from the cell phone he held in his hand. He had a vaguely familiar quality about him, like maybe I'd seen him around town.

The guy looked at his phone, then back at me. "I was told Ashlee lives here," he said uncertainly.

"Come on in," I said, stepping aside. "She's getting ready. I'm her sister, Dana."

"So this *is* the right apartment," he said as he walked past me. "I thought she'd given me a bogus address." From the way he said it, it wouldn't have been the first time.

He surveyed the room, not bothering to hide his curiosity, before turning back to me. "I'm Ryan."

The moment he said his name, I recognized him, even without the baseball cap. This was the guy who was fighting with Millie at the commune. This was the guy with the big ideas for bringing everyone into the twenty-first century. This was the guy who might have overheard Jan give Zennia's address to Birch.

And this might be the guy who'd killed him.

Chapter 14

I gestured to the couch. "Have a seat," I told Ryan. "Can I get you anything to drink?"

"A soda, if you've got it."

I guess he wasn't into wholesome living as much as others at the commune probably were. I went into the kitchen, found a clean glass in the cupboard, and dropped in ice. After grabbing a soda from the refrigerator, I brought everything to the coffee table. "I'll let Ashlee know you're here."

He mumbled a thanks, and I went to rap on Ashlee's door, making sure to count to three so she'd have time to throw on clothes if she wasn't decent. I stuck my head in.

Ashlee stood before her closet, looking much like the last time I'd seen her, only without the cardboard partitions between her toes.

"Your date's here."

She whirled around. "Already? Crap."

"I thought you were expecting him."

"None of the guys I go out with ever show up on

time." She grabbed an armful of clothes out of the closet, threw everything on the bed, and started rifling through them.

"Tell you what. I can stall him for you." While she got herself dolled up, I could ask him about the living conditions at the commune, see if he knew how precarious the financial situation was.

She glanced up. "That'd be awesome. You can talk to him about all that organic stuff. I think he likes that."

"Yeah, sure, that's what I'll do." Right after I was done asking my questions.

I pulled the door shut and returned to the living room, where Ryan waited on the couch. He was swinging his knee back and forth as if keeping time to a song in his head. He held his phone in one hand and was thumbing through the contents on the screen.

"She'll be right out," I said, although considering she was still picking out her clothes, I knew she'd be a while.

"No rush. I got all night."

At least *he* had all night. I needed to plan tomorrow's menu before I could even think about going to bed. I sat in the stiff wing chair I'd bought at the thrift shop a while back and leaned forward. "Didn't I see you at the commune yesterday?"

His leg stopped swinging, and he looked up from his phone with what I'd swear was a guilty expression on his face. "You were at the commune?"

"Visiting with Zennia."

"Don't know her."

"She knew Birch."

At this, he fumbled with his phone, almost dropping it in his lap, and set it on the coffee table. "Sucks what happened to him. I still can't believe it."

From the other room, I heard Ashlee's hair dryer kick on. "Were you two good friends?" I asked.

"Not exactly friends, but I respected his wisdom. Closest thing I've had to a mentor."

"Is he the one who introduced you to the commune?"

Ryan laced his hands behind his head and resumed his leg swinging, back to Mr. Casual. "No, I found it on my own. I was involved in a couple of startups back in the city, working eighteen-hour days and most weekends. I even slept under my desk a couple of times when a deadline was looming. After a few years of that, I needed downtime to get my head on straight. I started looking for a quiet place up in this area and stumbled on Evergreen by accident. Birch showed up a couple months later."

Listening to Ryan talk about his hectic work schedule reminded me of how much I appreciated my slower-paced life at the farm, even when it involved cooking for the guests. "How long are you planning to stay at Evergreen? A commune in the woods must seem pretty quiet compared to San Francisco and its nightlife."

Ryan shook his head. "There was never time to enjoy the nightlife. I was lucky if I managed to sleep four hours a night. I like it here. The people need me. I can make that commune money."

"Sounds like you've got big plans," I said. "What did Birch think?"

The hair dryer shut off, and Ryan reached for his phone to look at the screen. "What's keeping Ashlee?" So much for Ryan having all night to wait.

"I'm sure she'll be out in a few minutes."

He slurped his soda and let his gaze drift down to his phone again.

"How about the other members of the commune?" I pressed. "Are they excited about your ideas?"

Ryan was still studying his phone. "I need to make a call."

I didn't know if he was telling the truth or trying to escape this conversation. Either way, he was on his feet and heading for the door.

"What about Ashlee?" I asked.

"I'll be right back," he said over his shoulder and stepped outside.

Well, that was a fast exit.

Not knowing how long he'd be gone, I went over to the kitchen counter and picked up one of the cookbooks I'd borrowed from Mom. I carried it to the kitchen table, sat down, and flipped it open.

I was still browsing the appetizer section when Ashlee's door opened. She pranced out, with her head held high and her boobs perky. Clearly she was putting on a show. When she noticed the empty couch and no sign of Ryan, her shoulders drooped.

"God, Dana, what did you do? Scare him off?"

"Of course not," I said.

"Then what happened to my date?"

I gestured toward the front door. "He stepped out to make a phone call."

"I thought you were going to keep him entertained." She stalked toward the door. "He'd better still be out there," she warned.

She placed her hand on the door just as it swung inward. Her scowl instantly switched to a smile. "Hi, Ryan. I'm ready to go now." Ashlee batted her eyelashes. I rolled my eyes.

Ryan moved to the side so Ashlee could step out and join him. At that moment, it occurred to me that my sister was about to go on a date with a possible murder suspect.

My heart skipped a beat. "Wait! Where are you guys going?" I called, but I was talking to the closed door.

I debated whether I should run after them. Was Ashlee actually in danger? Even if Ryan killed Birch, and I had no reason to think he did, it wasn't a spur-of-the-moment killing. I mean, sure, Ashlee could be annoying, but not enough for anyone to murder her. Right?

I went back into the kitchen and boiled the hot dog I'd set aside when Ryan arrived, trying to keep thoughts of Ashlee and Ryan out of my mind. Once I'd finished eating, I sat back down at the table and spent the evening studying recipes, looking for the ones that required the least amount of time and ingredients. All the while I kept one ear open for the sound of Ashlee tromping up the stairs.

After I'd dog-eared several pages for possible lunch items, I slammed the cookbook shut. First thing in the morning, I'd pick one of the recipes I'd marked and swing by the store on my way to work.

I stood up and stretched, my neck muscles feeling tight after hunching over the book all that time. I unearthed a pint of chocolate chunk ice cream from where I'd hidden it behind the frozen pizzas and snack foods, took a spoon from the drawer, and settled on the couch.

After an hour of really bad television but really good ice cream, I turned off the TV and stowed what little remained of the ice cream back behind the other frozen food. I wanted to go to bed, but Ashlee still hadn't returned. I turned off the kitchen light, lay down on the couch, and pulled the throw blanket over me, wondering if this was how Mom felt when Ashlee and I were out on dates as teenagers.

I'd barely closed my eyes when I heard footsteps on the stairs. I hadn't realized how worried I'd been until a wave of relief washed over me. A moment later, Ashlee unlocked the front door and came inside. She flipped on the light, and I sat up on the couch.

She gave a little start. "Geez, Dana, scare me half to death, why don't you."

"You're awfully cranky. Bad date?"

"It was okay. Only, Ryan is a vegetarian." When I didn't respond, she said, "He doesn't eat meat." She flopped down in a kitchen chair and kicked off her heels. The shoes did a cartwheel and came to rest in the middle of the kitchen floor, where they would no doubt remain until I moved them in the morning.

I left the couch and came over to sit down across

from her. "I know what vegetarian means. Why is that a problem?"

"I've never dated a guy who eats healthier than me. I mean, the whole time I was eating my burger, he was looking at me like I was chewing a mouthful of kittens."

I laughed. "It couldn't have been that bad, but if Ryan can't handle dating a carnivore, he won't call you again. Problem solved." Which wouldn't be a bad thing if he was involved in Birch's murder. "Did you know Ryan lives on a commune?"

"He mentioned that at dinner. Another strike against him." Ashlee shuddered. "I can't date anyone who doesn't own a TV. What would we talk about?"

I spread my arms wide. "World events? Your goals in life? Exciting things that happened at work that day?" I rested my arms on the table. "But who says he doesn't own a TV? The commune has electricity, computers even. They're not living in the Dark Ages, you know."

Ashlee picked at a cuticle. "You wouldn't know that from the people who bring their pets in to see us."

"You mean Ryan isn't the only member of the commune who's a customer?"

"Heck no, but most of them are old and totally out of it. That's why I was surprised when he told me he lived out there. He's way too hip. Anyway, they probably come to us because we're one of the cheaper vets in town."

"Or maybe it's your sparkling personality that draws them in."

"Could be," Ashlee said, taking my comment at face value. "But they'd better get their act together or they won't be customers for much longer."

"Why's that?" I asked.

"Their checks keep bouncing. My boss was yelling about it the other day. He said from now on we're only allowed to treat the animals if the people from the commune pay up front and in cash."

"Did Ryan mention money troubles while you were out with him?"

Ashlee gave me an incredulous look. "You're kidding, right? Like a guy is going to tell me he's broke on our first date? He's trying to score a hookup here, you know."

"Good point. Only Jason mentioned the commune is in financial trouble, and I'm wondering how many people are aware of the problem."

"Don't know and don't care." Ashlee rose from the table. "I'm off to bed."

"Right behind you," I said. "It's been a long day, and I'm expecting tomorrow to be much the same."

I flipped off the kitchen light once more and headed for my room. I hadn't been kidding when I'd told Ashlee tomorrow could be a challenge, considering how badly breakfast and lunch had gone today. But at least I wasn't wondering if my next check would bounce, like the people at the commune. I'd have to ask Jason if he knew who was in charge of the finances at that place. If it was Birch, that might be the reason he was dead.

Chapter 15

The next morning, I bounded out of bed before my alarm even rang. I showered, got ready, and was out the apartment door before Ashlee had even woken up. Who knew where this extra energy was coming from? But I wasn't going to question it. I needed all the help I could get while preparing today's meals.

The Meat and Potatoes market was bordering on deserted at this early hour. I made my way through the aisles. Before leaving the apartment, I'd settled on vegetable soup with sourdough bread, a lunchtime meal I'd seen Zennia serve often. I finished my shopping in less than fifteen minutes and was soon on the highway, heading to work.

Once at the farm, I followed the side path past the vegetable garden, turned at the cabins, and cut across the patio before entering through the back door. Zennia was such a standard fixture in the kitchen that I felt a pang in my chest when I saw the empty room. I forced myself to hum as I unpacked the groceries with the idea that it might alleviate the silence, but everything still felt off. The energy that had propelled me forward all morning was noticeably lower as I folded the reusable bags and stuck them in the pantry. Maybe I'd call Zennia later today and see how she was feeling and whether she was ready to return to work.

With that thought in mind, I got busy and finished breakfast prep before the first guest even walked into the dining room. By the time people were done eating, I'd washed most of the dishes and even foraged in the garden for lunch ingredients. Maybe yesterday was merely a case of first-day jitters, and the cooking would be easier from now on.

Yeah, right.

I was chopping zucchini when Gretchen came in the back door. "Hey, Dana, how's it going?"

"Better today. I didn't even burn the eggs at breakfast. Of course, that's because I didn't cook any eggs." I scraped the zucchini into a bowl and set it aside. "How's business at the spa?"

"Hectic. I worked right through my lunch break yesterday. I ended up eating a stale granola bar I found in the bottom of my bag. Looks to be just as busy today."

"If I remember, I'll bring you a bowl of soup after I've finished serving the guests."

"That'd be great, if you're sure it's not too much trouble."

"No problem. I'll stop by later."

I finished chopping the vegetables, added them to the pot with the rest of the ingredients, and put the soup on to simmer. On my way to the office, I texted Jason to see how his day was going.

My phone chimed before I could set it down, and I read his reply. "Gr8. C U 2nite?"

I thought about my plans for the evening. I wanted to do a trial run on one of the recipes I'd picked out last night before subjecting the guests to it. What better way to test a new dish than with a guinea pig?

I texted Jason back and offered to cook him tofu stir-fry for dinner. I left out the part about him being my guinea pig.

He took so long to reply that I worried I'd scared him off with my offer to cook, but my phone finally chimed. "C U @ 6."

I put my phone in my pocket and focused on the day's marketing work. For the next few hours, I argued with editors over ad placement, tried to think up a new theme for the Web site, and fine-tuned a postcard I'd been working on. I saved my work and went into the kitchen to complete the final preparations for lunch. Esther came in the back door at the same time I walked into the kitchen.

"Dana, I have a few minutes and thought I'd give you a hand. What can I do?"

"Could you fill one pitcher with ice water and the other with lemonade? That'll give me a chance to add a few more things to the soup."

"Is that what smells so delicious?"

I moved to the stove and stirred the contents of the pot. "I found an easy recipe in one of my mom's cookbooks, but I don't think I've ever chopped this many vegetables in my life."

Esther picked up a pitcher and started to fill it with ice. "Gordon told me what a wonderful job you've been doing in Zennia's absence."

My eyebrows shot up. "You heard those actual words come out of Gordon's mouth?"

Esther laughed. "You sound surprised. He may not tell you often enough, or at all, but he thinks you're a real asset here. Those were his exact words."

I felt a swell of pride. "How about that."

I sampled the soup to make sure I didn't need to add any salt and then grabbed a stack of bowls. While Esther finished filling the water pitcher, I ladled out the soup.

Esther hefted up the pitcher. "Be back in a jiff to do the lemonade."

"I'm right behind you." I grabbed the two nearest bowls, double-checked to make sure I hadn't sloshed any soup on the rims, and followed Esther to the dining room. More of the tables seemed to be occupied than at breakfast, and I did a quick count to see how many bread baskets I would need. Ten people sat at six tables. My biggest crowd yet, if you could call ten people a crowd.

Esther started to make the rounds with the water pitcher while I carried the two bowls to the closest table. Even before I reached it, I could smell the cigarette smoke wafting off the diner whose back was to me.

She turned her head as I approached, and I saw it was Olive, Birch's sister. Either the smoke still clung to her from working a shift at the casino this morning, or she smoked as much as the patrons there did. I set the soup in front of her and her companion.

"Thanks again for bringing me out here," Olive said to the woman she was dining with.

The other woman, who had painfully brittle

bleached-blond hair and a weathered face, yanked her napkin from under the silverware. "You need a day where other people take care of you," she said. "You're working too hard. Plus, I got a coupon."

I wanted to linger and see what else Olive and her friend would talk about, but the other diners were waiting. I went back to the kitchen to retrieve more soup. I finished delivering the meals and noticed that Esther was still making the rounds with her original pitcher of water, seemingly stopping at each table to talk to the diners at length. It was nice to see her spending more time with the guests.

Since Esther was busy, I prepared the pitcher of lemonade and carried it to the dining room. I returned to the kitchen to make a fresh pot of coffee and wipe down the counters. Esther came in as I was hanging up the dishrag.

"These guests are the nicest people," she gushed. She set the empty water pitcher on the kitchen table. "Everyone kept talking about how much they love walking the trails and seeing the animals. One woman swore she and her husband would be back every year for their anniversary."

"Fantastic. Any complaints about the food?"

"Not a word. One woman even told me her lunch was delicious."

I almost missed the cup I was pouring coffee into. "Really?" I'd been so worried about people being unhappy with the food that I hadn't even considered receiving compliments.

"Yes, she couldn't believe how crunchy all the vegetables were."

Was that a good thing for vegetable soup?

I took a sip of coffee to make sure I'd made a decent pot, and then carried the carafe out to the dining room. More than half the guests had abandoned their tables, including Olive and her friend, and it didn't take long to serve coffee to the rest. I cleared the tables while Esther started washing dishes. As I was packing up the leftovers, I set aside a serving for Gretchen.

When the kitchen was almost as shiny as Zennia normally kept it, I thanked Esther for her help.

She patted my hand. "I'm glad I could be here for a change."

"How's your friend in the hospital doing?"

"The doctors mentioned complications today, which means she's not out of the woods yet. That reminds me I'd better get back and check on her. She's probably awake from her nap by now."

As soon as she left, I picked up Gretchen's container of food and headed out the back door. I stopped at Wilbur's pen on my way by. He eyed the container in my hand and snorted in a tone that definitely sounded like begging.

"Sorry, buddy, not for you."

He sighed and threw himself down in the mud.

"Taking it a little hard, aren't you?"

His only reply was a twitch of his tail. I shrugged and continued past the chicken coop and over to the spa. When Esther first told me that we'd be erecting what was essentially a giant tent for the spa, I'd questioned the durability, but once I'd seen the thick vinyl walls, the real doors and windows, and the heating and cooling system I'd changed my mind. The place was even carpeted.

As I stepped into the lobby area of the spa, I could hear Gretchen talking in the nearest partitioned section. I set the soup on the small mosaic-tiled table between the two rattan chairs.

I wasn't sure how long Gretchen and her client would be, but I had a few spare minutes, so I settled into one of the chairs and texted Ashlee to remind her to take out the trash. She immediately responded that it wasn't her turn. We argued back and forth until I suddenly noticed the voices were getting closer, signaling an end to Gretchen's session. I stood up and tucked my phone out of sight as Gretchen appeared around the corner. I did a double-take when I saw Olive and her friend in tow.

"I haven't felt this relaxed in years," Olive was saying. Gretchen murmured a thanks and moved to the hostess stand. Olive's friend pulled her wallet out of her purse, and Olive laid a hand on her arm. "At least let me cover the tip." She began to rummage in her own bag as she walked toward the stand.

Before she could reach Gretchen, her foot caught on the carpet, and she lost her balance. She jerked her arms out, but it did nothing to stop her forward momentum. I could only watch in helpless horror as she fell to the floor with a thud.

Chapter 16

Olive hit the floor, catching herself with her shoulder, while her friend let out a shriek. I rushed to Olive's side, fearing she might be seriously injured, but she was already pushing herself up. Gretchen moved to Olive's other side, and together, we eased her to her feet.

"Talk about a klutz," she said, her voice shaky. She was leaning heavily on my arm, and I could hear her labored breathing.

"Let's get you to a chair," I said.

Gretchen and I guided Olive toward the rattan chair I'd been sitting in a moment before. We lowered her down while her friend hovered in the background, shifting her weight from one foot to the other.

"I'll get a glass of water," Gretchen said. She darted out of the room.

I knelt down in front of Olive. "Are you hurt? Would you like me to call a doctor?"

She let out a little laugh. "Please don't bother.

I'm okay." She put her hand to her face. "Only embarrassed."

"Nothing to be embarrassed about," I said, "but I want to make sure you're all right."

Gretchen returned with the glass of water and handed it to Olive. She accepted it with a mumbled thanks and took several gulps.

Olive's friend moved over to where Olive had tripped and inspected the carpet. "Gosh, Olive, you sure took a tumble. These places need to be more careful with their older clientele." She looked pointedly at Gretchen and me.

"I'm not an old lady, Connie. I barely qualify for Social Security." Olive lifted one foot. "It's these two left feet of mine. I never was very graceful."

Gordon entered the spa as Gretchen retrieved the empty water glass from Olive. When he saw our clients, he fixed the knot in his tie and gave Olive and Connie a large smile that reminded me of the Big Bad Wolf. "Good afternoon, ladies. I hope you're enjoying our services here at the O'Connell Organic Farm and Spa."

Olive perked up under Gordon's attention. "Gretchen is a wonder. I almost fell asleep right in the middle of the massage. It's my first one, you know."

"We're honored you chose our humble spa for such an experience."

I suppressed a chuckle. When Gordon wanted to keep the clients happy, the charm flowed out of him like water from a faucet.

"Well, I'm not too glad we did," Connie griped.

Gordon gave an almost imperceptible flinch, only

detectable by a tiny facial tic. "Are you displeased with the service?"

Connie waved her arm toward where Olive sat in the chair, studying her hands. "Olive here fell flat on her face a minute ago. Must have been a bump in the carpet."

Gordon's usually tan face paled. He turned to Olive. "Are you injured?"

She shook her head and gave Connie a pleading look, clearly not wanting to dwell on her fall. "Connie's making a fuss over nothing. I was digging around in my purse and not paying attention to where I was walking." She waved toward the hostess stand where she's tripped.

Gordon went over to the spot, bent down, and ran his hand over the carpet. "I don't feel anything." He stood and returned to Olive. "Still, your visit here today is on the house." He twisted his pinkie ring. "Gretchen, if they've already paid, make sure you refund their money." He smiled again at Olive and Connie, though this time it looked strained. "I hope that will help with this unpleasantness."

Olive stood. "You really don't—" she started, but Connie cut her off.

"It's the least they can do. You can be sure I'll be keeping my money right here in my wallet."

"But, Gretchen, you should still get that tip," Olive said.

Gretchen started to respond, but I missed what she said as Gordon took me by the elbow. "A moment of your time, please." He kept one eye on the women as he led me out of the spa.

"We need to do something about this," he hissed when we were out of earshot.

"The massage was free. Shouldn't that be enough?"

Gordon ran his hand through his slicked-back hair, and I wondered if his fingers would come away greasy. "The lady who fell might accept that, but her friend seems like the type who holds a grudge. She might convince the other one that we're negligent. Next thing you know, she'll hire a lawyer, and we'll be out of business."

"Not that I think she's going to sue, but don't we have liability insurance?" I asked.

"Of course, but once you file a claim, the rates skyrocket." He twisted his ring again. "You should offer them a complimentary dessert, as well."

My heartbeat quickened as I mentally visualized the contents of the pantry and refrigerator. Nothing sweet came to mind. "Dessert?" I asked, hoping I'd heard him wrong.

"Maybe organic brownies. That's a real thing, right?" He snapped his fingers. "Wait, what are those cookies Zennia bakes with all those seeds and nonsense?"

"I have no idea," I said, wondering if I could even locate her recipe, let alone the ingredients. "How about a tour of the farm instead?" The suggestion came out of nowhere, but as I thought about it, the idea started to bear fruit. "I could walk them through the gardens, talk about what ingredients I used for today's soup. I bet they'd love to meet Wilbur and his pig pals." And I'd love to talk to Olive about Birch, since Zennia and I had learned nothing at the casino.

Gordon nodded as I spoke. "Be sure to throw in

how Esther was forced to convert her farm to a bed-and-breakfast after her husband died so she wouldn't lose her land and her livelihood. That should guilt them into not suing. I'd love to have both sign a waiver, too, but that might be pushing it."

I held up my hands as if that would stop him. "No way. You don't want to give them the idea of suing if they haven't thought of it themselves."

"Trust me, they already have, but maybe we can help them forget."

Gordon gave the knot in his tie one last adjustment and led the way back inside the spa. Olive and Connie were laughing at whatever Gretchen had said. If any ill will lurked beneath the surface, I couldn't sense it.

I approached the trio. "If you're finished here, how about a tour of the farm? We have a variety of gardens that are all thriving this time of year, plus several farm animals and two nature trails that wind through the back of the property."

"I don't know," Connie said. "My knees have been acting up lately." She turned to Olive. "And you shouldn't be on your feet after that tumble you took."

So much for taking their minds off Olive's fall.

"A small tour would be nice," Olive said. "I'm trapped indoors all day with my job. Getting fresh air might be just what the doctor ordered."

"All right. A short tour, as long as it's not too hard on my joints." Connie bent her knees slightly, as if testing to see if they were healthy enough for a tour.

Gordon walked over to the hostess stand and came

back with two coupons. He handed one to Connie and the other to Olive. "I'd also like to offer you both a complimentary return trip to the spa. I would love to accompany you on the tour as well, but duty calls." He moved quickly toward the exit as if he wanted to break into a sprint but was holding himself back. Guess he was done with customer relations for the day.

"Wish I could join you," Gretchen said, "but I have another client arriving any minute."

I grabbed the container of soup from the small table where I'd almost forgotten it and handed it to her. She thanked me and headed toward the back of the spa, most likely to set up.

Olive and Connie followed me out and down the path to the vegetable garden, where several ripening strawberries were peeking out from under the plants. The nearby lettuce leaves were such a vibrant green that they practically glowed.

"This garden is the source for almost all the salads served here at Esther's place," I said.

Olive squatted next to the nearest strawberry plant and inhaled so deeply that I thought she'd suck a strawberry right up her nose. "Homegrown strawberries are much tastier than the ones they sell at the supermarket."

"You've got that little plot of land behind your trailer," Connie said. "You should try growing your own."

"Birch got the green thumb in our family. He could coax anything to grow."

My ears perked up at Birch's name, but I was careful not to let my interest show. "Sounds like my mom," I said. "Except she grows flowers, rather than vegetables."

"Birch had the same luck with flowers, too. I swear, the sickliest plant would spring back to life when he started singing to it."

"Make sure you don't sing to any flowers, Olive," Connie said. "With your voice, you'd kill 'em dead."

Olive looked stricken, and Connie patted her arm. "Geez," Connie said, "poor choice of words." She turned to me. "Her brother was murdered a few days ago."

Olive stared at her feet.

"I'm sorry. That's awful," I said. "Do the police know who did it?" I doubted Olive had more information than Jason, but it couldn't hurt to ask.

"They haven't told me if they do," Olive said softly.

She checked her watch, and I realized we'd gotten completely sidetracked from the tour. Oops.

"If you'll follow me," I said, "I'll show you our herb garden over by the kitchen. It's the secret to all of Zennia's delicious concoctions." I didn't know if this was true, since I rarely ate Zennia's meals, but I'd seen her add plenty of herbs to her dishes. She must believe they served a purpose.

Olive and Connie trailed behind me as I walked back toward the spa and turned at the guest cabins. A woman swam in the nearby pool, but she didn't break stride as we passed by.

I stepped onto the gravel that covered a small plot near the kitchen door and plucked a sprig of lavender off the closest bush. I handed it to Olive.

She sniffed it and gave it to Connie. "Reminds me of my sleep mask. Not that it helps me sleep."

"You're working too hard," Connie said. "You don't have enough time to unwind."

"I need the money. I have bills to pay. You know that."

Connie threw the lavender on the ground. "Tell that cheap boss of yours to give you a raise."

"Not with that fancy new casino opening up over near the coast." Olive pressed her lips together. "Everyone's talking about how that's going to hurt business."

"Have you worked there long?" I asked.

"Almost four years. That casino's gotten me through tough times, but management wants the young, pretty waitresses to draw in the gamblers. The only guys ogling me these days are the ones too weak to carry their oxygen tanks to the tables with the cuter waitresses." None of us laughed at her joke, probably because there was too much truth behind it.

"Enough of this smelly stuff," Connie said, gesturing at the lavender bush. "Didn't you mention animals?"

"Yes, pigs and chickens. Right this way." I led them past the redwood tree and onto the path near Wilbur's pen.

When Wilbur saw us, he lumbered to his feet and came over, with his curlicue tail wagging. If Olive and Connie hadn't been with me, I'd have run back to the kitchen for a treat.

Olive walked straight up to the fence rail and leaned over to pat Wilbur on the head. "What a beautiful pig."

At Olive's words, I'd swear Wilbur dipped his head as if taking a bow.

"I used to have a pig like this when I was a girl. Birch and I raised them for 4-H." She sighed. "I wish I could have made peace with my feelings about Birch. If only I'd known what would happen to him."

I'd heard the sentiment from other people and always thought of my dad and what I wouldn't give for one more chance to tell him I loved him. "I'm sure he knew how much you cared for him," I said.

"I'm not sure about that," Olive said. "We didn't get along much the last few years, not after what happened. Even after he moved back to the commune, I rarely saw him." She looked me in the eye. "I blamed him for my husband's death, you see, even if the police didn't agree with me." She grasped the fence rail. "And now I can't help but wonder if God has stepped in and returned the favor."

Chapter 17

At Olive's declaration, Connie threw her arms around her friend. "Stop getting yourself riled up. It's all over now. No sense overworking your heart."

Olive's face was almost as red as Zennia's strawberries as she extricated herself from Connie's embrace. "I'm sorry. I don't know what came over me." She grabbed my wrist with a firm grip. Her fingers felt clammy, and I involuntarily shivered. "You must be wondering what's wrong with me."

I placed my hand on hers. "Not at all. Your brother died. It's bound to bring up a lot of emotions. The same thing happened to me when my father died."

"Still, I don't normally share such thoughts with strangers. When you're a waitress, you get used to listening to people rather than talking to them." She released my wrist. "I guess Birch's death got me thinking about my husband."

My skin prickled. "What happened to him, if you don't mind my asking?"

Olive opened her mouth to answer, but Connie spoke up. "Let's not drag up those horrible memories. You need to move on."

I hid my disappointment as Olive said, "You're probably right."

"Speaking of moving on, let's see how the chickens are doing." I patted Wilbur on the rump and led the way to the coop where Berta and the other chickens spent their days and nights.

A dozen chickens pecked the ground or rested in the fenced-in outdoor area. Several had hatched back in early March, and I still marveled at how fast they'd grown in the last three months. I didn't see Berta among the flock. She must have been inside the coop.

Olive and Connie spent a few minutes talking about their personal experiences with chickens, though Connie's mostly involved frying them up and eating them. I mentioned how the birds provided the eggs for the morning omelets and Zennia's baked goods.

When the women seemed to lose interest in the chickens, I said, "How about a nice walk along the Henhouse Trail? It doesn't go back far, but the last time I was out that way, I saw a red-tailed hawk and a jackrabbit."

"I wish I could, but I should be going," Olive said. "I've got work tomorrow and all my uniforms are in the laundry basket waiting to be washed."

"And my knees can't handle much more exercise," Connie said.

"Well, then, I'll walk you to your car," I offered, but Olive shook her head.

"Please don't bother. You've gone out of your way to show us around. I enjoyed the tour."

"Yeah, it wasn't half bad," Connie said.

My skills might not get me a job as a tour guide at Universal Studios, but the women seemed happy. "Would you like to take a few strawberries with you?" I asked.

Olive's eyes lit up. "Could we?"

"Of course. Let me run in the house for a container, and I'll meet you over there."

I hurried to the kitchen and grabbed two disposable containers. By the time I got to the vegetable garden, Olive and Connie were waiting. I picked the ripest berries on the plants and handed each woman a container. "I hope you'll visit us again." *But watch your step next time,* I silently added.

"Thank you," Olive said, while Connie mumbled her own thanks. They headed back toward the spa and the path that led to the parking lot, while I turned toward the house. In the kitchen, I stopped at the sink to wash my hands. While I lathered on the soap, I thought about Olive and how she blamed Birch for her husband's death. That might be motive to kill him, but the accident had happened a few years ago. Why kill him now?

Gordon came into the kitchen as I was drying my hands. "I saw those two ladies leave. The old battle-ax was even smiling. Can I assume it went well?"

"As far as I know. They seemed to especially enjoy the animals. Plus, I gave them each a container of strawberries to take home."

"Good thinking." Gordon checked his watch.

"You've had a full day. Why don't you knock off early?"

While I would love to believe Gordon was concerned about my well-being, I knew his main interest was not paying me overtime if he didn't need to. "Not a bad idea. I wanted to try out a tofu recipe tonight before I serve it to the guests tomorrow."

Gordon pinched the bridge of his nose, as if suddenly struck by a headache. "Since this is for work, I suppose you can expense the ingredients."

"Thanks. I hadn't even thought to suggest it." I saw Gordon wince and knew he wouldn't be volunteering to cover my expenses in the future. He left the kitchen, still looking pained.

After wrapping up a few items in the office, I updated my time card and drove to the store, the ingredients list for the tofu stir-fry clutched in my hand. I wandered up and down the aisles until I located a small tofu selection practically hidden in the produce department.

I waffled over the choices. Silken? Firm? What did these even mean? Which one had the recipe specified? I grabbed a pack of each, wishing Zennia was here for guidance. I thought about calling her right then but decided to wait until later. I needed to figure these things out for myself.

After finishing my shopping, I drove home. I stepped in the door and emitted a groan when I saw the sorry state of our clothing-strewn apartment. Since Jason would be here later, I needed to clean the place before I could even consider starting dinner.

By the time I'd finished scrubbing the kitchen

and bathroom and vacuuming the living room, what remained of the afternoon had slipped away. I dashed into the bathroom for a quick shower and was drying my hair when I heard the muffled sound of knocking over the hum of the hair dryer.

I hurriedly finished my hair, swiped on a touch of lip gloss, and went to answer the door. Jason waited on the other side with a bottle in his hand.

He held it up. "Not sure what goes with tofu, so I picked a white."

I took the bottle and gave him a kiss, catching a whiff of his cologne. "Whatever you brought will be great. It's the dinner I'm worried about. I haven't even started cooking yet."

Jason followed me into the apartment and shut the door. "Then let me help. You can blame me if dinner tastes terrible."

"You've got yourself a deal." I removed my only two wineglasses from the kitchen cabinet while Jason uncorked the bottle. I almost turned on music but knew I'd need all my concentration to cook anything resembling a meal, even with Jason's help. "Let's get this party started." I opened the cookbook to the page I'd marked and skimmed the recipe.

Jason read over my shoulder. He grabbed a bell pepper from the bag on the counter, rinsed it off, and started slicing. I retrieved a package of tofu out of the fridge and cut open the plastic cover. The white square glistened in the overhead light. I poked it with my finger, and a small dent appeared where my nail cut it.

"Afraid it's going to jump up and bite you?" Jason asked with a smile.

"I've never cooked tofu before. Is there a special method I should use?"

He shrugged. "I think you just slice it up."

I picked up the package and reached in to pull the block of tofu out. The block fell apart and crumbled all over my fingers.

The squishy texture made me cringe. "Yuck." I grabbed a paper towel to dry my hand. "How am I supposed to slice this?"

Jason paused in his cutting. "Is that the only kind you bought?"

"I also have a firm type. Not sure what the difference is, but it's got to be better than this blob." I went back to the refrigerator and grabbed the other package. The moment I opened it, I could tell this tofu was more stable. Still, I sliced the block up as fast as I could, before the tofu could change its mind and melt into a puddle.

Jason had finished with the bell pepper and moved on to an onion. I made the sauce while he finished chopping everything.

I double-checked the recipe. "Guess I'm ready to cook." I stared at the pile of vegetables and sliced tofu. Suddenly nervous, I gulped down half a glass of wine.

Jason put an arm around my shoulders and gave me a squeeze. "It's only a stir-fry," he said.

"Right." I grabbed the large skillet that Mom gave me back when I left home for college, placed it on the burner, and cranked the heat to high. I poured a small amount of oil in the skillet.

Jason stood to one side and drank his wine. "Need any help?"

"Thanks, but I need to learn this on my own."

While I waited for the skillet to heat up, I filled Jason in on Olive's trip to the spa this afternoon and our conversation about her brother.

"I ran across news about the accident when I was researching Birch's background today," Jason said. "Apparently Birch was driving down the highway, lost control, and hit a tree. According to the article, he didn't remember the accident, so he may have fallen asleep. I couldn't find a follow-up article. That must have been the end of any investigation."

I added the tofu to the skillet. Oil spit in all directions when the tofu hit the hot surface, and a loud sizzle sounded. I pushed the tofu around with the spatula. "But why would Olive say that Birch killed her husband? Doesn't sound like that was even a possibility based on what happened," I said.

"If Birch did fall asleep, maybe she blamed him for that."

I retrieved the cutting board full of vegetables and carried it to the stove. "Maybe." I scraped the vegetables into the skillet.

Jason was silent while I worked, but I could feel his eyes tracking my movements. After a minute, I stirred the bowl of sauce one last time and dumped it in the skillet with everything else. A cloud of steam puffed up, followed by a surprisingly enticing scent of salty goodness. I inhaled deeply, and my stomach growled in response.

I turned off the burner.

Jason was the first to break the silence. "Can't wait to try it."

"Oddly enough, neither can I. I never thought I'd look forward to tofu and vegetables."

"Must be because you made it yourself. I've read that's how parents get little kids to try new foods by having them help cook."

"Great. I'm like a little kid in your eyes?" I said.

"Oh no, you're all woman."

I felt my whole body flame up at his comment. "Wow, you sure know how to get a girl all hot and bothered." I busied myself with removing plates from the cupboard. "Better eat before the food gets cold," I said over my shoulder.

Jason moved next to me to spoon up a serving, and I could sense the closeness of his body, which did nothing to cool mine. I had a feeling that if he touched my skin, it would sizzle like the vegetables.

I almost fanned myself as I said, "Find yourself a seat at the table." I scooped up my own helping, dug out a couple of forks from the drawer, and retrieved two napkins. We settled at the kitchen table, and I smoothed a napkin in my lap.

We each speared a piece of tofu, and together, we took a bite. The salt from the soy sauce hit my tongue, sending my taste buds soaring. I waited for Jason's reaction.

"This is good," he said. For a second, I wondered if he was simply being nice, but his green eyes held nothing but sincerity.

"It is, isn't it?" I took a bite of vegetables. "The broccoli isn't bad either."

We focused on our eating. When I'd swallowed

the last chunk of carrot, I chased the food down with wine. "You know, I'm usually full when I finish dinner. I can't say the same here."

"You could serve the stir-fry over brown rice tomorrow."

"Of course. I can't believe I didn't think of that myself." I looked over my shoulder toward the kitchen cabinets. "If we're still hungry later, I have packaged cupcakes."

Jason chuckled. "The perfect way to finish a healthy meal." He stood up and carried his dishes to the sink.

I followed with my own plate and silverware. Jason rinsed the dishes and placed them in the dishwasher.

"Since we're being healthy tonight, how about a walk?" I asked.

"Count me in."

After slipping on a sweatshirt, I locked the apartment door and led the way downstairs. The evening air was cool but not too chilly. A smattering of clouds were visible in the late-evening sky.

I was still reveling in my mealtime success as we crossed the parking lot of the apartment complex and stepped onto the paved walking trail that wound through the neighborhood.

"I can't believe how well my stir-fry turned out," I said. "Who knew vegetables could taste this good?"

"Those of us who regularly eat vegetables."

I swatted Jason's chest with my fingers, noticing how firm his body felt. "So Zennia keeps telling me."

"How is Zennia?" he asked. "Any chance she'll be coming back to work soon?"

"Not that she mentioned," I said. "She enjoyed

our visit to the commune, but she's still clearly having a hard time dealing with Birch's death. I don't know if it's because she loved him all those years ago or because he was murdered in her yard."

"Could be both."

"Either way, I need her back at the farm soon. I'm running out of different ways to prepare the vegetables." We passed a woman walking her Chihuahua, and I nodded a greeting. "Speaking of eating vegetables," I said, "Ashlee went on a date last night."

I realized that made no sense at the same time that Jason said, "What do vegetables have to do with Ashlee's date?"

"The guy's a vegetarian. That's not the interesting part, though. She was on a date with Ryan, the guy from the commune who's pushing for more technology."

Jason reached over and took my hand as we walked, interlacing his fingers with mine. "Don't tell me Ashlee has run out of guys to date in Blossom Valley and drove to the commune to find more."

I laughed. "She doesn't go through guys quite that fast. Ryan brought an animal into the vet clinic. I guess a few of the residents at the commune take their pets there, and Ashlee said they've been bouncing checks so much that her boss will only accept cash now. You were right about their iffy financial situation."

"Everyone I've talked to keeps mentioning it."

We reached a massive oak tree with an impossibly wide trunk. Whoever paved the walking trail had split the path in two to run on either side of the tree. We took the path on the right, circled the oak, and headed back toward my apartment.

"Did she tell you anything about Ryan?" he asked. "Like where he went to college?"

"Not that I recall. She just complained about his eating habits and how he lives on a commune. Which reminds me, I've been wondering how such a place handles its finances," I said. "Does everyone pay their own electric bill or do they donate a portion of their income? What if they don't have any income?"

"I've been asking those exact questions. Everyone pays a preset monthly amount, plus they're expected to contribute to the livelihood of the commune in some way. If they have no source of income or can't pay, then they have to provide extra labor to make up for that. Apparently Frank's contribution is that he handles the bill paying, taxes, and investing. He's been doing it for the last fifteen years, but the person I spoke to mumbled that he wouldn't be doing it much longer if he kept making mistakes."

The sky had darkened by this time, and I almost wished I'd brought a flashlight. I kept my eyes on the ground as I walked. "Any chance he's skimming off the top, and that's why the place is running into these cash flow problems?"

"Didn't sound like it. Rather, he's getting sloppy. I also don't know how much money the commune is bringing in, but you'd have to sell a lot of jams and honey to support such a large place."

We'd reached the stairs to my apartment, and I led the way up. Once inside, I shed my sweatshirt and draped it on the back of a kitchen chair.

"Care for coffee?" I asked. "I wasn't kidding about those cupcakes either."

"Coffee only, if it's not too much trouble."

"No trouble at all." I dumped the remnants of the morning's pot and made a fresh one.

As the machine started chugging away, I heard a key in the lock, and the front door swung inward. Ashlee stood in the doorway, clutching one broken high-heeled shoe in her hand. Half her hair was piled on top of her head, while the rest spilled down in a tangled mess. I could see twigs and leaves sticking out.

At the sight of her, my insides filled with panic. What had happened?

Chapter 18

My feet felt stuck to the kitchen floor as my mind took in Ashlee and her disheveled state. Out of the corner of my eye, I saw Jason rise from the couch. Before either of us could ask what happened, she spoke. "I've done it!"

"Done what?" Jason asked.

"Scared off that cat." She limped into the apartment on one heel, looking like a pirate with a too-short peg leg. She sat down in a kitchen chair, dropped her broken high heel on the floor, and slipped off the other one. "That stupid animal has been using my tire as a bathroom for weeks. The thing was even waiting for me when I pulled in a minute ago. But I freaked it out. There's no way he's coming back."

"You didn't hurt it, did you?" I asked.

"I wish. I threw my shoe at him, but he moved out of the way too fast."

"If all you did was throw your shoe, why are you such a wreck?" I plucked a leaf from one of her blond curls.

She reached up and felt around her hair, pulling out two twigs and another leaf. She dropped the foliage on the table. "When I missed the cat, I chased it all over the complex, even in the bushes, which wasn't easy with only one shoe, but now that dumb cat knows I mean business."

Somehow, I doubted the cat was all that frightened of a one-shoe Ashlee. A picture sprang to mind of her hobbling down the road, yelling at a cat she'd never catch. I tried to suppress my smile, but couldn't quite manage. I glanced at Jason as he sat down at the table and saw that he was trying not to smile, too.

Ashlee noticed our expressions. "I'd like to see you guys catch it," she growled.

"He's not using *my* car for his bathroom," I said. "Where were you tonight anyway? Seeing Ryan again?"

She wiggled out of her jacket without standing up and tossed it over the back of the couch. "No way. I still don't know if I'm going to bother with that guy again. Blossom Valley isn't exactly swamped with vegetarian restaurants, and I don't want to deal with the hassle of finding a place where we can both eat."

"I hear he lives at the Evergreen commune," Jason said.

"Yeah, that's another problem. What if things get serious and he wants me to live out there with him?" She patted the part of her hair that was still piled on top of her head. "I know it's hard to believe, but I don't always look good in tie-dye."

I managed not to roll my eyes as I filled two cups with coffee. I carried them over to the table and handed one to Jason. "I didn't think you wanted to get serious with anyone right now."

"I don't, but you should never say never. That's when fate comes and bites you in the butt."

My sister, the philosopher.

"I guess you don't have to worry about it, since Ryan hasn't called you for another date," I pointed out.

Ashlee stuck her tongue out at me.

"When you were on your date with Ryan, did he tell you anything about himself?" Jason asked.

Ashlee scooted her chair back and inspected the bottom of her foot, which was blackened by her run through the parking lot.

"What didn't he tell me? The guy talked about himself nonstop. All about his fancy IT job when he lived in San Francisco, how he got his degree in only three years at San Francisco State, blah, blah, blah." She put her foot back down.

Jason suddenly sat up straighter and leaned toward Ashlee. While I knew he wanted to find out information about Ryan, his reaction seemed more intense than her comment warranted. What had he found so interesting?

"You're sure he said SF State?" he asked.

"Pretty sure, although by that point, my eyes were starting to glaze over. I mean, get a clue, buddy. Everybody knows you don't do all the talking on the first date." She slapped her palm on the tabletop. "You know, the more I think about that date, the less I want to see Ryan again." She stood up. "Thanks for helping me make up my mind."

"No problem," I said.

She gave us a little wave and went into her room,

leaving her shoes on the floor and her jacket on the couch.

Once I heard her bedroom door shut, I asked Jason, "Why were you interested in Ryan's college background? You asked me about that earlier, too."

He drained the last of his coffee and set the cup down. "Someone else told me that Ryan attended SF State, but I can't find his name in their records. Could be a simple clerical error, but I like to know my facts when I'm working on a story."

"What story are you working on? Is it related to Birch's murder?"

"No. Your curiosity about the commune got me thinking other readers might have a similar interest. I thought I'd catch up with the people I originally interviewed to see how many are still there and how their lives have changed, if at all. I need to run the idea past my boss, but I was doing preliminary research and looked into Ryan's history while I was at it. For a guy who keeps promoting the wonders of modern technology, he's managed to keep a low online profile." He checked his phone. "It's time I got home."

I walked him to the door. "Thanks for helping with dinner tonight and being my taste test guinea pig."

"Anytime. I'm here to serve."

Though he was partly kidding, hearing those words gave me a fuzzy feeling in my chest, and I gave him a long kiss before he headed down the stairs to his car. I locked the door behind him and straightened up, leaving Ashlee's shoes and jacket for her to deal with in the morning. As I turned out the kitchen light and headed to the bedroom, I remembered that I'd forgotten to call Zennia to check on her. Oh well, my call would have to wait until tomorrow. I just hoped she was all right.

The next day flew by in a blur. I managed to feed everyone both breakfast and lunch without destroying the kitchen or poisoning any diners. The tofu stir-fry even earned rave reviews from two of the guests. I spent the rest of my time finessing a magazine ad, catching up on e-mails, and cleaning out the pigsty, an occasional chore that I'd managed to avoid since I'd started filling in for Zennia. Somehow I didn't think I should be cleaning up after the pigs in the middle of cooking for the guests.

By the time midafternoon rolled around, I was ready to call it quits for the day. I knew Gordon would be thrilled if I only worked eight hours and he didn't have to pay me overtime.

After updating my time card, I grabbed my purse and jacket and went out the kitchen door. I swung by the pigsty to pat Wilbur good-bye and then followed the path past the guest cabins. As I turned toward the vegetable garden, I heard a "yoo-hoo" coming from the spa tent. I looked over my shoulder and saw Esther waving at me.

I changed course and joined her at the entrance to the spa.

"Dana," she said, "Gretchen and I are experimenting with making scented soaps, and we can't agree on which scent we should pick. Gretchen swears the citrus smell is better, but I like the floral one. Would you help us out?"

"Sure, I have a minute." I followed her inside to find Gretchen at the hostess stand with two small blocks of soap before her.

She perked up when she saw me. "I'm glad you're here. We could use another opinion." She held up both blocks.

I sniffed the first one and caught a whiff of lemon, or maybe it was grapefruit. "That's nice," I said, and Gretchen smiled.

Esther grabbed the other block of soap from Gretchen and held it beneath my nose. "Try this one."

I'd barely inhaled when a heavy, cloying floral scent obliterated any other smells I might have detected. My great-aunt had worn a perfume that smelled like this, and I was instantly transported back to her afternoon teas, where I'd have to sit perfectly still in my frilly dress and Mary Janes, not daring to speak unless my aunt asked me questions, usually about school. I suppressed a shudder, not wanting to offend Esther.

I pointed to the lemon-scented soap. "Definitely the first one."

Esther looked so crestfallen that I patted her on the shoulder. "The floral one is nice, too," I lied, "but I think the citrus will have a more universal appeal. What's it for anyway?"

Esther's face brightened. "My composting classes have proven to be popular, and I thought we could add other ones. Gretchen volunteered to teach guests how to make the soaps."

"What a great idea," I said. When Esther first started holding classes on composting a few months back, I was hoping it might lead to more. Up until that point, she'd left almost all decisions related to the farm up to Gordon, choosing to take a backseat while he ran the place. I was thrilled to see her moving into a more active role. "How about you, Esther? Will you be hosting other classes? You're such a good teacher."

Her cheeks instantly turned pink at the praise. "I might, if I can find the right one."

"Or maybe Zennia could teach cooking classes when she returns," Gretchen said. "Has anyone heard from her lately?"

I shook my head. "I meant to call her yesterday but got sidetracked. Have you heard from her, Esther?"

She put a hand to her mouth. "For heaven's sake. I promised Gordon I'd bring Zennia her paycheck at lunchtime, and I plumb forgot. Now what am I going to do?"

"I'm heading home right now," I said. "I can stop by her place and drop it off."

"Would you mind?" Esther said. "I'm supposed to visit my friend in the hospital later today. They might be discharging her soon, which means I can get back to helping more here at the farm."

Gretchen grabbed the soap from the hostess stand and held it out. "Could you bring her this, too?"

I took the soap. "Maybe by now she's made a decision on when she's coming back." I didn't want to get my hopes up, but I had no clue what I'd be serving the guests for breakfast and lunch tomorrow. Or the next day, for that matter. The sooner she returned to work, the better for all of us.

"I hope it's soon," Esther said. She gave me a sheepish look. "Not that your cooking isn't wonderful, Dana, but every time I walk into the kitchen, I feel like we're missing a member of the family."

"I know exactly what you mean. If you'll give me her paycheck, I'll go see her right now."

Esther and I walked back to the house, where she retrieved Zennia's paycheck from the office. I slid it in my purse for safekeeping and headed out.

Being late afternoon, traffic on the highway was light, not that it was ever heavy, and I reached Zennia's house in minutes. A small, older-model compact sat in her driveway, so I parked on the street. As I got out of my car, I glanced at the house on the corner and saw the blinds slip back into place.

Feeling like I was now under scrutiny, I walked up Zennia's driveway. Someone, presumably the police, had removed the crime scene tape, and her yard was once more a haven for flowers, birds, and bees alike.

I rang the doorbell. While I listened to it chime inside, I wondered who the car in the driveway belonged to. I hoped I wasn't interrupting anything.

A moment later, Zennia answered, dressed in a floor-length housecoat. Bags hung under her eyes, but she smiled when she saw me.

"If I'd known I'd be this popular today, I would have gotten dressed."

I held out the soap. "Sorry I didn't call first. I was on my way home and wanted to drop this off from Gretchen. She's trying her hand at making scented soap."

Zennia took it and waved me inside. "You're always welcome here, especially considering all you've been doing for me lately."

I dug around in my purse and pulled out the envelope. "Before I forget, here's your paycheck, too."

She took it and closed the door behind me. "Payday already? I've lost all track of time."

"You need to meditate," said a voice from the direction of the wicker chairs. "Center yourself."

I jumped at the unexpected sound, belatedly remembering the car in the driveway.

Millie rose from one of the chairs and turned toward me. "A pleasure to see you again, dear heart."

"Um, you, too," I said.

Zennia gestured toward the other wicker chair. "Please, sit down. Millie and I were catching up."

"I don't want to interrupt," I said.

"Nonsense," Zennia said. "You might find this interesting. Millie was telling me about the changes at the commune in the last few months."

A frown crossed Millie's face. "And none of those changes are good. We've got a rat in our midst, sneaking around and gnawing at the very fabric of our community. And I'm getting ready to exterminate him."

I took the seat Zennia had pointed to, eager to hear more. Somehow, I just knew that rat was Ryan.

Chapter 19

Zennia chuckled at Millie's outburst. "Millie, you always have such a way with words."

Millie rose from her chair and stepped into the sunlight coming through the window. She jutted out her chin. "I speak the truth."

"I know you do," Zennia said. "That's what I love about you."

"Who's the rat you're trying to exterminate?" I asked.

Millie stepped closer and gestured for me to stand up. I did so, and she looped an arm around my elbow. "Come, let us walk around the garden."

I allowed her to lead me outside, curious to see if she would identify this rat by name. Zennia walked beside us, though I saw her step falter as we approached the lawn and the spot where she'd found Birch.

Millie noticed her hesitation, too. "Come, Zennia, you must face any lingering evil energy and vanquish it, so you can see the beauty once again."

"I'm trying." She moved ahead of us and stepped

onto the grass. She spread out her arms, as though walking on the grass wasn't a big deal, but I could see how tense she was. "There now, see?"

"The first step is the hardest," Millie said.

Zennia sank onto the nearby bench. "I think I'll take a moment to collect myself." She stared off into the distance.

Millie and I left her and continued walking along the edge of the lawn. I tried to keep my mind on the bright, colorful flowers, but my thoughts kept returning to Millie and the problems at the commune.

She stopped before a small cluster of flowers inside a stone circle. "What do you see here?"

I felt like I was back in school and the teacher was waiting for answers to a test I hadn't studied for. "Flowers?"

A slight shake of Millie's head indicated that I'd failed the test. She touched the petal of a large purple flower I didn't recognize. "And what do flowers represent?"

Not sure what she was looking for, I opted for multiple answers. "Nature? Life? Beauty?" One was bound to be correct.

This time, Millie nodded. "Right you are. All three. When I first joined the commune, almost thirty years ago, that's all anyone ever wanted. To embrace nature and live off the land. Of course we would occasionally sell our products to nearby farms and even a few shops in town, but we could take pride in our work. These were foods and goods that we crafted with our own hands." She held up her hands. Though they were gnarled and bony, they were obviously still strong. "We could see that people appreciated the fruits of our labor. Even when we moved to filling mail orders, there was still a personal touch. I could almost imagine the customers opening their boxes and smiling with joy as they took out a jar of honey that came from our bees." Her voice had been soft, almost musical as she spoke. Now a sharp edge cut through her next words. "Now these damn computers are here."

I'd grown up with computers and the Internet, and I'd always seen both as a convenient tool, a way to communicate and gather information faster than ever before. Still, I'd come across this attitude before and was ready to counter. "Won't computers make your job easier?" I asked. "You can fill more orders, keep track of shipments and payments, and have customer information all in one place."

Millie snapped her head around and gave me a look that made my insides wilt like the farm's lettuce at high summer noon. "We could do that before. These machines are too impersonal. You get no sense of who is placing the orders. I might as well work in a factory and spend my days in front of a conveyor belt."

"But having an online presence will increase your sales," I argued. "People from all over can order your jams and jellies. With the proper advertising, you can reach an entirely new set of customers. I can tell you from personal experience that having a Web site for Esther's farm has been invaluable. I doubt the farm would still be in business without our online advertising, not to mention our reservation system. People want things easy and fast these days. The commune could benefit from that."

Millie grimaced. "You sound like Ryan. I don't care about money. I care about a peaceful coexistence with nature without all this computer mumbo jumbo."

I watched a bee land on a nearby blossom. Perhaps it would collect pollen to take back to the hive. Or it might sting one of us. You never knew. "I'm not saying you should strip the land and dam up the streams. But I've heard about the money troubles at the commune, and the Internet could help rescue the place."

Millie crossed her arms, and her expression turned dark. "I knew Ryan was spreading rumors around town, but things aren't nearly as dire as he wants everyone to believe. Admittedly Frank made a few mistakes, but he's been keeping the books for years, and his work is usually impeccable."

"But you're behind on your property taxes. The government could seize your land."

"How do you know about that?" She went on before I could answer. "Besides, that's all nonsense. We have benefactors who will help us if it comes to that. I know enough people. Plus, we still bring in money at the farmers markets and selling goods to our regular customers through our catalog service. We'd have even more money if Ryan would stop pressuring everyone to upgrade our Internet service and buy a bunch of fancy new software.

We need that money for groceries, electricity, and other bills."

She'd worked herself into such a frenzy that I could hear her panting. She paused to catch her breath.

"I didn't mean to upset you," I said. "The financial situation of the commune is really none of my business. I just think that technology isn't always a bad thing. Sometimes it can be a lifesaver."

Millie waved her hand at me. "Bah. You've been brainwashed, like Birch was."

"Birch was in favor of Ryan's ideas?" Zennia asked from behind me. She must have abandoned her bench while Millie and I were talking.

"Does that surprise you?" I asked.

"Absolutely. The Birch I remember was as in tune with nature as Millie here. I can't imagine him wanting to use computers to sell his goods."

"You and Birch lived at the commune in the early nineties, right? That's around the time E-commerce was only getting started. Isn't it possible that Birch changed his mind, especially after running his own shop in Oregon?"

"I suppose anything's possible, but I find it hard to believe."

I wanted to remind Zennia that she barely knew Birch after twenty-five years, but that seemed insensitive considering the poor guy had just been murdered.

Millie spoke up. "I didn't want to believe it at first either, Zennia. I remembered Birch from when you two lived there, and he would have laughed if someone told him we'd be shipping our honey halfway across the world thanks to a little box with a keyboard. But Ryan has all his fancy ideas and college education. The moment Birch returned to Evergreen, Ryan started pressuring him to support his plans. He'd monopolize Birch's time every chance he got, running the numbers and talking about these Internet companies down in San Francisco and how they'd struck it big. Before I knew it, Birch was pushing for all these changes, too."

"What did everyone else have to say?" I asked. "Birch and Ryan didn't run the commune alone."

"No, but Birch influenced the older residents, and Ryan was working on the new kids."

"But you've been there much longer than Birch. People will listen to you, too."

"Perhaps," she said, but she still looked troubled. "Frank's another long-timer that's got a lot of pull, and I thought he was on my side. Now I'm not sure. We had a long talk last week about how we might slow Ryan down, but this morning he acted like he couldn't remember the conversation. That's not the first time either. Makes me wonder if Ryan's pulled him over to his side, and Frank doesn't have the guts to tell me."

"Frank doesn't strike me as a wimp," I said, remembering his confrontation with Detective Palmer the first time the two men met.

"He's usually not," Millie agreed, "but something's off-kilter, and I need him on my side. I'm convinced that Ryan and Birch had won over the majority and were planning a group vote. But now with Birch dead, there's a chance Ryan won't win."

I eyed Millie a little more closely. Sure, she looked like a wise grandmother who would use kind words and reason to voice her arguments, but she obviously felt the future of the commune was at stake. Was Birch dying so close to the group vote a coincidence? Or had Millie killed him so he couldn't sway the voters?

Chapter 20

Zennia's eyebrows came together. "When I was talking to Pearl at the commune, she didn't mention any of this tension. Made it sound like Evergreen was still just this side of heaven."

"Pearl pays attention to her knitting and the tea she constantly brings everyone. She ignores the political side of life," Millie said. "Speaking of Pearl, she found some old photographs that she thought you might like. They have both you and Birch in them, if I remember correctly."

Zennia looked down at Millie's empty hands as if the photos might be there. "You didn't bring them?"

"Pearl might keep herself in the dark about any political disturbances at the commune, but she's the resident worrier about all other things. She's convinced the pictures won't reach you unless she hands them over personally. She promised to keep them in a safe place until the next time she comes into town or you make it out her way."

"Maybe I'll run up to Evergreen tomorrow,"

Zennia said. "I don't have any photographs from my time at the commune, and I'd like to see them. Plus I didn't get a chance to talk to everyone when I was there last time."

I didn't even stop to think before I asked, "Can I come with you? I loved the behind-the-scenes peek when we were there, but I still don't feel like I know what an average day on a commune is like." Besides, didn't Jason say he was working on a follow-up story about the place? Maybe I'd find a human-interest angle he hadn't thought of. "If you don't mind waiting until the afternoon, that is," I added.

"I'd be thrilled to have company. Think we can leave around three?" At the mention of time, Zennia glanced at her watch, and her eyes widened. "Millie, I'd better hurry up and change, or we're going to be late." She turned to me. "You're welcome to join us, Dana. When Millie graced me with a surprise visit this afternoon, I called a few friends to see if they were available to meet for dinner."

"Thanks, but I'll have to pass," I said. "I still need to plan the menu for tomorrow's meals at the farm." Besides that, I was beat.

A worried expression appeared on Zennia's face. "I hope I haven't created too much extra work for you in my absence."

I felt a pang of guilt at complaining in front of Zennia. She was dealing with enough, although the fact that she was having dinner with friends was a promising sign. "It's no trouble," I said. "In fact, I made a rather tasty tofu stir-fry for lunch today. You'd be proud of me. One of the guests even left me a tip." A one-dollar tip, but still, I took it as recognition of my efforts.

Zennia's eyes sparkled. "Good for you, Dana. I knew there was a healthy cook lurking under all those cheese puffs and ice cream sundaes. Wait here a minute. I have a few recipes you might find useful." She dashed into the house, leaving me alone with Millie.

After the debate Millie and I had over technology's benefits and evils, I struggled to come up with more normal conversation. "Do the people at Evergreen have family in the area?" I finally asked. What I was wondering was where people would go if they couldn't live at the commune any longer, but I didn't dare say that to Millie.

She shrugged. "I can't speak for everyone, of course, but I have several nieces and nephews nearby, plus plenty of cousins. Birch had his sister, and Frank used to have a brother, though I believe he joined his creator a while back. Ryan has relatives in the Bay Area. With any luck, he'll leave the commune soon and go live with them."

I hadn't meant to get her back on the topic of Ryan, but luckily, Zennia emerged from the house before Millie could say more. She'd changed from her housecoat into a coral-colored ankle-length dress. She handed me a small stack of index cards. "That vegetarian chili recipe on top is fast and easy. I also included a breakfast casserole recipe and a few others for you as well." She grabbed my hand and leaned in. "I promise I'll come back to work as soon as I feel able. This second trip to Evergreen may bring my chakras into alignment."

"Take as long as you need. I'll manage." Now

why did I say that? I pulled my keys from my pocket. "Have fun at dinner."

I scanned the chili recipe as I walked down the driveway. Not only was it as simple as Zennia said, but it reminded me of the vegetable soup I'd made for yesterday's lunch. Like that recipe, most of the ingredients were growing in the farm's vegetable garden or stocked in the kitchen. And the breakfast casserole looked almost easier than scrambling eggs.

With a sense of relief at knowing what meals I needed to cook, I got in my car and drove home. I was in such a good mood that I didn't even mind that Ashlee had parked over the line, leaving me to squeeze out of my car. Someday she'd learn how to park. And drive, for that matter.

Humming to myself, I climbed the outside stairs and opened the door to the apartment. I immediately clapped my hands over my ears at the noise coming from the television.

Ashlee lowered the volume when she saw me. "Hey, sis, what's up?"

I lowered my hands, marveling that she wasn't deaf by now. "The usual," I said. I slipped off my shoes and placed them in the coat closet before shrugging out of my jacket. "Got any plans tonight?"

"Brittany's coming over. It's maintenance night," she said in a tone that implied I should know exactly what that meant, which, of course, I didn't.

"Remind me again what maintenance night is?"

She sighed. "I'm going to deep-condition my hair, redo my manicure, and exfoliate, all those extra details that I need to do to keep myself in shape. Making guys notice me doesn't happen by accident, you know." She gave me the once-over. "I'm surprised you got Jason, what with those patchy elbows."

I slapped my hands over my elbows. "I do not have patchy elbows." I rubbed my elbows to make sure the skin was smooth, annoyed with myself for nibbling at her bait like a trained seal. "I don't," I repeated.

"Maybe not today, but someday you're not going to be so lucky."

I sat down on the couch and picked up one of Ashlee's fashion magazines, briefly wondering if it contained an elbow exfoliation article. "I'll start worrying about my patchy elbows when they cause holes in my long-sleeved shirts."

"If Jason's still around by then."

"He's not exactly dating me for my elbows," I said.

"You'd be surprised. It's the little things that make or break a relationship."

Good grief, this conversation was going nowhere. I dropped the magazine back on the coffee table and wandered into the kitchen to see if anything was readily available to cook for dinner. I'd been so busy grocery shopping for the farm the last few days that I'd let my own food supply suffer. Luckily, a frozen meal of fried chicken, mashed potatoes, and a brownie waited for me in the freezer.

Five minutes later, I removed my dinner from the microwave and carried the tray and a fork over to the table. I took several bites and frowned. The fried chicken felt greasier than I remembered, and I was willing to bet these weren't real potatoes. Funny how I'd never noticed the fake flavor before. Was cooking at the farm starting to affect my taste buds?

I decided to text Jason while I ate to take my mind off my mediocre meal. I asked him if he needed any information while I was at the commune tomorrow afternoon, but he didn't have any suggestions. Undeterred, I promised to report back anything of interest.

The doorbell rang, and Ashlee answered it.

"Hey, Ash. Hey, Dana," Brittany said as she breezed in. She dropped her handbag on the kitchen table and started pulling out a collection of nail polish. "Ready to make yourself even hotter?" she asked Ashlee with a giggle. No matter how many times I saw Brittany, I could never get used to the giggling.

"How's it going, Brittany?" I asked.

"Awesome. Are you going to join us for maintenance night?" she asked.

Ashlee went through the bottles of polish. "I asked, but she said she's fine the way she is. No one ever kept a man that way."

Brittany openly studied me. "She doesn't look too bad. It's good to have confidence in yourself."

"Exactly," I said, not entirely sure if Brittany was complimenting me or not.

"Whatever." Ashlee set down the bottle of polish she'd been holding. "I'm just cranky because of that speeding ticket I got today."

"Could have been worse," Brittany said. "He could have seen you run that stop sign." She giggled again.

They moved over to the couch while I went to my room to read. After a couple of hours, my eyes started closing against my will, and I found myself reading the same paragraph over and over. I marked my place and switched off the light, already looking forward to my visit to the commune. I didn't know what might happen out there, but I had a feeling something would.

The next morning, I swung by the Meat and Potatoes market on my way to work, surprised at how familiar I was becoming with the vegetable aisle. The early morning produce clerk had even started addressing me by name.

Once my shopping was finished, I drove out to the farm, where I assembled the breakfast casserole and popped it in the oven. The timer dinged as the first diners sat down, and I was soon knee-deep in serving duties. Afterward, I cleared the dining room tables, put away the leftover food, and tackled the dishes. As I was wiping down the kitchen table, Gordon walked in, dressed in his usual suit and tie. His dark hair was slicked back and gleaming in the light.

He scanned the kitchen. "You seem to be getting more efficient with your cooking assignment while Zennia is away. Excellent work."

"Thanks." I pointed to the counter. "That still needs to be wiped down if you'd like to help."

His face remained impassive. "I wouldn't want to disrupt your system. I came in to ask if you'd care to be involved in a taste test."

I paused in my wiping. "What kind? Wine? Chocolate?"

"Of course not wine. I prefer the employees not

drink during work hours," he said with a pointed look, as if I kept a bottle of whiskey hidden away in a cupboard. "It's organic jam. I'm meeting a gentleman shortly who's interested in partnering with us. We would sell his jams and a few other products in the front lobby, and he'll give us a small cut of the proceeds. One more endeavor to keep this place afloat."

I straightened up. "Is the farm in trouble? I thought we were doing okay these last few months."

"We are, but every dollar counts when you're running a place this small, and I'd like to bolster our savings account for the leaner times of the year." He adjusted his watch. "Still, I'm not willing to compromise our reputation by peddling subpar goods, which is why I need help with the taste test."

"Sure, I'll help. Let me know when he gets here."

Gordon left me in the kitchen, and I got started on the counter. When I'd wiped up every last crumb, I stepped into the hall, intending to catch up on the farm's blog in the office. Before I could get there, however, Gordon appeared at the other end of the hall and gestured for me to join him.

I bypassed the office and entered the lobby, where I stopped short. Ryan stood at the counter, a collection of jars spread before him.

He gave me a quizzical look. "Hey. Ashlee's sister, right?"

"Right," I said, staring. Why on earth was Ryan touting the commune's jams and jellies here? What happened to his plan of taking over the world through online sales?

Gordon cleared his throat. "You two know each other?"

"He had a date with Ashlee a few nights ago," I said.

"I'm planning to call her," Ryan said hastily. "I've been busy. You know how it is."

Wasn't that every guy's excuse? "Sure" was all I said. I could have let him know Ashlee wasn't exactly waiting by the phone, but on behalf of all the girls out there who still were, I decided not to let him off the hook.

"This isn't going to affect your opinion of the jams, is it?" Gordon asked.

"I can still be impartial," I said, but I saw Ryan's Adam's apple bob up and down, as if he was nervous.

"Excellent. Gretchen is seeing to a client right now, but let me find Esther and solicit her opinion as well. One moment." He headed for the stairs, which led to Esther's bedroom and sitting room on the second floor, leaving me alone with Ryan.

Ryan busied himself with straightening the jars.

"I'm surprised someone else from the commune isn't handling this," I said. "I heard you were interested in ramping up the online sales side."

Ryan pushed his glasses back with a finger. "Few of the residents at the commune have any business sense. I know for a fact that the future of the commune lies in online sales, but we still have a lot of work ahead of us. While I get that side up and running, I'm exploring other ways to drum up business. We're even planning a booth at the fair this weekend."

"Is the commune in that much trouble? The

place has managed to support itself for decades,"
I said.

He started to roll his eyes but caught himself.
"The majority of regular customers have been
buying from us since the commune opened, but
they're starting to die off, and we're having trouble
attracting new customers. At the same time, costs
continue to climb, and every one of those buildings needs major improvements. We can't survive on what we sell at the farmers markets and
that mail-order business, no matter what the old-
timers say."

I heard the floor creak upstairs and knew my
time was about up. I hurried on. "I notice you say
'we' a lot. For someone who's only lived at the commune a short while, you've really put yourself in
the middle of things. How do the long-term residents feel about the way you seem to be taking
over?"

His jaw tensed, and I wondered if he'd let something slip in his anger, but as I'd feared, Esther
and Gordon came downstairs right then, saving
Ryan from having to defend himself. He brushed
past me and stepped over to Esther, his attention
on her.

"I'm Ryan. It's a pleasure to meet you." He shook
Esther's hand. "I've brought all of our top sellers
today for you to try. Blackberry preserves, lemon
curd, clover honey . . ." His voice trailed off.

"It all sounds delicious. I think this is a wonderful idea to sell your jams and whatnot here."

"How about we try them first?" Gordon said.

Ryan moved back to the counter and pulled out

a plate and a box of organic nine-grain crackers from a tote bag. I noticed he managed to look everywhere but at me.

While we watched, he opened the box, unscrewed the lid on a jar, and spread the contents on the crackers. He arranged everything on the plate and passed it around. We each took a cracker.

I ate my portion, savoring the sweet blackberry flavor. Esther ate her bite and proceeded to lick each finger, which I took as a sign she liked the jam as well. Even Gordon managed to say, "Not bad." Next, we sampled the honey, followed by the lemon curd.

"I like everything I've tried," I told Ryan and Gordon. "I might even buy the lemon curd for myself, although I have no idea what to do with it."

"Put it on breakfast items, like pancakes, scones, or blueberry muffins," Ryan said, finally making eye contact, though his gaze instantly dropped.

"I always like to fill those premade tart shells with the curd," Esther said. "It makes an easy dessert."

Gordon went behind the counter, reached down, and came up with his clipboard. "If everyone's finished comparing recipes, Ryan and I have business that needs attending to. Esther, it might be a good idea if you stayed as well to finalize the details."

I guessed that meant I wasn't welcome. I'd been hoping to ask Ryan more questions, but maybe I'd luck out and he'd be at the commune when Zennia and I stopped by later.

"If you don't need me, I'll be in the office," I said.

"Thanks for your help, Dana," Esther said.

I went into the office and caught up on correspondence before I returned to the kitchen to prepare lunch. Zennia's vegetarian chili recipe took no time at all to make and even less time to clean up. Before I knew it, three o'clock arrived. I updated my time card, gathered my belongings, and walked to my car.

A few minutes later, I pulled into Zennia's driveway, where she was already waiting, purse in hand. I'd barely managed to slow to a stop before she pulled open the passenger door and got in.

She shut the door and turned to me, breathless. "I dreamed about Birch last night."

What could have been in this dream that had her so excited? "What was it about?"

"Birch came to visit me in the garden and assured me that he's at peace now. He said I should look toward healing and stop dwelling on his death."

I put the car in reverse and backed out of the driveway while she clicked her seat belt into place. "Birch is right, you know," I said, feeling slightly silly for agreeing with a dead man, and one in a dream, no less.

Zennia patted my knee. "I told you this second trip to the commune is exactly what my heart needs. This dream confirms it." She looked so earnest that I could only nod in agreement.

Then I crossed my fingers and prayed that Zennia wouldn't be disappointed.

Chapter 21

Since Zennia had driven to the commune on our last trip, I offered to drive this time. As we drove past the Mighty Eagle Casino, I wondered if Olive was working today or if management had found an excuse to fire her and the other older workers, like she'd been worried about the other day at the spa.

After the series of twists and turns and narrowing roads, I drove across the small bridge and pulled into the commune's parking area. Off in the meadow, I could see half a dozen children playing, but I didn't see any grown-ups working in the rows of vegetables on the other side of the barn.

The doors of the low-slung building stood open. As I got out of the car, I could hear loud voices coming from inside.

I nodded toward the building. "Sounds like people are riled up in there. Sure you want to interrupt?"

She tilted her head, considering. "Let's at least take a peek to see if Pearl's in there."

Wondering what awaited us, I entered with Zennia right behind me. The room was packed. All the seats at the round tables were occupied, and more people were standing along the walls. Everyone seemed to be speaking at once, while Frank stood on the small stage and tried to quiet down the crowd. Even from across the room, I could see the sweat circles under his arms. Looking around at the angry faces, I didn't envy his position.

"Hey," he shouted, "we're not going to accomplish anything at this rate. You have to pipe down."

The noise level dropped a smidge. I heard a voice shout from the side. "I didn't move here to be a computer start-up like in Silicon Valley. I came to live off the grid."

A man near me, wearing a plaid flannel shirt and dirty jeans, raised his own voice in counterpoint. "We need to make more money. We have bills to pay, mouths to feed."

A few "yeahs" followed his remarks, and then the crowd broke into an uproar. Frank placed his fingers in his mouth and let out a shrill whistle that brought silence to the room.

"You all know majority rules here," he said. "Let's stop talking and start voting." A few angry murmurs rippled through the crowd, and Frank waited a moment until there was quiet. "Everyone in favor of Ryan's online sales plans, raise your hand." A young woman near the front put hers up, and the people on either side of her did the same.

As hands rose around the room, I tried to take a quick count, but Frank spoke again before I'd had a chance to finish.

"Those opposed," he said.

All the hands that were up lowered, while others rose. I couldn't be sure, but the two sides appeared evenly split. Based on the way his shoulders slumped, Frank seemed to agree with me. "That didn't help," he said.

"We need a leader," an older woman in a peasant top shouted. "If Birch was here, he'd know what to do." More voices backed up her statement.

"Well, Birch isn't here," Frank said, pacing around the front of the small stage. "We need to figure this out on our own. I want everyone to go back to their cabins and think about what's best for the commune. We'll meet here again tomorrow night and conduct a written vote to make sure everyone is counted. Be here at seven."

He stepped down from the stage, and conversation broke out throughout the room once more. Zennia and I stayed against the wall while most of the assembly filed out. A few people were arguing, while others were whispering to one another.

At the table closest to where I stood, a pair of older women were sitting and talking in low, urgent voices.

". . . don't know if I can still live here," I heard one woman say.

"But where can we go?" was the other's reply.

When the departing crowd slowed to a trickle, I leaned toward Zennia. "Did you spot Pearl?"

Zennia shook her head. "I was keeping a close eye on everyone as they left. She must not have been at the meeting. Remember what Millie said about how she avoids politics?"

"True. Any idea where she might be?" I scanned

the remaining members, but Pearl wasn't among them.

"I think that's her car in the parking lot, the one with the I LOVE TEA bumper sticker. Perhaps she's in her cabin. We'll have to ask someone where that is."

Millie suddenly appeared at Zennia's elbow. "Ask what?"

"Where Pearl lives," Zennia said. "I want to see if she has the photos."

"I told her you might be stopping by," Millie said. "She's in the old Stewart cabin toward the back of the property. I'd go with you, but I want to talk to Frank about this vote tomorrow night."

"That's all right. I think I remember the way," Zennia said.

She and I exited to the brick patio out back and were greeted by a gust of wind. I clasped my upper arms at the sudden chill. "I should have brought my jacket."

"The wind will die down once we're among the trees."

Together, we trudged across the open field. A white butterfly flitted along with us for a short while before veering off and fluttering away.

"I wonder how the vote will turn out," I said. "Everyone seems to have such strong feelings about it. Most likely half the people here aren't going to be happy with the outcome."

"They'll have to make peace with what the majority decides," Zennia said. "I wouldn't be surprised if a few abandon the commune when the vote doesn't go their way, but most will stay."

"Where will the others go?" I asked.

"Wherever fate takes them. Perhaps to another commune. There are several up north."

We reached the low slope that led to the quilting house, as I liked to call it. Zennia led the way around the building. She picked a path that eventually took us to a small meadow filled with beehives. I could hear the buzzing of the bees and kept an eye out for any errant members who might fly my way, but we reached the other side without incident.

Here, three new paths branched off from the edge of the meadow, but Zennia picked one without hesitation, and we continued on. As we walked, the woods became denser. The closeness of the trees, with their thick and tall trunks, almost blocked out all sunlight, creating an atmosphere similar to dusk. The smell of dust and decaying wood filled the air.

"Can you imagine walking back to your cabin at night?" I said. "It must be unbelievably dark, even on nights with a full moon. What about wild animals?" My voice trembled, and I coughed to cover the sound.

"There might be a few, like mountain lions or the occasional bear," Zennia said. As she spoke, she stepped in a small depression in the dirt, and I saw her foot wobble. "But I'd be more worried about twisting my ankle."

"Good point, especially for people of Pearl's age."

After a few more minutes, we came upon a small cabin almost hidden among the trees. Beyond the cabin, I saw a tiny building that was probably an outhouse. It even had a crescent moon cutout in the narrow door. Right then, I knew I'd never live on a commune, unless they could guarantee me a cabin with indoor plumbing.

I climbed the two steps up to the porch and knocked on the door. All I heard in response was silence. The place was small enough that Pearl should have answered within seconds if she was home. Turning to Zennia, I said, "Looks like she's out."

She glanced around at the enormous trees that kept the area dark and gloomy. "I guess we could wait," she said doubtfully. "Although if she's working on a sewing project, she might not be back until after supper. Let's start at the building where everyone does their sewing and the barn after that. I don't know why we didn't check those places first and save ourselves the trip out here."

We followed the path back to the bees. A rustling sound came from my right, and I peered into the thick bushes filling the nearby landscape but didn't see anything. It was probably a squirrel or a bird, but I still remembered how Frank had surprised me the last time I'd wandered into the woods.

We emerged from the canopy of trees and into the bee meadow. Sunlight streamed down on me, and I squinted at the sudden brightness.

"What a difference," I said.

"I don't remember that cabin being in such a dark location," Zennia said, "but I'm sure the trees have grown in the last twenty-five years."

When we reached the quilting house, I went up the steps and opened the door without knocking. Pearl sat inside by herself, sewing. She jerked her needle with a start when she saw us.

"Goodness, I wasn't expecting anyone," she said. "I thought everyone was at the meeting."

"I hope we didn't startle you," Zennia said as she moved past me and into the room. "Millie told me you found some old photographs that I might like."

Pearl reached in her sewing bag and pulled out a wrinkled brown envelope. "I knew you'd want to see them. Millie said you might stop by today, and I've been carrying them around with me." She handed the envelope to Zennia. "Can I get you any tea while you look at them?"

What was this woman's obsession with tea?

"No, thank you," Zennia said as she sat in the nearest chair. I noticed her hands were trembling as she lifted the flap and pulled out the photos. I took a seat next to her and waited while she went through the stack. Occasionally, she would run her finger along one of the images, as if she could touch the people in the picture.

She held one up. "This was when Birch and I first arrived here." The photo showed a much younger Zennia, with her long hair hanging well past her waist. She wore a short summer dress and cowboy boots. Though I'd only met him once, I easily recognized Birch as the man with her. He looked exactly the same, only with darker hair. He even sported the beard. Zennia was laughing and gazing at Birch with obvious adoration.

"You both seem so happy," I said.

"Best time of my life. Looking at this photo, I can't imagine why I ever left."

She continued through the pile, passing each photo to me as she finished with it. When she handed me the last one, she closed her eyes for a long moment. When she opened them, I could see tears pooling in the corners of her eyes. "Poor Birch," was all she said.

Pearl murmured in agreement from where she sat, still sewing.

A loud clanging noise interrupted the quiet, and I looked questioningly at Pearl.

"Supper bell," she said. "Won't you join us?"

Zennia laid a hand on my arm. "Could we, Dana? I'd love to see who else will be there."

My stomach clenched at the thought of what might pass for dinner here. Pine needle soup? Dandelion salad? But I'd survived plenty of Zennia's healthy fare. Eating one meal at the commune wouldn't kill me.

"Sure. Why not?" I said.

I put the photos back into the envelope and gave it to Zennia. Together, the three of us left the quilting house and walked down to the main building. I noticed that Zennia carried herself straighter, and her step seemed lighter. Perhaps this trip to the commune had helped her after all. Maybe she'd found that inner peace she'd been searching for.

And on a selfish note, maybe she was one step closer to returning to her position as the farm's cook.

We reached the building, crossed the brick patio, and entered the main room. The place was crowded but quiet, as if people were tiptoeing around the topic of online sales. The aroma of spices filled the air, and I felt a pang of hunger.

Whatever we were having couldn't be all bad if it smelled this good.

A small group waited for their turn at the buffet table, and Zennia, Pearl, and I got in line. When I reached the front, I grabbed a plate and silverware and scooped up what looked to be stew with brown rice. When we'd all loaded our plates, Zennia led the way to a mostly empty table. I picked a chair and Pearl sat next to me, with Zennia on the other side of her.

I was halfway through my plate full of food, which was surprisingly tasty, when Frank sat down in the adjoining chair with a thud. He gave me a curt nod that didn't invite conversation before he began shoveling food into his mouth. He chewed with his mouth open, and I turned slightly away, tuning into what Pearl was saying.

"You can't imagine the amount of change," she told Zennia. "I pictured my golden years quilting and enjoying the great outdoors. You and Dana must feel the same way, what with you both working at an organic farm. But if Ryan gets his way, we'll all have to work shifts filling orders. I'm not cut out for that kind of life."

A woman I hadn't met leaned across Zennia toward Pearl. "You know the rules. Everyone has to contribute or else they get kicked out."

I wondered how the less tech-savvy members of the group would be affected if Ryan's changes were implemented. Surely there were plenty of other ways to help at the commune. "Has that always been the rule?" I asked.

The woman nodded emphatically. "Since the beginning. Everyone has to help out, no matter how little. We kicked out a member a few years ago, because he wasn't pulling his weight. What was his name? George?"

Frank started coughing. The woman offered him her water, but he waved her offer away.

His coughing subsided, and the woman said, "Anyway, you need structure and organization. Otherwise the whole plan falls apart. Ever read *Lord of the Flies*?"

"No, but I've heard a bit about it."

"Same thing. Bunch of kids get stranded on an island with no adults and no guidance. Oh sure, everything's swell in the beginning, but soon after, the group splinters, and what little organization they have collapses, leading to tragedy."

"But that book's fiction," I said, slightly alarmed at her grim picture of the future.

"Yes, but it's based on human behavior." She tapped her temple. "I know this commune can't stay together if we allow ourselves to split like those kids on that island. We need to make a decision, and everyone who stays needs to accept and embrace it."

Pearl shoved her plate away. "I don't know if that can happen. I'm worried."

Zennia patted her hand. I glanced over and saw Frank eyeing the four of us. I wasn't sure if he was listening to the conversation, but if he was, he didn't join in.

He scooped up another forkful of stew, but then let it fall back on his plate. The fork made a clanking sound as it hit the side of the dish. Several diced vegetables spilled off, but Frank didn't seem to notice. I followed his gaze toward the other side of the room and almost dropped my own fork.

Detective Palmer stood at the door. He surveyed the occupants one by one, clearly looking for someone in particular.

"What's he doing here?" Frank growled.

Good question.

Chapter 22

I sensed a ripple effect as people became aware of the detective's arrival. First, the ones closest to the door stopped talking, followed by the tables farther in. As those diners quieted down, others on my side of the room noticed the change until eventually everyone was staring at Detective Palmer. He must have visited the commune on a previous occasion, because they all seemed to know who he was.

He gave a bemused smile. "Now that I have everyone's attention, I need to speak with a few of you in private." He consulted a piece of paper in his hand. "Frank Hamilton, I'll start with you." An audible sigh of relief seemed to rise up from the diners.

Frank let out an expletive under his breath, rose from his place at the table, and threw down his napkin. He crossed the now-silent room to join the detective while everyone else watched his progress. Detective Palmer said a few words to him, and they made their way toward the hall. I assumed they were heading to the office where Zennia and I had spoken to Frank on our first visit.

As soon as they went out the door, the room erupted into loud talking.

At my table, Pearl laid a hand on her chest. "Phew, I'm glad he didn't call my name."

"I wonder who else is on his list besides Frank," I said.

She fanned her face, as if she might faint. "Not me, I hope. I couldn't possibly handle a real-life police detective asking me questions. Besides, I don't know anything."

"You'd be surprised how much people know without realizing it."

Pearl didn't reply. I looked around the room and noticed Ryan come in the door. He headed straight to the buffet table, where he filled his plate. He scanned the nearby tables, most likely for an empty seat. When his gaze landed on our table, I gave a small wave. He lifted his chin in acknowledgment but looked longingly at an empty chair at the next table, where two children were squabbling over a spoon.

I wasn't sure if Ryan was more worried that I might harass him about not calling Ashlee or that I might ask him questions about his increasing role at the commune. Either way, he must have decided that facing me was easier than dealing with the kids, because he headed over to my table.

The moment Ryan set his plate down next to Frank's empty spot, a woman across the table glared at him, grabbed her own plate with its half-eaten meal, and stalked away. I could guess which side of the online sales fight she was on.

I saw a flush creep up Ryan's neck. "I'm starting to feel like a social pariah these days," he said.

"Some residents obviously feel strongly about keeping the commune in its current state," I said.

Ryan's phone chimed. He tapped a few buttons but kept talking. "What state is that? Broke? If we're going to survive, they need to accept the change and move forward."

"Change is hard. A lot of people find it unsettling," I said. "If that weren't bad enough, having the detective here is only reminding everyone of Birch's death."

Ryan's head whipped up, and his eyes searched the room. "The detective is here? Now?"

I'd swear I heard a tremor in his voice and wondered at the sudden anxiety. Was there something Ryan didn't want Detective Palmer to know?

"He's talking to Frank, but I think he had a list of people to speak with."

Ryan's phone chimed again. He read the screen, and then said to me, "I don't know if I have time to talk to the good detective. I'm a busy guy." As if to prove his point, he picked up his phone and began texting. After a moment, he put his phone down and checked around his plate. "Forgot my fork."

He walked away, and I heard the now-familiar chime coming from his phone, which lay on the table. I looked at Ryan's retreating back. He wasn't even halfway to the silverware caddy. Beside me, Pearl and Zennia were deep in conversation with the *Lord of the Flies* lady and paying no attention to me.

Without giving it another thought, I shifted over to Frank's vacant chair and stretched my neck until I could read the screen on Ryan's phone. The message said, Count me in. It's going to be huge. I'll take the first available cabin.

My head swirled with questions. Was whoever had sent the text talking about a cabin here at the commune? How could Ryan secure one when he was such a newbie? And what was going to be huge?

I reached for the phone to scroll up to the previous messages, but just then, I sensed someone moving closer to me. I glanced up to find Ryan glaring down.

Oops.

I moved back to my own seat and pointed at the phone. "It kept chiming. I thought the message might be important." Not the best excuse, but it'd have to do.

Ryan snatched up the phone to read the screen, and I'd swear he paled a little. He placed the phone facedown on the table and muttered, "Everything's fine." He sat down and took a bite of stew, not looking at me as he ate.

I turned toward Pearl and Zennia and was surprised to see that Pearl was now alone. "Where's Zennia?"

She motioned to a corner of the room. "Over there. I think she knows someone."

Across the room, Zennia was surrounded by five or six people I didn't recognize. She was talking and waving her hands, more animated than I'd seen her in days.

"I think those photos really helped," I said.

Pearl beamed, reminding me of Esther when anyone praised her. "It was pure luck that I uncovered them. I've been collecting old photos for years with the idea that I'd make a giant scrapbook to record the commune's history, but I've never gotten around to it. I was digging around for an old tea set when I came across a shoebox with the photos. That one where they're rowing across the pond is my absolute favorite."

I searched my memory. "I don't think she showed me that picture."

"It's absolutely adorable. I hope I didn't . . ." Pearl pressed her hand to her cheek. "Oh no, I forgot to bring it. I must have left it on the desk somehow when I was putting the others in the envelope. I'm such a dumb bunny."

The last sentence flew out of her mouth so casually that I knew she must berate herself on a regular basis. "It could happen to anyone. You can get the photograph now, can't you?"

"I suppose. Only with my arthritis, it's becoming such a burden to walk to my cabin. When I moved in all those years ago, I absolutely loved the place, with its seclusion and immersion in nature. But I may need to move to a cabin closer to this building, with all the trouble I've had walking lately." She bit her lip. "Do you think it would be all right if I gave Zennia the picture the next time she's out here? I know she would love to have it."

"I'm not sure if she's coming back. Besides, it seems like a waste not to get it now when we're already here." I looked back at Zennia, who was still talking. These photos could be that final bit of closure she needed. "I can get it. I know where your cabin is, and it shouldn't take me more than fifteen minutes to get there and back."

"I couldn't ask you to go to all that trouble. I'm the nincompoop who forgot it."

"I don't mind. You say it's on the desk? Do I need a key?"

Pearl shook her head. "Heavens, no. I never bother to lock up."

"All right. I'll be back shortly. Do me a favor and let Zennia know where I've gone. I don't want her to worry." I grabbed my empty plate and silverware and carried them over to the pass-through window where stacks of dirty dinner dishes waited. I glanced back at Pearl on my way out the door. She was poking at her food and frowning, probably giving herself a mental lecture for forgetting the photo. Nearby, Ryan had finished eating and was standing up, plate in hand. I headed out the door.

The temperature outside was considerably cooler than inside the main hall. The breeze hadn't died down any, and I wished once more that I'd thought to bring a jacket. Maybe the walk to Pearl's cabin and back would warm me up.

I started across the field at a quick pace, noticing how the sun was much lower in the sky now. The barn where they stored all the jams, quilts, and other goods the commune members sold cast a long shadow across the meadow. When I reached the other side, I hurried up the small slope and turned toward the beehives. The area was eerily quiet.

At the fork in the trail, I paused. Which one had we taken before? The middle one or the one next to it? With Zennia leading the way, I hadn't paid much attention. Now, in the dim light of dusk, the paths all looked the same.

I considered going back to ask Pearl, but that would waste a lot of time, and the woods would only be getting darker. I decided to forge ahead. If nothing seemed familiar, I'd know that I'd picked the wrong trail. Besides, they all probably met up near the same place. I'd be able to spot Pearl's cabin easily.

I picked the middle trail and started down the path, noticing how much darker it was here among the trees. Why hadn't I thought to ask for a flashlight before I'd so gallantly volunteered to retrieve the photo? At least I had a flashlight app on my phone.

Pulling my phone from my pocket, I opened the app. Instantly, the surrounding trees and ground lit up under the glare. I resumed my errand.

The ground beneath my feet was bumpy, and I had to keep my phone and my eyes trained downward, while glancing up now and again to see where I was going. After a few minutes, I admitted to myself that I didn't recognize anything. Surely I would have remembered that fallen tree leaning against that redwood, wouldn't I?

Quickening my pace, I doubled back to the start and picked another path, positive it was the correct one this time.

A noise in the bushes made me gasp, and I swung the beam of my phone in that direction. I heard what sounded like a small animal scamper away, probably more scared of me than I was of it.

Zennia told me there were most likely no dangerous animals to worry about in these woods.

Still, what if she was mistaken?

I resumed walking and ducked under a low-hanging branch that covered the path. I immediately stopped. I definitely hadn't encountered this branch on the way to Pearl's cabin earlier.

With a sigh, I retraced my steps back to the start. At any rate, only one path remained. It had to be the correct one.

A little less confident and a lot more spooked, I headed out, shivering as a bird flew overhead and let out a screech. As I trudged along, following the trail before me, doubt crept in my shoes and crawled up my legs. Had it taken Zennia and me this long to reach the cabin before? Had we walked by this massive tree that blocked out the rapidly dwindling light?

Just as I was thinking about going back to the dining hall empty-handed, I spotted Pearl's cabin up ahead. Relief made my fingers and toes tingle as I practically skipped to the porch. I bounded up the steps and turned the knob.

As promised, the door was unlocked. A gust of icy wind swept up the porch behind me, and I quickly went in, closing the door.

The inside of the cabin was pitch-black. I kept a firm grip on my phone as I used it to look around the room. A desk sat next to the door, and I spotted the photograph sitting on top. I picked it up. Pearl was right to declare it her favorite. Zennia sat in one end of a rowboat, holding an umbrella, while Birch rowed from the other end. The pond was covered in lily pads, and the whole scene looked like a painting.

A soft thump outside made me freeze. It sounded like a footstep on one of the porch risers. Maybe Pearl had noticed how long I'd been gone and decided to come out here after all.

"Hello?" I called out. My voice squeaked, and I cleared my throat. "Pearl? Is that you?"

Silence.

"Pearl?" I called a little louder.

My heart raced. I could almost sense a presence on the other side of the door, waiting.

The seconds ticked by, while I held my breath. When I didn't hear anything more, I started to wonder if I'd imagined the sound. God knew I let my imagination run wild at the worst times.

I closed the flashlight app on my phone. The blackness was immediate, save for the tiny dots of light as my eyes adjusted to the dark. I strained to hear, but was only met with more silence. I inched over to the door, eased it open, and peered out.

Nothing but trees. The steps were clear, and the porch was empty. Whatever had made that noise was long gone. Much like I wanted to be.

I carefully slid the photo into my jeans pocket and pulled the door shut. With a last look around the porch, I trotted down the steps and hurried over to the path, which was barely discernible now. I started to work myself up to a jog, knowing I'd been gone way too long. It was a slow jog, though, since I could barely see and didn't want to risk falling down and spraining an ankle. Then I might be stuck in these woods all night, unless Pearl came looking for me. I forced myself to slow to a brisk walk, my gaze glued to the path.

I heard a sound off in the trees. For a half second, I almost stopped, but I told myself it was a little rabbit, no scarier than Peter Cottontail himself. I didn't have time to entertain more crazy ideas if I wanted to reach the main building before the sky was completely dark.

Another sound, this one of snapping twigs, did make me halt. Unless that rabbit was exceptionally large, the noise I heard wasn't coming from a rabbit. I was suddenly aware of how alone I was out here. How close was I to the bees in the meadow? How much time had passed since I'd left Pearl?

A crunch came from almost directly behind me, like someone stepping on a pile of twigs and leaves. A shard of fear pierced my heart. Maybe I wasn't as alone as I thought.

I started to run.

Chapter 23

I careened down the path, half blind with terror. Crashing sounds came from behind me, and I realized that for once, my overactive imagination wasn't to blame. Someone *was* chasing me through the woods.

I glanced behind me as I ran, but all I could see were trees. I turned my attention to what was in front of me. Surely I was close to the end of the path by now.

The tip of a branch smacked me on the cheek with a sharp sting. I sensed the path growing narrower, but that couldn't be right. Had I wandered off the main trail?

The pressure in my chest grew as I blundered ahead, knocking branches out of the way. Twigs clawed at my arms and tried to hold me back.

When my lungs felt like they might explode, I stopped. I strained to listen, but the only sound I could hear was my own gasping. I struggled to breathe deeper and slower, knowing I needed to steady myself before I could run again.

Finally, my breathing started to return to normal. I took a moment to listen again, but the woods were now silent. Maybe whoever was after me had lost track and given up.

Even so, I didn't know where I was. I needed to find the main building, or a cabin, or anything else that might help me figure out my location. With my ears at the ready for any suspicious sounds, I started walking in what I hoped was the right direction.

Far off to my left, I heard a shout that sent what felt like an electric current through my chest.

Someone was still out there.

I started to trot in the opposite direction from the sound. Could I find my way back to Pearl's cabin?

Another shout.

I must have been hallucinating, because this time, I recognized my name. There it came again. A man was definitely yelling, "Dana!"

I opened my mouth to holler back, but snapped it shut before I did.

What if the guy calling my name was the same person who was following me? Maybe he was trying to trick me into revealing my position. How did I know if he was one of the good guys or not?

With my feet rooted to the forest floor, I was torn between yelling out in the hopes of being rescued and staying mum until I knew for sure who was doing the rescuing. My heart thudded as I heard the yelling grow louder. Surely my stalker wouldn't risk exposure by making so much noise.

Another shout sounded. Unless my panic was affecting my hearing, this time, someone else was yelling.

I needed to take a chance and expose my location if I wanted to get out of these woods. I sucked in a lungful of air to steel myself and practically screamed, "I'm here!"

Behind me, in the opposite direction of the voice, pine needles crunched. I whipped my head around, but couldn't see anything. Maybe my yelling hadn't been such a good idea.

I took three steps to the side, trying not to make a sound while I cursed my impatience. I should have waited until I knew for sure who was searching for me. Now I was about to be found, and possibly by the one person who I didn't want to find me.

Hoping to blend in with the shadows, I pressed my back against the trunk of a large redwood. Inch by inch, I sidled around to the other side of the tree, ready to bolt if anyone tried to grab me.

Instead, a beam of light shined straight into my eyes, blinding me. I threw up my arms, flailing at the source of the light. My hand banged into something, and the object fell to the dirt with a thunk. I looked down to find a flashlight at my feet.

"What the hell are you doing?" a man asked.

"Detective Palmer?"

I was so relieved to recognize his voice that it was all I could do not to throw my arms around him and squeeze him with all my might. Luckily, my self-control kicked in before I could embarrass myself.

Detective Palmer stooped and picked up the flashlight, which was still working. He kept it pointed at the ground. "Are you all right? What happened?"

Puffing, I said, "I went to Pearl's cabin to pick up a photograph for Zennia. When I was leaving, I heard someone following me, and I took off. I must have hooked up with another path and gotten lost. I was trying to find my way back when I heard you calling my name." I tried to suck in more air after all that rambling.

"You were followed?" He shone the flashlight around, but the light only picked up the vast tree trunks. The sounds I'd heard earlier were long gone.

I heard another shout, and Detective Palmer yelled, "Over here." To me, he said, "Why would anyone be following you?"

"Your guess is as good as mine. All I know is that when I went inside Pearl's cabin, I heard footsteps on the stairs. I ran away as fast as I could."

"Did you see anyone?"

Great, I knew he was going to ask me that. "Well, no."

"Any chance you imagined the footsteps?"

I felt anger flare up in response to the doubt in his voice. "No. I was chased. I could hear them running through the brush behind me."

"More likely, you heard one of us out searching for you."

I looked around. For the first time, I noticed

several flashlight beams flickering through the woods. "Is that who I heard calling my name?"

"When I went to interview Pearl," Detective Palmer said, "she told me she was worried about how long you'd been gone. A bunch of us in the dining hall grabbed flashlights and went out looking for you. You must have heard one of the searchers and thought you were being followed."

I wasn't ready for Detective Palmer to dismiss my fears so easily. This time, I spoke slowly for emphasis, as if that might help convince him I wasn't being paranoid. "I heard someone outside Pearl's cabin. When I called out, they didn't answer. Then, when I started down the trail, I heard them behind me." Even in the dim light from the flashlight, I could see Detective Palmer get ready to speak, and I hurried on. "If it was a member of the search party, why wouldn't they call out and let me know they were there?"

Before he could answer, a light popped into view from behind a tree, and Millie stepped up next to me. "I wonder if it was me you heard. I was following a small track that a deer has made in recent weeks. I thought you might have stumbled upon the same path. I followed it in hopes of finding you."

The answer sounded logical enough, but in my gut, I knew someone had been coming after me. Only the yells of the search party had scared them away.

I felt like explaining this to Millie and Detective Palmer, but I could tell they were happy to believe that I'd gotten disoriented in the dark and scared myself silly. Besides, I could see the other flashlight beams getting closer. My pursuer might be among that group at this very moment, pretending to be one of the searchers.

Better to tell Jason everything when I got back to town. He'd believe me. And then I could tell him who I thought had been chasing me.

Chapter 24

By the time I got back to the main hall with Millie, Detective Palmer, and the other searchers, everyone was laughing and joking, in high spirits after their game of flashlight tag. Several people had teased me about how I'd gotten lost when I should have stayed on the trail. I didn't bother telling them that I'd been chased, most likely by Ryan.

He'd caught me reading that text, plus he could have easily overheard me when I'd offered to run out to Pearl's cabin. He left at the same time I did. With everyone talking, no one would have noticed his exit. My only question was why. Was the text really that important? What did he think I knew?

As soon as I stepped in the door, Pearl ran over to me and clasped my hands. "Dana, what have I done? I never would have allowed you to go off on your own if I'd known this would happen. Can you ever forgive me?" She was near tears.

I squeezed her hands. "There's nothing to forgive. I'm okay."

She reached up and touched my cheek. "But you've got scratches."

"Nothing too serious."

My answers seemed to pacify her but did little to quiet my own nerves. What would have happened if Detective Palmer hadn't found me when he did? Would he have found my body in the woods the next day instead?

I shivered at my overblown imagination. Detective Palmer noticed but misunderstood the reason and led me to the coffee urn.

"This will warm you up," he said as he poured me a cup.

I accepted the coffee, more to give myself something to do than to actually drink it. No one was near us in the corner, so I leaned toward him and asked, "How's the investigation going into Birch's murder?"

Detective Palmer gave me a patient smile. "I see you're feeling better."

"I'd feel a lot better if you'd arrest the killer. Then maybe Zennia would return to work and save me from cooking up more tofu recipes." And people wouldn't be chasing me in the woods either.

"The department is working on it."

"Have you considered Ryan?" I asked point-blank.

"We're looking at everyone related to the commune," said Detective Palmer in that way he used, where he answered every question I asked without telling me anything useful.

"Look at him especially hard," I said.

Detective Palmer studied me for a moment. I drummed my fingers on my coffee cup.

"He doesn't have a motive," he said finally.

"He might. He got a text tonight from someone asking for a cabin here at the commune. I think he's planning to sell them or at least rent them out."

"You got all that from a text?" Detective Palmer asked.

"That and all the other changes he's trying to make around here. The guy obviously has a plan. I have a bad feeling about him."

Detective Palmer let out a sound that was close to a laugh. "We don't arrest people based on the feelings of random citizens who read other people's texts."

I felt my face grow hot. "I'm not a random citizen. I'm a victim who was chased through the woods." Whoops. I hadn't planned on bringing that up again. "I'm trying to figure out why."

"Leave the detective work to me," he said, not unkindly. "Speaking of which, I still have a few people to interview. Excuse me."

I drained the rest of my coffee and went to find Zennia. She was sitting at a table with Millie.

"Are you about ready to go?" I asked. "We have a long drive back."

She glanced at the clock on the wall and gave a start. "My, it's gotten late. I imagine you'd like to get home after your misadventure." She rose from her chair and gave Millie a hug. "Thank you for a delightful evening."

"You're welcome here anytime," she said.

Zennia pulled her sweater from the back of the

chair and picked up the envelope with the photos. Seeing them reminded me of the one in my pocket, and I pulled it out, grateful it wasn't too badly wrinkled.

I handed it to her. "Here's one Pearl forgot to give you."

She studied the picture, and a faraway look came into her eye. "I remember this day. Birch was always such the romantic." She slid the photo into the envelope. "I'm grateful to Pearl for saving these for me. I must have thanked her a thousand times tonight."

"Was she with you the whole time I was gone?" I was ninety-nine percent sure Ryan was the one who had followed me, but I might as well find out where the others were.

"Yes, right up until Detective Palmer called her name to interview her."

"Who else did Detective Palmer talk to?" I asked.

"I hardly paid attention, since I wasn't expecting him to call my name. After all, he has my contact information and can call me at home whenever he likes."

"You didn't see him talking to Ryan by any chance?" I asked, not holding out much hope.

"I'm afraid not. He seemed to be calling names on a steady basis, but I didn't notice whose names. Sorry I can't be of more help."

"That's okay. Let's head home."

An hour later, I dropped Zennia off at her house. As soon as she'd gone inside, I pulled out my phone and texted Jason. I confirmed that he was still awake and able to see me.

With renewed energy, I backed out of the driveway and turned my car in the direction of his place. I couldn't wait to hear what he thought about tonight's events.

I reached his duplex where he was waiting on the sidewalk. The moment I shut off the engine, he opened the driver's side door and helped me out. Then he pulled me close for a long embrace.

I leaned against his chest, enjoying the warmth and comfort. He rested his chin on my head. After a minute, he pulled back and held me at arm's length.

"Are you all right?"

Even in the dim lighting of the street lamp, I could see the concern on his face, and I couldn't help but be touched. "How do you know anything's wrong?"

He put an arm around me and led me up the walk. "As much as I love surprise visits, you've never stopped by this late. Plus, your face is scratched up."

I automatically put a hand to my cheek, where I could feel faint welts. "I'll tell you inside."

Once in the house, we walked straight to the living room. I sank onto his leather sofa and recounted the events of the evening.

As I spoke, Jason paced back and forth in front of the television, his speed increasing when I got to the part about hearing footsteps outside Pearl's cabin. By the time I'd finished telling him about being chased and rescued, I was starting to worry that I'd have to replace his carpet.

Jason rubbed his goatee. "Okay, I'm going to sound like Detective Palmer for one minute. Are you positive you were followed? It couldn't have been an animal? Or the wind? Or your imagination?"

"I know what I heard."

"Good enough for me," he said "Where does that leave us?"

I pressed a hand against my temple as the threat of a headache loomed. "We need to focus on Ryan, figure out what his motive might be."

"Let's back up," Jason said as he sat down next to me. He rested his hand on my thigh. "How do you know it was Ryan? Did you see him go outside?"

I recalled the scene in my mind when I'd dropped off my dinner dishes and turned back to wave at Pearl. "No, but he stood up as I was walking out the door. I assume that's when he followed me."

"Did you see him come out the door behind you?"

"No, but why would he stay?" I shifted slightly to look directly at him as I pled my case. "He told me how uncomfortable he was feeling. If he stuck around, someone was bound to start an argument about his Web site ideas."

Jason rubbed my knee. "Did you notice where everyone else was when you left?"

"Frank was talking to Detective Palmer in the office down the hall, Pearl was sitting at the table where we'd eaten, and Zennia was with a group of friends on the other side of the room. I'm not positive, but Millie might have been with her."

Jason held up his hand. So you can only account for Frank, Zennia, and Pearl for sure," he said. "There were dozens of people in that room. Any one of them could have followed you out. Or even left after and caught up with you, including those three."

I crossed my arms. "But no one else is connected to Birch's murder."

"We don't know that," he said. "We've identified a few people who knew Birch well, but plenty of other people could have killed him. And who's to say the person following you had anything to do with Birch's murder? Plenty of creeps in the world, even ones who live at communes, would jump at the chance to catch an attractive girl alone in the woods."

"No," I said. "I'm positive that whoever followed me is somehow connected to Birch's murder, and I still think it's Ryan. I didn't tell you, but he got a bunch of texts when he first sat down to dinner. When he left the table, I read one."

Jason groaned and hung his head in mock despair. "Please tell me he didn't catch you."

I paused, then said, "He did."

He groaned again. "What were you thinking?" He waved his hand. "Never mind. What did the text say?"

"Something was going to be huge, and the texter wanted a cabin."

"A cabin at the commune?" Jason asked.

"I'm assuming," I said, "but I don't know how

anyone could claim a cabin like that. Zennia explained the rules to me, and cabins are assigned based on seniority and family needs. Ryan might not get a cabin for years, let alone whoever texted him."

"Unless Ryan is planning to change the rules."

"How? By convincing the commune residents they need to rent out their cabins to keep the land from being seized?"

"That's not a bad idea."

I shook my head. "Millie would never go for that."

"Millie might not be able to stop him. Majority rules out there. He'd only need to convince half the commune plus one."

"It's crazy, but I guess if he can talk the members into adopting online sales, it's not too much of a stretch to convince them to rent the cabins, too." All this thinking was wearing me out. I leaned my head against Jason's shoulder. "Didn't you tell me you were having trouble finding information about Ryan?"

"I did," Jason said, "at least concerning his education. Turns out he attended SF State but didn't graduate. He has half the credits he needs. I also located his most recent employer but a representative from the company would only confirm when he started and when he left. No details on his actual position."

"I got the impression he was a coding genius or an IT guru."

"That's what he said, but since he lied about graduating, he may have exaggerated about his job as well. For all I know, he worked in the mail room. I've put out feelers."

I smiled. I loved it when Jason used his newspaper lingo. "Okay, he shows up at the commune a few months ago, purportedly burned out at his tech job and looking for a place to unwind. He doesn't know anyone at the commune but manages to befriend a few of the residents. Once Birch arrives, Ryan latches on to him, and Birch seems to love his ideas. But if they were in agreement, why would Ryan kill Birch?"

"He wouldn't. Unless there's more to the story. Did Birch change his mind about Ryan's plans? Did Millie convince Birch that Ryan was wrong?" Jason rubbed his goatee again. "And let's not forget about Frank and his financial problems. Birch might have found out, and Frank killed him. Then again, Millie had a bigger motive to murder Birch. His support of Ryan's ideas threatened her entire way of life."

"But she couldn't be the one who chased me. I'm almost positive she was with Zennia when I left." I touched a finger to my lips. "Although . . ."

"What?" Jason asked.

"She was right behind Detective Palmer when he found me. She could have easily hidden when she heard him coming and acted like she was simply one of the searchers." I sighed. "I don't know what to think now." My certainty over Ryan being my pursuer was starting to waver. There were simply too many unknowns.

Jason mirrored my doubts. "That's the problem. Anyone could have been in those woods without the others knowing. We can't be sure it was Ryan." He hugged me again and then pulled back to look at me. "The important thing is that you're safe. That's all I care about."

He brushed an errant strand of hair away from my face, leaned over, and kissed me slowly. All thoughts of Ryan, crazy people in the woods, and murder vanished.

When we broke apart, I said, "This thing between us is pretty good, don't you think?"

"Better than pretty good," he said, his voice husky.

We kissed again. I checked the time on my phone and flinched. "I don't know how I'm going to get up in the morning. Think the guests will be upset if they don't get breakfast?"

"Tell them it's the first day of a fast."

I laughed. "Not bad, but I don't see Gordon agreeing to that. Guess I'd better get to bed."

"You could always stay here tonight, rather than drive home."

Now there was a tempting offer. I debated with myself before standing and pulling out my keys. "As much as I'd like to, I can't leave Ashlee alone. She needs constant supervision."

Jason stood up as well. "She sounds like an untrained puppy."

"I often think of her that way."

"She may be more grown-up than you realize," he said. "She's not a kid anymore."

"I'm not so sure. I'll talk to you tomorrow."

He walked me to the door and gave me a kiss before I went out to my car. On the way home, I thought about tonight's adventure. Ryan was still my top choice for who chased me, but what had he been planning to do once he caught me? Maybe he'd only wanted to talk, although if that were the case, he probably would have called out to me. But maybe I'd never been in as much danger as I'd thought.

I glanced in the rearview mirror. All the same, I'd be watching my back.

Chapter 25

The next morning, I hit the snooze alarm twice before I convinced myself to get out of bed. Even if I only served cold cereal and fruit, I still needed to be at the farm before the first guest showed up in the dining room.

I cut my usual shower time in half and pulled my hair back in a ponytail so I could skip the blow drying. Knowing I shouldn't, I stopped by the Daily Grind to grab a white mocha before I headed out of town.

When I reached the farm, I grabbed my half-drunk coffee out of the cup holder and rushed inside to find the dining room empty. Thank goodness.

I made my way to the kitchen, where a bowlful of fresh eggs sat on the table, a sign that Esther had been up early and out visiting the chicken coop. Now that I'd woken up a bit more, I decided to scramble the eggs for breakfast. I'd even cook up facon, the vegetarian version of bacon that Zennia occasionally served.

Within minutes, the first diners appeared, and I hustled to serve the steady stream of guests. Within the hour, everyone had eaten and left. I cleaned up the kitchen and dining room, eager to get that chore out of the way. Once everything was finished, I sat down in the office to compose the day's blog and deal with any online correspondence.

By ten, I'd reached a stopping point in my marketing work and could plan my next move, namely lunch. I knew the entrée would be pasta with roasted vegetables, but I needed rolls to accompany the meal. If I went to the store right now, I'd have just enough time to shop and get back for lunch preparations.

I grabbed my purse from the bottom desk drawer and removed a handful of bills from the petty cash container. On my way through the lobby, I stopped to tell Gordon I was taking money to buy lunch ingredients and headed out.

A few minutes later, I pulled into a parking slot in front of The Health Nut. A woman with a full bag exited the store as I went through the door.

Inside, the owner, Jan, was placing money in the cash register. When she saw me, she smiled. "You're the girl who works with Zennia, right?"

"Right. I'm Dana."

"How's she doing? I've thought about calling her, but I didn't want to intrude."

"She's hanging in there."

Jan slid the cash register drawer shut. "I keep meaning to pay Birch's sister a condolence visit as well, but I'm terrible at handling death, especially a murder. What could I possibly say that would make anyone feel better?"

"You know Olive?" I asked.

"I see her around town every now and again. In fact, I saw her the very morning Birch was killed."

My eyebrows went up. "Here? In Blossom Valley?"

Before Jan could answer, a guy in a gray work shirt pushed a handcart loaded with cardboard boxes into the store. I internally cursed the interruption as Jan hurried around the counter and went over to greet him.

While she was busy, I walked over to the bread section for the rolls and then browsed the other offerings while I waited for her to finish. When the deliveryman wheeled his load of boxes toward the back, I went up front with my rolls.

Jan was jotting in a ledger, but she looked up as I approached. "All set?"

"Yes. Only the rolls today."

She rang me up, and I handed her the money. I could faintly hear the guy working in the back.

"You were telling me how you saw Birch's sister in town the same day he was killed," I said.

"Was I? That's right." She handed me my change. "She was getting coffee at the Daily Grind, same as me. I remember because when I heard Birch had been killed, I wondered if Olive might have sensed bad things were going to happen to him and felt drawn to come into town. You know how they always talk about psychic connections between siblings."

I stuffed the money in my pocket. "I've heard that about twins, not siblings, but it is quite a coincidence that Olive was in Blossom Valley right when Birch was murdered."

Jan leaned forward and nodded. "Exactly. Like maybe she had a premonition that Birch was in trouble."

I was thinking more along the lines that Olive found out Birch would be in town that morning and came here to kill him, but I didn't say as much. "Something like that," I said instead.

"Of course, Olive lives just outside of town, and I run into her on occasion. I'm sure I'm making a bigger deal out of it than I should."

"I didn't realize she lived that close." I felt my rush of excitement at finding out Olive had been in town crumble like a stale cookie.

The delivery guy came up front with an empty handcart and handed Jan a clipboard. I grabbed my bag of rolls, thanked her, and left. All the while, I was wondering how often Olive came to town for coffee. What were the odds she'd be in town the same morning her brother was murdered there?

Back at the farm, I cut through the lobby and walked down the hall toward the kitchen. As I got closer, I could hear dishes clanking. Maybe Esther had decided to help me with lunch.

I entered the room and stopped. My mouth dropped open.

"Zennia!" I tossed the bag of rolls on the table and rushed over to hug her. "What are you doing here?" I didn't dare voice what I was hoping she'd say.

She smiled serenely, looking like the Zennia I knew so well. "I believe I've finally come to terms with Birch's death. While I was puttering around my garden this morning, I realized that my place is here in this kitchen. I've already let Esther know that I'm back."

I grabbed her again and squeezed even harder this time. "I'm so glad!" I couldn't seem to stop smiling.

When I let her go, she said, "You act like I've been gone for months. Listen, I can resume my duties whenever you're ready, but I don't want to step on your toes if you've been enjoying yourself in the kitchen."

"Are you crazy? You can start right now."

Zennia grinned. "I had a feeling you'd say that." She picked up the recipe card for the pasta that I'd left on the table this morning. "Is this what I'll be making?"

Now that I only needed to worry about my marketing duties, the rest of the day flew by. I caught up on all the non-critical issues I'd shoved aside once I'd started cooking.

Around four, I went outside to clear my head and say hi to Wilbur. He and the other pigs were soaking up the afternoon sun.

When Wilbur saw me approach, he rose and joined me at the fence, sniffing and snuffling around the rail. I pulled my hand from behind my back and showed him a cluster of grapes.

"For you," I said as I pulled the grapes off their stems and dropped them inside the pen.

Wilbur snorted his thanks and gobbled up the fruit. When he was finished, he pushed his snout through the split rails in search of more, but I only shrugged. "Don't want to spoil your dinner."

With a piggish grunt, Wilbur turned his back on me as my cell phone rang. I pulled the phone from my pocket and answered.

"Hey, babe, how's my favorite girl?" Jason said.

I leaned against the top rail. "Not too shabby. I'm just talking to Wilbur."

"I worry about you sometimes."

I laughed. "I'd much rather talk to you, if that helps."

"It does, but seeing you is even better. I'd like to take you to dinner, since you had a rough night last night."

"Sounds great," I said. "We can celebrate Zennia's return to work."

"Zennia's back? You must be ecstatic. With that kind of news, I'll let you pick the restaurant."

I knew Jason would have let me pick anyway, but suddenly I knew exactly where I wanted to go. "It's a bit of a drive, but we'll have after-dinner entertainment, too. You're a gambler, right?"

"What's this all about?" Jason asked.

"I'll tell you on the way over. How does six o'clock work?"

"Fine. Then you can tell me what you have up your sleeve."

Not patchy elbows, I thought to myself. "You'll find out."

We said our good-byes, and I went inside to finish a few items in the office. As I cleaned up my e-mail inbox, my mind was on my plans for the evening. With my attention on Ryan, I'd almost forgotten about Olive as a possible suspect in Birch's death. Talking to Jan had reminded me that I shouldn't dismiss Olive so readily.

Tonight, I wanted to find out what role Birch had played in the death of Olive's husband. And if it was reason enough for Olive to kill him.

Chapter 26

While Jason drove us to the Mighty Eagle Casino for dinner, I filled him in on my conversation with Jan that morning.

Jason kept his eyes on the road as he said, "If Olive lives close to town, it wouldn't be unusual for her to stop in regularly. Maybe she loves the coffee at the Daily Grind."

"But Birch was killed early in the morning, and Olive was nearby at the time."

"She might get up early every day. And that is the time of day most people drink their coffee."

I watched the towering redwood trees whiz by my window. "But she seemed upset when she mentioned her husband's death the other day," I said. "Like her anger is still fresh."

"Her brother's murder could have dredged up those old memories."

"I guess," I said halfheartedly.

"I'm not trying to discourage you," Jason said as he eased into a turn. "But being spotted at a restaurant around the same time Birch was killed

isn't much reason to believe she's the murderer."
He slowed as he neared the casino's driveway.
"You don't think Olive chased you in the woods,
do you?"

"Absolutely not, but you yourself said last night
that maybe Birch's death and my pursuit aren't
related."

Jason turned into the entrance for the Mighty
Eagle. I checked the side mirror and saw more cars
turning in behind us. The place probably drew the
after-work crowd, along with retirees and chronic
gamblers. I wondered how the new casino would
impact business.

Most of the front spaces were taken, and Jason
parked on the far side of the lot. As we crossed the
asphalt, a tour bus motored past. The stench of ex-
haust fumes filled my nose, a warm-up for the cloud
of cigarette smoke I knew awaited me.

The inside of the casino was teeming with gamblers. As I'd expected, a visible haze of smoke
hovered near the ceiling. Between that, the constant dinging of the slot machines, and the flashing
lights, it was sensory overload.

Jason took my hand, and we made our way to
the restaurant. Our progress was accompanied by
the occasional celebratory shout from the direction of the card tables and slot machines.

A hostess in a diamond-patterned vest, white
dress shirt, and short black skirt greeted us as we
approached the restaurant's entrance. "Table for
two?" She grabbed menus and led us across the
room. All the while, I cast an eye over the diners

and serving staff, but Olive was nowhere to be seen.

The hostess stopped at a table near the back corner, and I chose the seat that faced the dining area to more easily spot Olive. Jason sat down across from me.

"Your server will be right with you," the hostess said as she handed us our menus.

"Any chance it'll be Olive?" I asked.

Her penciled eyebrows came together. "I'm pretty sure her shift doesn't start until seven-thirty, but I can check if you'd like."

"That's all right." No need to draw attention to the fact that I was actively tracking down Olive. She might get spooked.

The hostess left, and a waitress came over to take our drink orders. By the time she'd brought my iced tea and Jason's glass of red wine, I'd decided on the fettuccine Alfredo while Jason ordered the steak. As we ate, we chatted about our workdays and the latest news.

I was nearing the last few bites of pasta when Olive came into the restaurant. As she passed the entrance, the hostess stopped her and pointed in my direction. I gulped down a noodle and felt it slither all the way to my belly. So much for keeping a low profile.

"Why do you look nervous?" Jason asked. He glanced over his shoulder and saw Olive making her way toward our table. "Is that Olive? I never could get an interview with her."

She reached us before I could reply. "This is sure

a surprise. Renee at the front said you were asking about me." Her smile faltered.

Gee, thanks, Renee. I hadn't worked out how I could ask Olive about Birch's involvement in her husband's death. I went with the first lie that popped into my head. "I remembered that you worked here and thought I'd say hi."

"How sweet."

I motioned to an empty chair. "Won't you sit down?"

She seemed surprised by the request, but pulled out the chair and sat. "Only for a minute. My shift starts soon."

I took a sip of iced tea to stall for time, and then asked, "How have you been lately? No ill effects from your fall at the spa?" Gordon would be furious if he knew I'd reminded her of that, but I couldn't think of anything else to say.

"No, I'm fine. It'll teach me to watch where I'm going."

An awkward silence fell over the table until I remembered my manners. "Olive, this is my boyfriend, Jason Forrester. Jason, this is Olive."

They shook, but Olive didn't release Jason's hand. "Forrester . . . are you the one who's been calling me? The reporter who's been writing those articles about Birch?"

"Guilty as charged."

Olive patted his hand and let it go. "I like your articles. You don't make Birch sound like a nut. A guy from another newspaper described Birch as a nudist hippie pot smoker who liked to talk to butterflies. He had the nerve to ask for an interview."

She clasped her hands on the table. "That's when I decided not to talk to anyone."

"Have you been getting a lot of calls regarding Birch's death?" I asked.

"Not too many. Most of the calls are from gossipers who barely knew Birch, sad as that is. It doesn't matter that he died. Just that he was murdered."

"His death matters to the people who cared about him," Jason said soothingly. "Would you be interested in doing an interview with me, since you know the type of articles I write?"

Olive traced the subtle eagle pattern on the tablecloth. "I'll have to think about it. Birch and I haven't always been close, and I might say something I'd regret."

Recognizing an opening, I leaned toward her. "I remember you said Birch was involved in your husband's death."

Olive glanced at Jason before answering me. "I don't talk about that much."

I wasn't sure if she was being vague because she honestly didn't like to talk about it, or she didn't want to mention the details in front of a reporter. I caught Jason's eye and jerked my head slightly to the side, indicating that he should make himself scarce.

He smirked at me, but rose from the table. "Please excuse me. I need to make a phone call."

As soon as he walked off, I tried again. "You said the other day that Birch's murder was God's way of getting him back for your husband's death. Do you really think the two are connected?"

Olive lifted the salt shaker and swept away errant

crystals that had been scattered around the base. "No. I was letting my anger get the best of me. You'd think I'd be over Tony's death after all this time, but as soon as I heard about Birch, it was like reliving the same nightmare."

"Does this mean you don't blame Birch for your husband's death?" In my peripheral vision, I could see Jason lurking near the hostess stand, but I kept my eyes on Olive.

"Oh no, I do. I just don't think Tony's death and Birch's death have anything to do with each other. Tony and I went up to Oregon to visit Birch for a little vacation, one of many trips we'd made. It should have been a fun and relaxing time, but Birch fell asleep at the wheel and crashed, when he never should have been driving in the first place. He knew he was too tired, but he insisted anyway because he wanted to play host."

"He must have underestimated how tired he was. It's hard to judge these things."

"But Birch was up all night working on a new T-shirt design for his shop. And a few days before the accident, he told me how he'd almost fallen asleep behind the wheel and that he needed to be more careful." Olive's scowl grew fierce. "To top it off, he drank a glass of wine that night. Not enough to make him drunk, but wine always made him drowsy. He knew the risks, but not only did he take away Tony's life, he ruined mine as well."

I could practically feel the anger radiating off of her. "You must have loved Tony a lot."

"You bet I did, but there's more to it. It's the life we shared. You know, eating out every week, taking a vacation once a year. We weren't rich, but we managed to get by. Since the day Tony died, there hasn't been a single moment where I haven't worried about money. I was forced to sell the house we'd bought together when we were first married and move into a tiny trailer. I haven't taken so much as a weekend getaway in the last four years. And now I find out that this job . . ." She checked her watch and rose. "Speaking of which, I should clock in."

She rose from the table with such effort that I found myself saying, "Have faith. Things will get better."

Olive looked down at me with a sad smile. "You're sweet. I remember being young and full of hope. And look where it's gotten me."

With a sigh, she walked away. I watched her go, a heavy weight seeming to settle on my shoulders as well. A moment later, Jason rejoined me at the table. The sight of him helped me shake off my melancholy gloom.

"Did Olive tell you anything useful?" he asked as he sat back down.

"Man, that poor woman has dealt with a lot in her life, but as for Tony's death, it seems pretty cut-and-dried. Birch fell asleep while driving, nothing more." I sucked up the last of my iced tea.

"And she blames Birch after all this time?"

"I think her grudge has more to do with her own life circumstances rather than her husband's death. Every time she has trouble paying a bill, she must be reminded of what Birch took from her. The only question is whether her resentment was enough for her to murder her own brother."

"Seems like a weak reason, but people have

killed for less." He looked in the direction Olive had gone. "I'd still like to interview her."

"Sorry, she didn't mention it."

"No problem. I'll call her tomorrow." He stood up. "Let's go win some money."

We paid our dinner bill and went out onto the casino floor. The crowd had increased while we'd been eating, and the gamblers stood two and three deep at the more popular tables. Most of the slot machine stools were occupied, while other gamblers hovered nearby, hoping to snatch the machine the moment the current slot-puller stood up.

We reached a fairly quiet row of machines, and Jason stopped. Three stools in the middle of the row were vacant.

Jason sat in front of a slot machine decorated with pictures of a miner and bags of gold. He fed a five-dollar bill into the machine and pushed a few buttons. When the reels stopped spinning, three lamps rested on the center line. The machine chimed as a dollar was added to his pot.

I took the stool next to Jason at a machine covered in images of pyramids, asps, and sphinxes and inserted a few dollars. Several spins later, I was out of money and reaching for my wallet. I set a twenty-dollar limit on myself. The rent was due in a few days.

After I lost another couple dollars, I switched to the machine on the other side of Jason. Surely the stampeding horses galloping across the top would be luckier than the pharaohs.

Before I'd even settled down on my stool, Jason's machine dinged as three genies hit the center row.

By the time the counter stopped spinning, he was up twenty bucks.

Grumbling, I put a five in the horse machine, but lost it in less than two minutes. I checked Jason's machine. Up another ten. Clearly he was sucking all the luck out of the row where we sat.

"I'm going to try the other side," I told him. He waved a hand in acknowledgment, never taking his eyes off the screen as the reels spun by.

With my luck running low, I found a penny slot and inserted several ones. I picked the max line bet and hit the button, watching the genie lamps spin around before settling completely out of sync.

My total dropped by three dollars, and I almost gasped. I'd lost three hundred pennies in one spin! I lowered the betting amount, but my credits still hit zero within minutes.

I checked the contents of my wallet and winced at the paltry amount that remained. I stuffed it back in my purse, all done gambling for the night.

Getting up from the stool, I scanned the area. With so many machines, I'd lost track of where Jason was sitting. I started to wander up and down the rows, pausing when someone hit a jackpot, which seemed to be everyone but me.

As I got close to a door marked OFFICE, it opened, and Millie walked out. Her eyes widened slightly when she saw me.

"Dana, such a pleasure. Out for a night of gambling?" she asked.

"Not anymore."

A man came out of the same door as Millie. He spoke in her ear before heading across the casino.

A look of affection crossed Millie's face. "I came

here straight from the meeting tonight. My cousin Jaye is going to help us with the commune's financial problems. I told you we have benefactors who won't let us struggle."

"That's great news," I said.

"Yes, as long as Frank doesn't mess up anything with the books again. Birch was planning to talk to him about that, but I don't think he got the chance. At least this money will give us the breathing room we need until the commune can get its affairs in order."

Loud cheers erupted from a nearby table. I raised my voice to be heard over the din. "Does this loan mean you didn't need to hold a vote during tonight's meeting?"

"I only heard of Jaye's offer a short while ago. That was after the vote." A gleam came into Millie's eye. "Ryan, the silver-tongued devil, convinced most residents to side with him, but little does he know the vote won't matter. I've got information that will change everything. Once the truth is revealed about what a scoundrel he is, he'll be forced to leave with his tail between his legs."

Millie practically cackled in victory. Goose bumps rose on my arms at the sound. I couldn't wait to find out what she knew.

Chapter 27

Millie seemed so certain that she'd be rid of Ryan that I half expected her to leave for the commune right that moment to help him pack. "What did you find out?" I asked.

She pressed her lips together. "As much as I despise the man, I'll give him one more opportunity to do the honorable thing and admit his lies. If he refuses, I'll call a meeting and tell everyone what I know."

Well, rats. I'd hoped she'd tell me first. "Does this have anything to do with Birch's murder?"

Millie shrugged. "Not directly, but if Birch uncovered the truth as I did, Ryan may have killed him to keep Birch from spreading the word."

A memory popped up on the outer corners of my mind, and I dragged it to the forefront. Hadn't Birch been planning to talk to Ryan that night after the farmers market? Was it connected to Millie's discovery?

"Should you talk to him alone?" I said to Millie. "It might be dangerous."

She shook her head. "You don't need to worry about me."

"There you are," I heard Jason say behind me. I turned around to find him stuffing a large stack of bills into his wallet.

"Done already?" I asked.

"Can't take all of the casino's money in one night. I should leave something for next time." He looked at my purse. "How'd you do?"

"I don't want to talk about it."

"That bad, huh? I'll split my winnings with you."

"No, thank you. I'll win next time." I turned back around to find Millie buttoning her coat. "Millie, this is my boyfriend, Jason."

Jason nodded to her. "We met at the commune. Nice to see you again."

"You, too, but I'm afraid I can't stay. I must hurry back to Evergreen if I want to talk to Ryan before he turns in for the night," she said. "Don't be surprised if he's not around the next time you visit." She headed for the nearest exit.

"What's this about Ryan?" Jason asked.

"Millie's uncovered dirt about him. She's positive that he'll leave for good once she talks to him."

"Think it's related to him lying about his college degree?"

"Maybe, or more likely it's connected to that text. Maybe she figured out his exact plans."

A crafty look came over Jason's face. "I still need to interview a few people at the commune for my human interest story. I may go sooner than I'd planned."

I looped my arm through his and snuggled up

close. "And I'm sure you need a lovely assistant to take notes, right?"

He gave my hand a squeeze. "We might be able to work something out. In the meantime, did you want to do any more gambling?"

"Good grief, I won't be able to pay my rent at the rate I'm losing. Get me out of here before I have to move back in with my mom."

Jason laughed. "If it comes to that, you could always move in with me."

The idea made my heart palpitate, but all I said was, "Aren't you the sweet talker."

He kissed me briefly, and we walked out of the casino. I spent the trip across the parking lot wondering about the closet space at Jason's place. Not that I needed much.

The drive home was uneventful, and before I knew it, Jason was pulling into my apartment complex. He walked me up the stairs and we stood outside my apartment where we engaged in a little lip-locking. After we pulled apart, he headed down to his car, and I put my key in the lock. I couldn't wait to roll into bed. The last couple of nights had been long ones.

My hopes for a quiet end to the day vanished the moment I opened the door. Brittany and Ashlee were sitting on the couch, booing at the TV and throwing popcorn at the screen. Pieces of popcorn were scattered over the carpet.

"What are you guys doing?" I asked as I dropped my purse in the chair and took off my jacket.

"Watching a dating show," Ashlee said. She pointed at the screen. "That girl totally picked the wrong guy. The other one is way better looking."

As if to emphasize her point, she threw another piece of popcorn.

"Maybe this guy has a better personality."

Brittany giggled. "No way, but he does have a more expensive car."

"I can't believe how shallow she is," Ashlee added, as if she hadn't just booed the girl for not picking the hottest guy.

"You know who else drives a cool car?" Brittany said. "That guy who was with Ryan today. Too bad he's so old."

My ears perked up. "Ryan? Did you see him again?" I asked Ashlee. Considering he was the front-runner for who might have followed me in the woods, the notion that they might go out again didn't exactly thrill me.

The dating show went to commercial break, and Ashlee muted the volume. "Kind of. Brittany and I ate lunch at the Breaking Bread Diner, and he was there with some guy."

"Did you talk to him?"

"Not at first. I was totally ignoring him. You know, laughing with Brittany, so he'd see how much fun I was having even though he hadn't called me."

"That's right," Brittany said with a giggle. "You don't need that loser."

"Anyway, we ended up leaving at the same time and got stuck walking out together," Ashlee said. "Since the other guy held open the door for us, it's not like I could pretend they weren't there."

"Any idea who this other guy was?" I asked.

"Never seen him before. Ryan told us he was his

uncle, but the dude looked totally surprised at that."

Brittany giggled again. "Did you see the way his eyes bugged out of his head? If that guy's his uncle, then I'm your sister."

Ashlee sighed. "I wish you were my sister. That would be so cool."

I waved my hand in front of Ashlee's face. "Hey! I'm right here."

"Chill. I didn't mean that Brittany would replace you. I meant she could be my sister, too. We could be, like, the Three Musketeers."

"Isn't that a candy bar?" Brittany asked.

"Plus it was a movie," Ashlee said, "with all those hot guys."

"And a book," I said. "The book came first."

But they weren't listening to me. Brittany was too busy rooting around in her bag. "I'd swear I saw a candy bar in here."

"See if you can find two," Ashlee said.

Brittany pulled a chocolate bar out and held it aloft. "I'm trying to get superskinny for that party next weekend, so I'll split it with you."

"If that's all you've got," Ashlee said, always the gracious one.

"Did Ryan tell you anything else about his so-called uncle?" I asked to get them back on track.

Ashlee took a bite of her candy bar half and held up one finger while she chewed. I tried to hide my impatience, knowing she'd take even longer to finish the bite.

At last, she swallowed. "Not to me."

"Or me," Brittany added.

"But I did hear the guy asking when they'd start moving on things, and Ryan got all fidgety and talked about how it would take time, maybe a lot of it." Ashlee inspected the remainder of her candy bar. "The other guy seemed put out by that, said he wanted results soon. Ryan said he was doing the best he could."

Were Ryan and this other guy talking about Ryan's big plans to increase online sales? Or was this connected to the text I'd seen about the cabin? Either way, if Millie got her wish, Ryan might be ousted as early as tomorrow. All his plans would be ruined.

"That's it?" I asked.

"What else do you want?" Ashlee said.

Oh, the reason Ryan lied about his education, what information Millie uncovered about him, maybe even a clue as to who killed Birch, but I didn't think Ashlee could help me with those, so I said, "Nothing."

"Then why did you ask?" Brittany asked with a giggle.

Ashlee glanced at the TV. "Crap, we're missing the final pick." Brittany stuffed the rest of her chocolate in her mouth while Ashlee fumbled with the remote control to turn the volume back on. With those two absorbed in the show once more, I made my exit, not that anyone noticed.

Once I'd brushed my teeth, I donned my pajamas, sent a good night text to Jason, and crawled into bed, wondering if Ryan was looking for a new place to live.

* * *

The next morning, I arrived at work only to find an empty kitchen. Panic gripped me as I wondered where Zennia was. Had she suffered another relapse? Decided she wasn't ready to come back?

I pulled open the refrigerator door and scanned the shelves, wondering what I could throw together for the guests. I was picking up the yogurt container to create the old stand-by of yogurt parfaits when the kitchen phone rang.

I almost dropped the yogurt but managed to shove it on the shelf before it could fall. I grabbed the phone. "Hello?"

"Dana, it's Zennia."

Alarm bells went off in my head. Why was Zennia calling when she should be here cooking? This couldn't be good. "Zennia, why aren't you at the farm?"

"I was getting ready to leave, but now I'm afraid I'm not going to make it in time for breakfast prep." I heard her take a ragged breath. "Dana, you won't believe what's happened."

The fear in her voice made my stomach plunge. For a moment, I even wondered if another murder had taken place on her front lawn. "What?" I asked.

"Someone shot at Millie last night. They tried to kill her."

Chapter 28

Zennia's announcement was so close to my guess about another dead body that my brain seemed to have trouble working. It took me a moment to realize Millie must still be alive.

"Wait. Is Millie all right?" I asked, just to be sure.

"She wasn't hurt, but she's quite shaken up."

Relief that Millie was unharmed mingled with confusion. "Who tried to kill her? Ryan?"

"It's a long story. My main concern right now is that I won't make it to the farm in time to cook breakfast."

I checked the clock and saw that she was right. "Don't worry, I can cover for you."

"You're a lifesaver, Dana. I didn't plan for you to cook in my stead again this soon, but I can't convince Millie to come with me, and I don't feel right leaving her alone."

I heard voices in the hall and tried not to watch the second hand sweep around the face of the rooster clock, a steady reminder that time was slipping away. "Is Millie with you now?"

"Yes, she showed up a short while ago. I have every intention of preparing lunch today, but I'd feel much better if Millie would join me at the farm."

"Okay, let me get breakfast out of the way, and then I can stop by your house. Maybe between the two of us, we can convince her to come out here." Anything to guarantee Zennia would arrive before the noon meal. I had no idea what I could fix for lunch.

I hung up and got to work assembling the parfaits. Within minutes, I had everything ready for the guests, some of whom were waiting. I shuttled between the kitchen and the dining room, trying to serve everyone as quickly as possible, but breakfast couldn't end fast enough. I almost refused one woman a refill on her coffee with the fear that she might linger.

Finally, everyone had gone, and the dining room was clear. I hurriedly stripped the tables, washed the dishes, and cleaned up the counters. That done, I updated my time card in the office and headed down the hall.

Gordon stood at the counter, typing on the reservation computer. He glanced up when I came in.

"I'm taking an early lunch today," I said.

"Be sure to update your time card."

"Already done," I called over my shoulder as I made my escape. A minute later, I was speeding down the highway.

I exited, wound my way through the streets, and pulled into Zennia's cul-de-sac. Her Prius and Millie's car, which I recognized from my previous visit, sat in the driveway. Several cars occupied spaces along the curb. I flipped a U-turn and parked at the corner. This was the same house I'd parked in front of the day of Birch's death. I automatically looked up at the second-story window to see if anyone was peeking down at me, but the blinds were drawn.

As I got out of my car, the door to the house opened. An older woman in a jogging suit walked out, holding a leash with a Pomeranian on the other end. Its tiny pink tongue hung out as it panted noisily.

The woman locked her front door and came down the walk.

"Morning," I said.

She shortened the leash until the dog was forced to stand at her heel. The woman frowned at my car. "I'm expecting company soon. I like my guests to be able to park in front of my house."

"I won't be long."

"Good. This whole neighborhood has been overrun with visitors ever since that man was killed."

"That's right," I said, feigning ignorance. "I read about his death in the paper. Happened right around here, didn't it?"

She waved in the general direction of Zennia's house, a slight curl forming on her upper lip. "Yes, over where that hippie woman lives with that overgrown garden."

I bit back a smile. Zennia would no doubt take her comment as a compliment, even if the woman meant it as an insult.

"I'd be nervous with a murder happening so close to where I live," I said.

"I've been double-checking the locks on my doors every night. Of course, Fluffy here will protect me."

I eyed the small dog panting up at her owner. The thing couldn't weigh more than five pounds and looked about as ferocious as one of the chicks at the farm.

"Were you home the day the murder happened?" I asked.

She shivered. "I missed seeing the killer by minutes. I was getting ready for Fluffy's walk when I heard a squealing noise. I looked out my window and saw this beat-up van stop in front of the hippie's house. Thank goodness the driver doesn't live around here. Those types of eyesores bring down everyone's property value."

I glanced around, noting several older and slightly shabby cars. Frank's van fit right in. "How do you know he doesn't live nearby?" I asked.

"The nice policeman mentioned that the dead man arrived in that van. Apparently a friend was dropping him off." The woman lowered her voice. "I got the impression the policeman wasn't supposed to tell me that. He got quite flustered after he said it."

Perhaps Detective Palmer had sent a rookie officer, one who hadn't learned the art of discretion yet, to interview the neighbors. "Did you see anyone else? Or another car?"

"Not a soul. I went downstairs a few minutes later to put Fluffy's leash on, and we started on our walk. A little after that, I saw the van go by, but no one else. The neighborhood was as quiet as a graveyard."

I flinched at the comparison, but the woman didn't seem to notice. Had the killer snuck into the cul-de-sac and murdered Birch while Fluffy was tinkling on the tulips down the street, or was Birch still waiting patiently in Zennia's garden at that point?

"Nothing when you returned from your walk either?"

The woman pursed her lips. "I already told the police no. I almost never run into anyone that early. I'd be done with Fluffy's walk today, except I needed to finish cleaning my house. Which reminds me, I need to start my walk if I want to be back before my guests arrive." She looked pointedly at my car.

"I'll be gone by then," I said. Maybe.

She yanked on the leash and started down the sidewalk. Fluffy trotted after her, the dog's short legs a blur as it tried to keep up.

I continued on to Zennia's house, wondering if the police had obtained more information from the other neighbors. With the early hour, it wasn't likely.

Zennia opened her front door before I could even knock. "Dana, you made it. Come in, come in."

I stepped in the house and spotted Millie in one of the wicker chairs. On the phone, Zennia said Millie was shaken up, but here, she seemed no more excited than if she and Zennia had been discussing the latest blooms in the garden.

"Zennia told me what happened," I said. "Are you all right?"

Millie smirked. "I've survived closer calls in life. He'll have to do better than that if he thinks he can scare me away. "

Getting shot at was about as close a call as I could imagine for myself. "You said, 'he.' Do you think it was Ryan?"

"I'm sure of it. I confronted him with my information as soon as I got back to the commune last night and told him I wanted him out or else I'd expose him for the fraud he is."

Zennia had disappeared into the kitchen, where I could hear her moving around. I settled into the chair next to Millie. "What did he say?"

"He tried to deny everything. When that didn't work, he threatened me. Told me I'd better keep my mouth shut or else." She slapped the chair arm, the first evidence of emotion I'd seen from her. "Not two hours later, I was walking to my cabin when someone took a shot at me."

"You're lucky you weren't killed."

Zennia entered the room carrying a tray with three mugs on it. "That's exactly what I said." She set the tray on the coffee table and handed me a mug. "But even after Millie repeated everything to the sheriff, he still refused to arrest Ryan."

I whipped my head around to face Millie, careful not to spill the tea Zennia had given me. "But he shot at you!"

"The sheriff couldn't find any proof," Millie said. "Ryan did a real snow job on the sheriff, even offered to let him search his living quarters. You can bet he'd already hidden the gun in the forest, and the bullet could be in any one of those trees."

"That's it? You're almost killed, and the police won't do anything?" I asked.

Millie steepled her fingertips, demonstrating a maddening air of calm. "No one claimed to hear the shot, and besides that, the sheriff pointed out it could have been a poacher in the woods. He said his hands are tied without any evidence."

No wonder Zennia was worked up. The sheriff wasn't even looking for the shooter, which meant whoever it was—and it was most likely Ryan—could try again.

"What are you going to do now?" I asked. "I don't think it's safe for you to stay at the commune."

"I immediately packed a bag and came to Zennia's. She's always had a good heart, and I knew she'd welcome me. I'll sleep here until Ryan moves out."

I added sugar to my mug and stirred so forcefully that tea sloshed over the side. I grabbed a napkin and dabbed it up. "It sounds like he won't leave quietly if he's resorted to attempted murder."

"He won't have a choice. I'm making my case at the commune this evening."

I almost choked on my tea. "Isn't that risky?"

Millie placed her hands on her thighs. "Once I reach the commune, I'll make sure I'm constantly surrounded by people, and I'll come back here as soon as it's over. Ryan won't have an opportunity to harm me."

"I'm going with her," Zennia added. "I'll make sure Ryan doesn't get anywhere near her."

Zennia didn't exactly strike me as the ideal

bodyguard, and there was no way Millie could guarantee she'd be safe, but the two women had clearly made up their minds.

"Besides," Millie said, "once everyone knows his story, Ryan will have no reason to harm me."

"Except if he wants revenge," I said, though I knew I was wasting my breath arguing.

"He'll be too busy running out of town with his tail between his legs to worry about me."

Zennia glanced at her watch. "If you two don't mind, I'm going to wash up the breakfast dishes. It won't take a minute." She left the room.

I set my mug down and slid to the edge of the chair. "Will you tell me now what you found out?" I was almost positive she'd learned of whatever Ryan planned to do with the cabins, but there was an outside chance she'd discovered something else.

"Perhaps the time has come, since I've given Ryan the option to bare his soul and he has refused me." She turned her pale blue eyes on me. "The man doesn't have nearly the skills and knowledge he claims."

"I know he didn't finish college," I said.

"That's only part of it. He proposes these glamorous plans, but has no real experience. My cousin told me how he's created several apps that go on cell phones. I'm not entirely clear on what an app is, but every one of his has been a flop. He even tried to start his own company, but no one would back him because they have no faith in his abilities."

I tilted my head. "But what about his fantastic job down in San Francisco?"

"Not fantastic at all. He worked in customer support on the lowest level and had absolutely no influence." Millie's face turned grim. "But that's not even the worst of his treachery. Pushing the commune into online sales is only step one of his plan."

Now things were getting interesting. "What's step two?" Did it have anything to do with that text I saw?

"He plans to kick the residents out of the nicer cabins and rent those for thousands of dollars a week. Evergreen will become a business retreat where technology developers from all over the world can meet and brainstorm, while Ryan pockets the profits."

Aha. Jason and I had been right. But Millie's idea that Ryan would keep the money didn't make any sense. "People in the commune won't agree to that plan, will they?"

Millie frowned, the lines in her face deepening into furrows. "I'd like to think not, but the money from my cousin is only a loan, one that will need to be repaid eventually. I worry that if Ryan can reverse the commune's situation with these online sales, people will do whatever he asks to guarantee financial stability. All he has to say is that it's for the good of the commune when really, it's for the good of his bank account."

"How could he keep the money? Isn't Frank in charge of the books?" Millie's ideas sounded completely farfetched, and I wondered how much was based on reality and how much was based on her fear that Ryan would succeed in changing the commune.

"Ryan is a sly dog. I'm sure he'll find a way to steal part of the money for himself."

"Honestly, I don't see how that could happen. Wouldn't any money be shared among everyone?" I leaned toward Millie. "At any rate, what sort of proof do you have? Any documentation?"

"My cousin is friends with several important businessmen. Ryan approached one of them about his ideas." Millie reached in her pocket and pulled out a crumpled-up napkin. "I also have this. Ryan threw it in the wastebasket, but I pulled it back out."

"What is it?" I asked, trying to get a good look.

She smoothed out the napkin and held it up. "Drawings. Of the commune. These are all cabins currently occupied by residents, but he's assigned other names to them. These must be his first customers."

"But where would the people living there now go?"

Millie pointed to a sketch of a building. "To the dorms. He must plan to rent out every cabin that has running water and electricity, and kick these poor souls out."

"Are you sure about this? These seem like big plans," I said.

"Let's not forget he tried to shoot me. That isn't the action of an innocent man."

Zennia came back into the room. "All done. Millie, what time did you want to go to the commune?"

"I called Frank earlier," Millie said. "He assured me that he can get everyone gathered in the main hall by five this afternoon, which doesn't give me much time. I must organize my thoughts and calm my soul before we drive out there." She looked at Zennia. "Perhaps I can sit in your garden and meditate."

"I'd much rather you came to the farm with me," Zennia said.

"I can't. I need the quiet to center myself."

Zennia laid a hand on Millie's arm. "Promise me that once you're finished meditating, you'll come back inside and stay here for the afternoon."

"If it will make you feel better," Millie said.

I rose from my chair. "I need to be going, too. Zennia, I'll see you at the farm. Millie, good luck this evening."

From the sound of it, she was going to need all the luck she could get. Even if Millie exposed Ryan's lies, there was no guarantee the residents would force him out. And if he stayed, what would he do to Millie?

Chapter 29

When I got back to my car, the woman who'd been walking her dog was placing a note under my windshield wiper. She saw me and yanked the paper back. "There you are."

"Did you need something?"

"Yes. You must move your car now. I was leaving you a note to that effect." She glanced guiltily at the paper clutched in her hand, and I wondered how offensive the wording was.

"You do realize this is a public street, right?"

She glared at me. "I told you I need that space for company."

I looked up and down the cul-de-sac. "Are they here yet?"

"I'm expecting them any minute."

"Great," I said. "Have a nice day."

I got in my car and slammed the door shut. I pulled away from the curb and forgot all about Zennia's cranky neighbor as my mind turned to Millie and her big meeting later today.

Even though Millie had uncovered damning

information about Ryan, people might be willing to overlook the fact that he'd exaggerated his education and experience. He could easily claim he was implementing his changes to help the residents. And for all I knew, maybe all of Ryan's grand plans actually were for the good of the commune. Millie had her work cut out for her.

When I got back to the farm, I typed up the day's blog, which I'd completely forgotten about in my rush to see Zennia and Millie. Once I'd posted it to the farm's Web site, I checked to make sure Zennia didn't need help with lunch. When she declined the offer, I returned to the office.

With nothing pressing at the moment, I called Jason to fill him in on everything I'd learned.

"I'm at the commune right now to finish those interviews," he said when I stopped babbling and allowed him a chance to speak. "The whole place is talking about how Millie's disappeared. I'm glad she's safe."

"People must be frantic after she was almost killed."

There was a pause. "Actually, no."

"Really?"

"No one heard the shot, and while the sheriff conducted a cursory investigation, he couldn't find any proof. A few people are suggesting she imagined the whole incident."

I stood up and shut the office door in case Zennia walked by. "You know, I do find it odd that no one heard anything. I've run through those very same woods at night, as you know, and I can tell you that it's insanely quiet out there. You could hear a shot for miles."

"I agree. And even as late as it was, I wouldn't expect everyone to be asleep." I heard talking in the background. "My interviewee has arrived," Jason said. "I might be here a while. I'll stay for the meeting and give you a call after Millie's speech."

"Hey, do me a favor and keep an eye on Millie and Zennia. I'm sure nothing will happen, but I'll feel better knowing you're there."

"Absolutely. Talk to you soon."

I put my phone in my pocket and spent the next couple of hours working on odd jobs around the farm. At three, Zennia left to take Millie to the commune. Though I knew the meeting wasn't scheduled until five, I spent the rest of the afternoon listening for my phone's ringtone. Twice I was convinced I heard it, only to yank my phone out of my pocket and discover the music was only in my head.

At five, I went out to check on the animals, trying to find anything to keep me busy. I was saying hi to Berta and the other chickens when my phone rang for real this time. When I saw Jason was calling, a knot formed in my belly.

"How did it go?" I asked as soon as I answered.

"I'm fine. Thanks for asking."

I laughed, and the knot slipped a bit. "Well, you must be okay since you were able to call me. But seriously, how did Millie's big announcement go? Is Ryan packing as we speak?"

"No. The whole thing was done in five minutes, and people seemed more confused than ever."

My instincts were correct. The villagers hadn't grabbed their pitchforks and chased the so-called beast out of town like Millie was hoping. "Millie must be furious."

"Absolutely. I saw her deep in talks with Frank a short while ago. Probably planning what she'll say tomorrow."

"Is Frank on her side?" As I spoke, Berta strutted over to the fence and glared at me. I took a step back in case she decided to peck me through a hole in the wire.

"As far as I can tell. Most of the old-timers are."

This situation was becoming more dramatic than one of those soap operas my mom loved to watch when I was little. "Remind me never to live on a commune," I said.

"I don't think they're all like this, but at any rate, I need to go. I just wanted to call and give you the latest."

"Thanks, I appreciate it."

I headed back to the house to grab my purse and keys. On the way home, I swung by the store for milk, Lucky Charms, Oreo cookies, and a few other essentials before driving to the apartment.

As I pulled into the complex, I did a double-take. Mom was stepping out of her car where it was parked in a visitor space. I whipped into my own space and got out to greet her.

After a quick hug, I said, "What brings you by?"

She smoothed out her sweater. "I haven't seen my two favorite girls in a while and thought I'd stop to say hello. I called Ashlee first to make sure I wouldn't be interrupting any plans."

I felt instant guilt for neglecting my mom. "Of course you're not interrupting, and you don't need to call first. I love to see you. Let's go up." I retrieved my groceries from my car and led the way up the stairs.

Inside the apartment, Ashlee was sitting on the couch in her pajamas. She held a pint of dark chocolate ice cream in one hand and a large spoon in the other. "Men!" she said as soon as she saw us.

"Trouble in the dating world?" I asked. I stepped all the way inside so Mom could enter, and then I closed the apartment door with my foot.

Ashlee jammed the spoon into the ice cream and set the carton on the coffee table. "Good ol' Ryan must have felt bad about not calling me, because he sent me a text message this morning to set up a date. I decided to say yes to show him what a generous and forgiving person I am, and he has the nerve to text me after lunch and cancel. Well, screw him."

"Ashlee," Mom said with a warning tone, "your language."

Ashlee winced. "Sorry, Mom."

I toted the groceries into the kitchen and talked to both of them over the counter while I unpacked. "I know for a fact Ryan was busy at the commune today."

"Then he shouldn't have asked me out in the first place," Ashlee said. She came into the kitchen, once more clutching her ice cream.

Mom followed her. "Maybe something came up," she said. "You're too lovely a girl for anyone to cancel without good reason."

"But his excuse was superlame," Ashlee said with a detectable whine in her voice. "He tried to tell me about an old lady out there making up lies about how he tried to kill her because she thinks he wants to make this big power grab to take over the commune. Does he honestly think I'd believe a story like that? I thought he was supposed to be smart."

"Surprisingly enough, he's telling the truth," I said, stowing the container of milk in the refrigerator. "Millie, the lady he's talking about, is trying to force him out before he can restructure the commune."

Ashlee screwed up her mouth. "And she's telling people he tried to kill her? That's dumb."

"He just may have," I said.

Mom put a hand to her chest. "Is Millie all right?"

"She's fine. She just had a good scare." I folded up the reusable grocery bags and put them away. "But, Ashlee, you should still drop Ryan."

"I agree," Mom said. "This boy sounds dangerous."

"There's a possibility he killed Birch, too," I said.

Mom gasped, but Ashlee said, "Bull pucky." She shoveled a large spoonful of ice cream into her mouth and talked around it. "The guy's a nerd, not an assassin. I'm an awesome judge of character."

I turned away so I wouldn't laugh in Ashlee's face as I thought about the guys she'd dated. But I had to admit that I was starting to doubt Millie's story.

What better way to smear an opponent's reputation than make up a tale about almost being killed? She might have been worried that not everyone would care about Ryan's lies, and she'd added the alleged shooting as a little insurance.

The only problem was that Millie seemed so honest. Would she make up such a crazy lie?

Mom said, "Ashlee, I'd feel much better if you moved on to another young man. Try to find someone more dependable, like Jason." She turned to me. "It's too bad he doesn't have a brother."

Ashlee pulled her phone out of her waistband. "I don't need Dana's help finding a guy. I'm already working on it. I met this totally hot guy when Brittany and I were clothes shopping the other day. I'm texting him right now." She headed to her room.

I shook my head at her retreating back. "Would you like to stay for dinner, Mom? I think I still have a frozen meal of meat loaf and mashed potatoes I could zap in the microwave for you."

"Is that the type of food you eat?"

"Not all the time. We also have hot dogs and Top Ramen."

She tried to hide her disapproval. "Tell you what. How about you go get Ashlee and we all go out to eat? My treat. I'll sleep better knowing you had at least one decent meal."

A hot meal that didn't involve a microwave or seasoning packets? She wouldn't get any argument from me.

The next morning, I entered the farm's kitchen. Zennia and Millie were already there and frantically trying to finish breakfast prep.

Seeing Zennia's flustered face, I asked, "What's going on?"

She wiped her forehead with the back of her hand. "I'm afraid we got here late this morning. Now we're playing catch-up."

"I told you to leave me at your house. Fear shall not dictate my life," Millie grumbled as she cracked an egg into a bowl.

"Humor me," Zennia said. "I feel better knowing you're not alone."

I spotted a pitcher of freshly squeezed orange juice on the counter. "I'll take out the juice and a pitcher of water, too." On my way to the cupboard for the second pitcher, I paused. "I heard another commune meeting is scheduled for today. Sorry your plan didn't work."

"He's slicker than I gave him credit for, but I'll get rid of him yet."

"Jason mentioned you were talking to Frank after the meeting yesterday. Did he have any ideas that could help?"

A dark cloud passed over Millie's face. "We didn't get a chance to discuss the meeting. Frank was too busy apologizing for misplacing the electric bill. He forgot to pay it for the third month in a row. The company is threatening to shut off the lights." She hit the rim of the bowl too hard with an egg. Bits of shell broke off and fell in. "People aren't going to listen to Frank if he continues to be this unreliable."

I pulled down the water pitcher and started dumping in ice. "I know Frank's lived there a long time, but do you think someone else should take over the books?"

Millie plucked pieces of shell out of the bowl. "Eventually. Birch and I had discussed that idea before he was killed, but I'm afraid I've put it on the back burner with these other problems."

"Well, maybe this loan you lined up will take the

stress off of Frank until everything settles down and you can find a replacement."

"Wouldn't that be nice? The last thing we need is for Ryan to insist on taking over the finances, too. Then he'll have even more power."

I filled the pitcher with water and carried it and the pitcher of orange juice out of the kitchen. In the hall, I almost bumped into Connie, Olive's friend.

I stepped to the side so she could enter the dining room. "Welcome back," I said as she walked past.

She stopped inside the door and smiled, showing yellowed smoker's teeth. "I know I said I'd never come back after you let my friend fall down like that, but dang, did that massage feel good. Figured I'd use one of the coupons that uptight guy in the suit gave me."

Gordon would be thrilled. Connie's return was further proof that he was the king of customer service. "And Olive? Will she be joining you?"

"I asked her, what with it being her day off, too, but she refused. I think she was embarrassed."

"Anyone could trip," I said as I led Connie to a table by the French doors. I poured her a glass of water and set both pitchers on the table. "She shouldn't feel embarrassed."

Connie sat down and plunked her purse on the floor. "She doesn't care about that. It's her job she doesn't want to talk about."

A diner at another table signaled to me, and I held up one finger to let him know I'd be there in a minute. "Has something happened?"

"I'll say. Turns out she got her layoff notice a full

week ago. She and about half the staff are out at the end of the month." She scratched a mole on the side of her neck. "I don't know why she didn't tell us when we were all talking, but I think she's ashamed that she'll be out of work in a couple more weeks. Who knows with her? She always was the sensitive type." She smacked her lips. "I sure am hungry."

"I'll go see if breakfast is ready." Before I left the room, I set the pitchers on the sideboard and stopped to see what the other diner needed, only half paying attention as he requested no added salt in his meal.

The layoff notice must have been what Olive tried telling me the other night at the casino, but I wasn't surprised she changed her mind. When I'd been laid off from my marketing job before moving back home, I'd needed a week to accept the news myself and another week to tell anyone else. Olive probably felt the same way.

I carried the first two breakfast plates out to the diners. When I got around to Connie's table, I set the plate before her and asked, "What are Olive's plans now? More waitressing?"

"That's pretty much her only skill. Life's been awful rough for her since Tony died." She picked up her fork. "When he got killed, Olive was left with hardly any savings. She stretched it out as long as she could, but there wasn't much to start with. That job at the casino was about the only one she could get, and that pay's so low, she can barely afford to rub two nickels together."

I dropped into the chair across from Connie. She gave me a funny look but didn't say anything.

"And pretty soon she won't even have that job," I said.

"Talk about the worst timing ever," Connie said.

"Timing?"

"One night she finds out she's going to be out of a job, and the next morning her brother gets whacked." Connie gulped down a drink of water. "Olive always said the day Tony died was the day that ruined her life, but the day her brother died must have been pretty low, too."

I stared at Connie, not sure I'd heard her correctly. "Birch was killed the day after Olive found out she was being laid off?"

At Connie's nod, I could only shake my head.

First her husband was killed in an accident caused by Birch, and now she was about to be fired from the only job that was keeping her afloat. Maybe getting fired from the casino was the last straw for Olive.

And that's when she'd snapped.

Chapter 30

With Zennia and Millie taking care of the clean-up from breakfast, I grabbed an apple for Wilbur and headed outside. I needed to organize my thoughts, and talking to that pig sometimes helped.

On my way to the sty, I inhaled the early morning June air and savored the warmth of the sun on my head and shoulders. The minute Wilbur saw me, he ambled over and stuck his nose between the fence rails. I petted his rough, bristly head and dropped the apple into the pen for him to snack on.

While he chomped on the fruit, I leaned over the railing. "You don't know any of these people, Wilbur, but I need a good ear right now."

Wilbur snorted in response, which I took as agreement.

"You see, this old boyfriend of Zennia's was murdered, and I just learned his sister received her layoff notice only hours before the guy was killed. That wouldn't be such a big deal except Birch—

that's the dead guy—killed Olive's husband in a car accident a few years ago, and this job is the only one she could get. Money was already tight for her, and I have to wonder if the layoff pushed her over the edge."

Wilbur nosed the remaining bits of apple, showing no interest in the conversation.

"Your lack of response tells me you don't think Olive's the killer. Am I right?"

Wilbur snorted.

"Okay, how about Frank and Millie? Frank's been messing up the books lately, and Birch wasn't happy about that. Plus, both Millie and Frank are dead set against the big changes Ryan wants at the commune, while Birch seemed to like Ryan's ideas. I'm not sure why one of them wouldn't kill Ryan instead of Birch, but maybe they figured Birch had more influence over the rest of the commune. Millie's starting to realize that Ryan has plenty of influence of his own, but she might not have known that at the time."

Wilbur snorted again, most likely because the apple was gone. Still, I said, "Who's Ryan, you ask? He's a new guy at the commune who's been telling everyone they should use the Internet to sell their goods. But I now know he really wants to turn the property into a techie retreat and charge sky-high prices to let people stay there. Maybe Birch found out, and Ryan killed him in hopes of keeping his plans quiet until he knew the residents would go along with him." I drummed my fingers on the fence rail. "And if Millie's telling the truth, though I'm not sure she is, Ryan *did* try to kill her after she figured out this retreat idea."

Wilbur gave me one last look before wandering over to his buddies and lying down in the dirt. I returned to the house, more certain than ever that Ryan was the most likely person to kill Birch. Thank God Ashlee didn't want to date him anymore.

When I got to the kitchen, I found Millie and Zennia at the kitchen table, flipping through a cookbook.

"I cannot believe the amount of butter these recipes call for," Zennia said. "Poaching the fish in a leek broth is definitely our best option for lunch." She closed the book just as Esther and Gordon walked in from the hall.

"The jars are practically flying off the shelves," Gordon said to Esther.

She settled onto one of the kitchen chairs and nodded at the rest of us in greeting. "People love homemade goods. I know I sure do."

"But if I'd known, I would have asked for a bigger cut of the profits," Gordon said.

I sat down in the other empty chair. "Are you guys talking about the jams and honey from the commune?"

At the mention of the commune, Millie sat a little straighter, her eyes on Gordon.

"We've almost gone through the entire delivery," Gordon said. "I need to call Ryan and have him send us more. Unless . . ." Gordon got that calculating expression on his face, the one that told me he was thinking up ways to make money. "Do you know anything about jams and jellies?" he asked me.

I licked my lips. "I know I like to eat them, but that's it."

"I put up preserves every year," Esther said.

"I often serve them to the guests with our scones or toast," Zennia added.

Gordon's eyes gleamed. "We could sell our own jars of preserves in the lobby. We'd make a fortune."

Esther immediately pooh-poohed the idea. "I don't make near enough. As it is, we usually run out halfway through the winter. If we started selling the jars, we'd be out in a month."

"You could make more," Gordon said. "Dana and Zennia could help you."

I tried not to show my concern. "Or we could keep letting the commune supply the jams. That method is a lot simpler, plus the commune could use the business."

"From your lips to my creator's ears," Millie said.

"Why worry about the commune when you have the farm to consider?" Gordon asked in typical Gordon fashion.

I glanced at Millie, but she didn't seem offended. Esther laid her hand on Gordon's arm. "I'm afraid we simply don't have enough blackberries and strawberries on the property."

Gordon glowered at all of us, as if we were to blame for not having the foresight to plant more berries. "Fine. We'll stick with the current plan."

"I don't know if you're aware of this," Millie said, "but we offer other items besides jams and honeys. We also have fudge and lemon curd, not to mention quilts and blankets."

"I've tried the lemon curd," Gordon said, "but not the fudge. It might be a good seller here."

"If you're going to the fair tonight, you can try

a sample," Millie said. "The commune is running a booth."

"Jason and I are already going," I said. "We'll have to stop by and say hi."

Gordon adjusted the knot in his tie. "Dana, why don't you sample the fudge on behalf of the farm while you're there? I have no fondness for those ridiculous rides and silly displays."

"You don't know what you're missing," I told him. He headed for the lobby, and I turned to Millie. "You're not helping with the booth tonight, are you?"

"Of course I am. I do my share to help the commune."

"But aren't you worried about Ryan?" I asked. "He may come after you again."

Millie pushed herself up from her seat and leaned on the table, her eyes ablaze. "I'd like to see him try."

As soon as I got home from work that evening, I went straight into the bathroom to take a shower and get ready for my date. I waffled between a light summer dress and skinny jeans with a long-sleeved maroon top, settling on the jeans since the evenings still ran cool. Besides, I'd hate to have a wardrobe malfunction if I wore a dress on those carnival rides.

When I emerged from my room, Ashlee was coming in the front door, dressed in her vet smock from work. She eyed my outfit.

"Going out?"

"I'm off to the fair. Jason's picking me up in a bit."

"You know, it's pretty cool that you never have to wonder where you're going to find a date. You always have Jason."

I took a step back in mock surprise. "Don't tell me you've found a benefit to staying in a committed relationship."

"Sometimes it's nice to know you've got a guy you can count on." For a second, she sounded wistful. Then she laughed. "At least until the next guy comes along. And I plan to find me one of those tonight." She looked down at her smock. "But first I need to get out of these grungy clothes."

She disappeared into her room while I hastily straightened the living room and tidied up the kitchen. By the time I touched up my makeup, Jason was ringing the doorbell. He gave me a swoon-worthy kiss the moment I opened the door.

"Hey, beautiful," he said when we broke apart.

I inhaled the spicy scent of his cologne and grinned. "Hey, yourself. Ready to go?"

Before we could step outside, Ashlee came out of her room. She'd changed into a short red dress with matching heels. Her hair held such volume that she could have been on her way to audition for a shampoo commercial.

"Wow," I said. "You'll definitely catch a guy tonight."

"That's the plan." She pulled her lip gloss out of a purse that looked too small to carry much else. "Have fun at the fair. Don't throw up from all that funnel cake."

I paused with my hand on the doorknob. "Do you want to come with us? The more the merrier."

"No way. Those rides are death traps," she said. "Besides, Brittany texted a minute ago and swears the new guy at the bowling alley is perfect for me. I'm going to check him out."

"Just think, this could be the guy you end up spending the rest of your life with," I said.

Ashlee snorted. "Please. That never happens anymore. Sticking with one guy is so old-school."

"I wouldn't say that," Jason said, giving my waist a squeeze.

"Me neither." I gave him a peck on the cheek, which prompted Ashlee to make a face. I grabbed my keys. "Have fun tonight," I told her.

"Try not to get killed when the Ferris wheel falls off the track," she called back.

I rolled my eyes. My sister said the most ridiculous things sometimes.

Still, maybe I'd skip the Ferris wheel. I was looking for a fun night, not a fatal one.

Chapter 31

We walked down to where Jason had parked his car in a visitor's space. The sun was starting to slide behind the hills, and the air was bathed in a warm, golden light. I knew darkness would fall soon enough, and that was fine by me. I loved the bright lights of the carnival rides as they twirled through the night.

Jason pulled out of the apartment complex, and I leaned back against the seat. "Remind me when we get to the fair that I need to sample fudge for Gordon," I said.

"Anything special about it?" he asked.

"It's from Evergreen. Their jams and honeys have been selling well at the farm, and Gordon wants to expand our offerings."

The traffic light switched from yellow to red, and Jason eased to a stop. "Who from the commune is going to be there?"

"I'm not sure, although Millie mentioned she'd be helping. I just hope Ryan has the good grace to either not show up or stay away from Millie if he does."

A few minutes later, we crested the small hill that led to the fairgrounds. I looked down to where the usual barren patch of dirt and three plain buildings had been transformed into a ride-and-show extravaganza. The Ferris wheel spun lazily in a circle, the lights shining brightly in the approaching twilight. Nearby, a dragon roller coaster sped along the track, while riders on the swings flew through the air, their feet dangling.

With the main parking lot full, the attendant directed us to the dirt overflow lot. The moment I opened my car door, the organ music that was so unique to carnivals reached me.

"Man, I love that sound," I said. "You know people are having a great time."

Jason came over to my side of the car and put his arm around my waist. "Let's go join the fun."

He bought our tickets at the gate, and we merged with the other fair-goers, most of whom seemed to be heading toward the closest building. Off to the side, a large grassy area held a petting zoo and a small collection of sheep and cows. Kids with their parents pointed to the animals and tried to pet them over the gates. The sugary sweet smell of cotton candy and the buttery rich aroma of popcorn filled the air.

With the building in my way, I couldn't see the rides, but I could still hear the shrieks of delight. My pulse quickened in anticipation.

Jason pulled me out of the throng of people and off to the side. "What would you like to do first?"

I surveyed the crowd, which seemed to be

growing by the minute. "Let's find the commune's booth. I can try that fudge before we hit the rides."

We entered the first building and wandered up and down the rows, passing booth after booth. Vendors were selling everything from car wax to mini blenders to dips and salsas. The aisles were narrow, and we inched along behind a logjam of shoppers.

After completing the circuit without seeing anyone from the commune, we headed for the exit. Outside, a light breeze blew by. It was a welcome relief after being stuck in the crowded building.

I led Jason to the second building, and we walked in. Like the first one, the place was dense with people and wares, and our search was just as fruitless. I kept a tight grip on Jason's hand as we struggled through the mass of people. After a quick trip up each aisle, I pushed my way through the crowd and back outside.

"Man," I said to Jason, "I think every resident of Blossom Valley is in those two buildings."

"Must be out-of-towners here, too, as many people as there are," Jason said. He pointed toward the third and smallest building. "Only one more to check."

The building sat off by itself behind a fenced area that usually housed old farming equipment but was currently being used to sell goods, while the outside had caged birds and reptiles for sale. Before going in, I took a moment to look at the animals in their cages, dreading how busy the inside was sure to be.

When I'd seen every gecko, mourning dove, and goose, I grabbed the door handle and turned to Jason. "Ready for this?"

"Let's do it."

I took a deep breath and pulled open the door, ready to face the onslaught of shoppers.

But I needn't have worried. While people were milling around the aisles, the crowd's size was a fraction of those in the other buildings. I started down the first row, quickly moving past the guy selling aluminum siding and the woman hawking face creams. I hung a left at the end, and moved up the next row.

Just as I started to wonder if Millie had been mistaken about the booth, I spotted Frank and Ryan in the far corner. Ryan was tapping on his phone, with his eyes glued to the screen. Frank stood with his arms crossed while he glared at the shoppers. No customers approached their booth, not that I was surprised with that kind of welcome.

I pointed them out to Jason. "There they are," I said. We made our way over. Ryan glanced up, grimaced, and returned to his phone. For a guy who may have killed Birch and tried to kill Millie, he certainly didn't act guilty. Mostly, he seemed annoyed.

I addressed Frank. "Have you seen Millie?"

"Her shift starts in an hour." He frowned as a woman moved toward the table. "Then I can get away from this zoo." The woman must have heard him, because she veered away at the last second. If this smaller crowd was too much for Frank to handle, I couldn't imagine what he'd do if he had to work in one of the other buildings.

I surveyed the offerings on the table. "Have sales at least been decent?"

"Not bad," Frank grudgingly admitted. He jerked

his head toward Ryan. "But I wish this yahoo would help when it gets busy."

Ryan looked up from his phone. "I don't even know why I'm here."

Frank started arranging the jars of honey. "That makes two of us," he mumbled to the table.

Ouch. I snuck a peek at Jason, and he raised his eyebrows in return.

Pearl walked up to the booth with a cardboard box in her hands. She wore jeans and a white button-up blouse, with a colorful scarf around her neck. She set the box on the floor and gestured to it. "Hi, Dana. Check out the fudge. It's selling like hotcakes." Her eyes widened. "Hey, maybe we should sell hotcake mixes. What do you think?"

"Not a bad idea for next year," I said. "You might have a real winner on your hands."

She beamed and began to remove little cellophane packages of fudge from the box. She placed them in an empty spot on the table. As she worked, her scarf would occasionally slip down and get in her way, and she would brush it back.

Jason put his hand on my back and leaned in close to speak in my ear. "I'm going to check out that booth of sports memorabilia over there. I'll be right back."

He walked off, and I turned back to Pearl, who was still setting up the bags.

"Does the farm have a booth here tonight, too?" she asked me.

"Nope, I'm here to enjoy the fair."

She paused in her unpacking. "It's the best, isn't it? Everyone has so much fun, and there are all these wonderful foods to enjoy. I always ride the merry-go-round at least once."

"What time does your shift end?" I asked.

"I don't have an official shift," she said. "I offered to help with the little things, like restocking supplies or fetching food for whoever's running the booth. I'm taking short breaks here and there when things are quiet. I even found a booth that sells hot herbal tea."

"How nice for you," I said. "I've noticed you're quite partial to tea."

Pearl smiled. "I've always found it so soothing. The world would be a better place if everyone drank more tea."

If only it were that easy. "Before I forget, I need to buy a little fudge," I said. "We might sell it at the farm." I picked up a bag. "How much?"

"On the house. It's the least I can do after that incident in the woods the other night." She blushed.

"I've already forgotten about that," I said, though of course I hadn't. "I'm stopping back here in a while to say hi to Millie. Maybe I'll see you again."

I put the fudge in my pocket to share with Jason later and joined him at the sports memorabilia booth, where he was shaking a man's hand. He plucked a card from the table and stuck it in his pocket.

He saw me and smiled. "Ready for some excitement?"

"Absolutely." We walked outside and over to the ride area, where a little kid was dragging his mom by the hand to the giant slide. The lights on the nearby Tilt-A-Whirl flashed in time to the music, and I watched the thrilled faces of the riders as they spun by. A shiver of excitement shot up my spine. While we waited in line at the nearest ticket booth, I studied the rides, trying to decide which one to start with.

"Let's go on the Viking first," I said, pointing to the giant pirate ship that was swinging back and forth. At one point, the ship swung up high enough that I thought it was going to turn all the way over, but at the last second, it swung back down. The screams of the riders reached us from across the blacktop.

"You don't kid around, do you?" he asked.

"You haven't seen anything yet. I plan to ride everything."

We bought our wristbands and made our way over to the pirate ship. While we waited for our turn, I handed Jason a piece of fudge and took a bite of my own. The creamy, smooth chocolate practically melted on my tongue. I'm pretty sure I moaned aloud at the rich flavor, but luckily no one could hear me over the jaunty music from the ride and all the people talking.

When we reached the front of the line, I followed Jason onto the ship and pulled down the lap bar. A gap remained between my thighs and the bar. I pushed down harder, but the bar didn't budge. The attendant came by to check that everyone was seated securely. She gave my bar a cursory tug and started to move on to the next rider, but I reached out and touched her arm. "Um, shouldn't this be a little tighter?" I asked.

"Naw, it's fine. No one's fallen off the ride yet."

Well, that was not reassuring.

I looked over at Jason. He was holding back a grin. "You're not nervous, are you?"

"Not at all," I said. "I was only checking."

The ride started to move, swinging back and forth slowly at first before picking up speed. As the boat started to rise, I felt myself stomach rise with it.

Beside me, Jason said, "This is great, right?"

I was afraid if I opened my mouth, I'd throw up on him, so I merely nodded. The boat continued to swing higher, and I used all my concentration to fight the queasiness.

After what felt like an eternity, the ship made its way back to port without my getting sick. I managed to navigate my way down the steps to the exit, where I allowed Jason to drag me off to the next ride. After the Hurricane, the dragon roller coaster, the fun house, and the Tilt-A-Whirl, I called for a time-out. I didn't remember the rides making me nearly this nauseated when I was a kid. Was this what it was like to get old?

I sank onto the nearest bench and let out a groan. Jason sat down next to me.

"What's wrong?" he asked. "I thought you wanted to go on all the rides."

I blinked twice to try and clear my head, but the ground still kept spinning. "I'm pacing myself."

"How about a funnel cake? It'll give us the energy to tackle the rest."

At the suggestion of the sugary fried treat, my stomach did a flip-flop. "I'll start with water."

"Coming right up." He moved over to the concession stand, while I leaned back against the bench and closed my eyes.

A slight pressure on the seat indicated someone

had sat down next to me. "Are they out of water?" I asked, opening my eyes.

But Jason wasn't sitting next to me; Olive was. I jumped a little.

"Oops, didn't mean to scare you," she said. She looked around. "I just love the fair, don't you?"

I put a hand on my stomach. "I'm not loving it right now. Not after the Tilt-A-Whirl. I don't remember it spinning that fast when I was a kid."

"I never go on any of those rides," she said. "Haven't you seen how rusty all the bolts and other parts are?" Maybe Olive and Ashlee should compare notes on the dangers of carnival rides.

"Are you here alone?" I asked.

"No, a friend and I rode over together. We're celebrating our luck. We've both landed jobs at the new casino that's opening."

I sat up straighter, my woozy stomach forgotten. "Congratulations. That's great news."

"Especially since I got my notice at the other place. I was too ashamed to say anything before, plus I was hoping management would change their minds. A bunch of us were talking about banding together and suing to keep our jobs, but that seemed like a lot of trouble and it's probably expensive to hire a lawyer. Besides, I want to work where I'm wanted." She stood. "I see my friend's out of the bathroom. Take care."

She walked off toward the restrooms as Jason joined me at the bench. He handed me a bottle of water and popped the top on his can of soda.

"Wasn't that Olive?" he asked.

"Yes, it was. You know, Detective Palmer should really come to the fair. I'm pretty sure every person associated with Birch is here tonight." I unscrewed the cap on the water bottle and took a drink. "Anyway, Olive was telling me how she got hired at that new casino over on the coast."

"Glad things are working out for her."

"Me, too." I checked the time on my phone. "Let's see if Millie's at the booth yet. Then I think I've recovered enough to face the Zipper."

Jason didn't look convinced. "Isn't that the one where they put you in a cage and then flip the cage around a bunch?"

"I can handle it." I laid a hand on my stomach. "I think."

"If you're sure." We walked back to the small building, where the crowd was still manageable, but growing. When we got to the back corner where the commune's booth was set up, I found Millie and Zennia there, with Frank and Ryan nowhere in sight. Zennia was busy talking to a woman who was reading the label on a jar of preserves, but Millie smiled as we approached.

"Did Ryan leave?" I asked.

"That scoundrel? He darted away like a frightened deer the moment he saw me."

The customer paid for her purchase, and Zennia came over to join us.

"Zennia, I didn't know you'd be here tonight," I said.

"After listening to you and Millie talk about it earlier today, I decided to come out and help. I haven't been to the fair in years."

"I bet it hasn't changed much," Jason said.

"Not a bit. All the same rides are here, and the food hasn't gotten any healthier."

"I'm sure I saw a place where they were selling salads," I said.

Zennia gave me a knowing look. "Right next to the deep-fried candy bar booth, I bet."

I was about to ask Jason if he wanted to try one of those candy bars now that I wasn't feeling as sick, but he was looking across the room. I checked to see what had caught his attention and saw an older gentleman in slacks and a polo shirt talking to a fair employee in coveralls.

"Do you know those guys?" I asked.

"The one in the polo shirt is the mayor. I've been trying to nail down his position on a Starbucks opening in town," Jason said, "but he's been avoiding my calls. I'm going to talk to him. I'll be right back."

"Sure, I need to make a trip to the little girl's room anyway," I said. "I'll find you when I get back."

Jason walked off, and I took a moment to enjoy the view of his backside before heading in the opposite direction to where the bathrooms were located. I made quick use of the facilities and washed my hands at the sink before stepping back out.

I scanned the area and saw Pearl down at the end of the row, standing near the exit. She noticed me at the same time and waved for me to join her. When I didn't immediately move in her direction, she started waving more insistently.

"Do you need help?" I called to her, though I knew she couldn't hear me from this distance.

A woman at the closest booth looked up from the pair of earrings she was holding. "No, I'm fine.'

"What?" I said, not realizing for a second that she was answering my question. "Oh, no, I was talking to that woman over there." I pointed at Pearl, only to watch her suddenly dart out the door.

With a feeling of unease, I headed after her, wondering if something was wrong.

Chapter 32

When I reached the door, I got tangled up in a small group of fair-goers who were entering the building. I tried to keep an eye on Pearl, but lost track of her as I made my way outside. I felt a moment of panic until I spotted her standing on the edge of a crowd watching a teenager ride a mechanical bull. As I walked over, I noticed she was looking around and frowning, but her face brightened when she saw me.

"Is everything all right?" I asked. "You were waving at me like there was an emergency."

She wrung her hands. "We're running short on fudge again, plus Millie would like more strawberry jam to sell. I was hoping I could get help carrying the boxes from the van."

Behind Pearl, the mechanical bull bucked the teenager off its back. Spectators whistled and clapped as the kid stood up and dusted off his jeans.

"Why did you run out the door like that?" I asked. "I thought I saw Ryan and was going to ask him to help, but now I can't find him. Can you help instead?"

I considered her request. Jason might be talking to the mayor for a while, plus he could always call my cell if he couldn't find me. "Sure, if it doesn't take too long. Where's the van parked?" I asked, hoping it was closer than Jason's car out in the overflow lot. I didn't want to schlep the boxes farther than I had to.

She pointed toward a fenced-in parking lot off in the distance. "In the employee lot. This won't take but a minute."

"All right. Lead the way."

I took a few seconds to text Jason about my plans and put the phone in my pocket. I followed Pearl past the mechanical bull as another teenager climbed on its back. We looped around the BMX demonstration, across a grassy area where workers were dismantling a small circus tent, and over to the employee lot. We could still hear the music and other noises of the fair behind us, but the sound was decidedly fainter.

Pearl opened the pedestrian gate marked EMPLOYEES ONLY, and we entered the lot.

Inside, tall parking lamps lit up the asphalt, illuminating the scraps of paper and cigarette butts that littered the ground. Cars and trucks of all sizes filled the rows.

"I'm afraid the van's parked at the far end," Pearl said. We started down the center aisle.

"Were you at the meeting yesterday?" I asked. "The one where Millie wanted to kick Ryan out of the commune?"

Pearl's step faltered, and she shook her head. "I never attend those meetings. Too much fighting."

"But how do you keep track of what's happening?"

"The women in my sewing circle let me know about anything important," she said.

We reached the van, which was parked between an SUV and a compact. Pearl reached in her jacket pocket. "Things have been so off-kilter lately, haven't they?" she said. "First Birch dies, then Millie claims someone tried to kill her, too." She pulled out a set of keys. "No one is getting along anymore."

She unlocked the back of the van and pulled open the door. The hinges let out a heavy groan. She reached up and hit the light switch on the ceiling, illuminating several large cardboard boxes filled with jars and cellophane packages. To the side was a stack of small, empty boxes.

"I think I'll fill up these smaller boxes," Pearl said, "We don't want to hurt our backs. It's a long way back to the building when you're carrying a load of jam." She set a small box next to a larger one and started transferring the jars. "You know, things were fine until Ryan got here. I've noticed he never drinks tea."

I moved up next to Pearl to help. "I'm sure once Ryan leaves or Millie accepts his ideas, everything will settle down again."

"I don't know," Pearl said. "It's not just Millie and Ryan who aren't getting along. Even Birch was mad at Ryan the night before he died. And Birch and Frank were fighting, too. I don't know what's happening to Evergreen these days."

My grip tightened on the jar I was holding.

"Wait. Did you hear Birch fighting with Ryan and Frank?"

Pearl paused in her transferring. "It's not like I was trying to. But the men were right outside the sewing room. With the way they were yelling, anyone would have heard them."

"Were they all three fighting together, or was Birch arguing with them at different times?"

Pearl pursed her lips. "I don't like to gossip. Girls at school used to do that when I was young, and I always thought it was mean."

"I'm not a fan of gossip either," I said, "but Birch is dead, and Millie almost joined him. What you overheard could be important."

"All right, I guess I can tell you. First Ryan and Birch were yelling about this silly Internet idea. That really surprised me, because Birch was always Ryan's biggest supporter. But that night, Birch said that Ryan had misled him and that Birch didn't like being tricked."

My breath caught. So Birch *had* discovered Ryan was making secret plans. I could almost feel the noose tightening around Ryan's neck. "What did Ryan say?"

Pearl set the final jar in the small box. I picked up the box and set it on the ground outside the van so she could fill up another one. A breeze blew through the lot and ruffled my hair. I heard a rustling sound off behind one of the cars, most likely from the wind blowing trash around the lot.

"Nothing," Pearl said, "or if he did, I couldn't hear it. Frank came up and asked what all the ruckus was about—you know how Frank is." She grabbed another empty box. "Let's fill one with honey, too. We're starting to run low."

I'd been gone long enough that Jason might have tried to contact me. I checked my phone to make sure I hadn't accidentally set it to silent mode, but it was on and showed no messages. I put my phone back in my pocket.

Pearl tried to shove the large box containing the rest of the jam to the side, but it barely budged. "Shoot, the box of honey is closer to the front. Would you mind?"

I stepped up into the back of the van, making sure to hunch over so I didn't scrape my back. I shoved the one box as far as it would go to the side before gripping the edge of the open box. I could see the jars of honey inside.

"What happened with Ryan and Frank after that?" I asked as I pulled the box forward.

"I think Ryan left," Pearl said, "because I could only hear Frank and Birch. Though mostly Frank was doing the talking. Boy, does that man have a temper." She leaned in and dropped her voice, though we were alone in the lot. "He's scared me once or twice, truth be told."

"I've seen that temper myself," I said, thinking of his initial meeting with Detective Palmer.

"It was in full force that night." She shivered. "I feel bad now, but at the time I was glad he was directing all that anger at Birch and not at me."

"What was he mad about?" I asked, stepping out of the van and wiping my hands on my jeans.

Pearl started pulling out jars of honey and putting them in the smaller box. "The books. Frank said he'd been handling the money for fifteen years and a couple of mistakes were no big deal. Then he said Birch better not think about forcing him out, because he'd make darn sure he didn't go anywhere."

A chill ran down my back. "You're sure this happened the night before Birch was killed?"

"Yes, that's why I was troubled to find out that he'd died the next morning. Can you imagine how unsettled his soul must have been with all that fighting? When I die, I hope it's in my sleep with all my affairs in order."

If Pearl hadn't been so positive about the specific night, I would have said she was mistaken. After all, Frank told me he hadn't seen Birch again that night after they returned from the farmers market. Why would Frank lie? Was it because he didn't want people to know Birch confronted him about his bookkeeping mistakes?

But others already knew that Frank kept messing up. Again, why lie? The chill that had run down my back now felt more like an icy dagger. There could only be one reason.

Frank's voice boomed out of the shadows. "Man, I can't catch a break."

I whirled around. Frank stepped out from the other side of the SUV parked next to the van.

Fear surged through me as I wondered how much he'd heard.

"Here I'm being a nice guy by helping you bring in the supplies, and what do I come upon? You two talking about me."

Next to me, Pearl stared at Frank, her eyes wide. "Oh dear, I knew I shouldn't have been gossiping. Please forgive me, Frank. I'm so embarrassed." She walked over to him and held out her hand in a conciliatory gesture, probably not realizing she still clutched a jar of honey.

In one swift movement, Frank smacked the jar out of Pearl's hand. It shattered on the pavement.

Pearl gasped. "Frank, I'm sorry. I didn't mean to upset you."

He glowered at the both of us as a feeling of dread weighed heavy in my gut. He waved his hand at me. "Even when I tried to scare you off in the woods the other night, you still kept asking your damn questions." He turned his hard eyes on Pearl, who seemed to shrink under his unrelenting stare. "And now I find out you overheard what Birch said to me."

Criminy. Frank was the one who chased me through the woods? And he must have killed Birch, too. Which meant he must plan to kill Pearl and me. I swallowed convulsively and scanned the back of the van for a weapon or heavy object I could use against him. All I saw were jars and boxes.

I glanced toward the gate, now a tiny rectangle on the other side of the lot. I could probably outrun Frank, but Pearl couldn't. I wasn't even sure she recognized the danger we were in. She seemed completely lost about the entire conversation.

Pearl cradled her hand. "What do you mean you chased Dana? Why would you do that?"

"He must have thought I suspected him of killing Birch," I said, earning a glare from Frank. I addressed him. "What did Birch ever do to you?"

"He just kept harping on my mistakes that morning. The whole way to Zennia's, he kept going on and on about how I needed to step down," Frank said. "I had to kill him before he suggested a vote to force me out. I can't lose my place at the commune. I have nowhere to go. The doc says I've got early Alzheimer's. What am I supposed to do?"

I couldn't help but feel sorry for Frank and his condition. The "stolen" calculator, the misplaced bills, the forgotten payments. All the pieces were there, but no one had put them together. He must have felt desperate when his doctor told him the news.

Then I reminded myself that he'd killed Birch, not to mention what he planned to do with Pearl and me. My pity turned to anger, and I focused once more on getting out of this mess.

"You didn't have to do it, Frank," Pearl said. "We'd never kick you out. We'll take care of you."

"Yeah, like you took care of George, right? Don't think for a second that I plan to end up like him, living with a cousin he can't stand. If I can even find any of my cousins. I haven't talked to them in years."

"But he didn't do any work at the commune," Pearl said. "He never lifted a finger. Not like you, Frank. You've always been a big help."

While I listened to them talk, my mind was trying to come up with an escape plan. Even if I could manage to call 911, the police wouldn't get here in time. We were on our own. I tuned back into the conversation.

"*You* think I'm a big help, but you're not running the show," Frank said. "Looks like Millie is. And once she gets rid of Ryan, I'll be the next one in her sights."

"Nonsense. She'll help you. In fact, let's go talk to Millie right now." Pearl stepped forward and reached for Frank's arm. At the same time, my cell phone started to ring.

A look of panic came over Frank's features, and he shoved Pearl backward. I tried to stop her fall, but I wasn't close enough. The ends of her scarf fluttered up in the air as she fell to the ground. With clenched fists, Frank loomed over her.

I grabbed the closest jar of honey from the box and hurled it at Frank's head. It clipped his temple.

Frank's hand flew to the spot I'd struck. His expression went black with rage. Pearl still lay on the ground, barely moving. He stepped over her, intent on coming after me.

Snatching up two more jars out of the box, I threw them as fast as I could. The first one sailed over his shoulder and broke on the ground. The second jar hit Frank square in the shoulder. He let out a grunt.

I picked up two more jars and threw them and then grabbed two more. Frank put up his arms to ward off the blows, but one of the jars managed to peg him in the forehead.

He stumbled backward in surprise, and his foot caught on Pearl. He tripped over her and went down. The back of his head bounced off the ground with an audible thud.

I rushed to Pearl, extricated her from under Frank's legs, and tried to yank her to her feet.

She did little to help me. All she could do was

sputter, "Why would he? Why . . ." but at least she was conscious. I heaved her up and practically dragged her across the pavement.

"We have to go," I said.

I looked back at Frank and saw that he was trying to sit up.

"Come on," I muttered. "Come on." We moved across the asphalt with painstaking slowness.

I checked over my shoulder again and saw Frank unsteadily rising to his feet. Once he regained his balance, he'd be on Pearl and me in a minute. I picked up my speed and kept one hand on Pearl's back to propel her forward. She almost lost her footing at one point, but I kept my grip firm and helped her along. Just as Frank started to run toward us, she made it through the gate, with me right on her heels. I grabbed the gate and swung it shut behind me.

Turning back, I saw that Frank was fast approaching. I tried to find a way to lock the gate but there wasn't any kind of latch. How the hell could I keep this gate closed?

My eyes settled on Pearl. "Your scarf!" I slid it from around her neck and swiftly passed it through the metal links, around the pole, and back again. With Frank only feet away now, I tied the scarf into a knot, managing to double-tie it as he grabbed the chain-link.

He yanked on the gate and howled. The scarf held, but I could see the material straining. He pulled again, and the scarf gave a little.

"We have to get help," I said to Pearl. She didn't move. She seemed to be in shock.

From behind me, I heard Jason's voice. "Dana, what's going on?"

I turned and saw him and Zennia coming toward us. Relief flooded through me. Still, I kept a tight grip on the scarf as I yelled, "Quick, over here."

Frank stopped tugging on the gate and snarled at Jason and Zennia. "For God's sake," he said. He turned around and lurched across the parking lot in the other direction, no doubt looking for another exit.

I fought the urge to chase after him. I hated to see Frank get away, but he was clearly making a run for it. Who knew what he'd do if we tried to stop him?

Jason rushed up to me and gestured toward Frank, who was halfway across the lot. "What's happening? Should I chase after him?"

I shook my head. "Let's call the police and let them handle it. Pearl has the keys to the van, which means he's on foot. And like Frank told me himself, he has nowhere to go."

Chapter 33

I hastily told Jason about what happened at the van and that Frank had killed Birch. He called the police while I checked on Pearl. She was sitting on the ground with her head between her knees. Zennia crouched next to her, and I squatted down on the other side.

Zennia caught my eye and said, "I'm going to run and get Millie. She might be able to help with Pearl."

Once Zennia was gone, I spoke to Pearl. "Are you all right? Frank gave you one heck of a shove."

"My bottom will be sore tomorrow, but otherwise I'm okay." She looked at me with a dazed expression. "Frank's lived at Evergreen as long as I have. Why would he do such a thing?"

I shrugged. "He must have seen his whole world crumbling and panicked." I sat down on the pavement. My hands were shaking badly, and I clasped them together. "I'm just glad he didn't succeed in killing us, too."

Pearl started to cry, and I patted her back.

Jason sat down on the other side of me and put his arm around my shoulders. "Are you all right?"

I nodded, afraid to speak in case I started crying like Pearl.

"The cops are on the way," he said. "Detective Palmer, too. They've got a bulletin out for Frank. I can't imagine he'll get far."

"Let's hope not." I leaned against Jason, and he put his other arm around me to envelop me in a hug. After a few moments I heard the sound of sirens far away. They came closer and closer until they suddenly went silent. Several uniformed officers swarmed into the parking lot, followed by Detective Palmer.

He bent down next to me. "You should really stop getting into these binds," he said by way of greeting.

I surprised myself by laughing. "Good advice. I think I'll take it."

He proceeded to ask me a series of questions. I filled him in, starting with what Pearl told me she'd overheard the night before Birch was killed and ending with when Jason and Zennia showed up. After that, Detective Palmer spoke with Pearl. She seemed to have recovered for the most part, though I'd have to make sure she had a ride back to the commune. No way should she drive herself, if that's how she'd gotten to the fair.

After a few more questions, Detective Palmer rose and flipped his notebook closed. "I'm glad you two are okay," he said. He walked off to join three officers near the van.

"Let's see if we can get Pearl up," Jason said.

He rose and helped me stand. I brushed off my

hands, and together, we pulled Pearl to her feet as Zennia, Millie, and Ryan came through the gate.

"Are you sure you're all right?" Jason asked me.

"Better by the minute," I said.

He rubbed my back. "I need to check with the detective. I've got a story to write. But I'm only a holler away if you need me." He gave me a kiss and walked off toward Detective Palmer.

Millie hurried over, with Zennia right behind her. Ryan stayed near the gate and shoved his hands in his pockets, seemingly at a loss.

Shaking her head, Zennia said, "I can't believe everything that happened tonight."

"At least we know who killed Birch," I said. "That's a bit of comfort."

"I never would have guessed it was Frank, though. He and Birch were always so close. To think, after all these years . . ." She let her voice trail away as tears glinted in her eyes.

"If this Alzheimer's diagnosis is true, he may have been acting like a completely different person. Plus, he must have been terrified about his future. Is he right that the residents would kick him out of the commune?" I asked.

"Absolutely not," Pearl said fiercely, showing a sudden spark of energy. "That was all in Frank's head. Too bad he didn't ask for our help. Poor Birch might still be alive."

Millie balled one hand into a fist and slapped it into her other palm. "He knows we always work out our problems. Though some are harder than others," she added with a backward glance at Ryan, who was still waiting at the gate.

"What's he doing here anyway?" I asked.

"He was helping me in the booth for a few minutes when Zennia returned and told us what happened. Before she came up, Ryan and I had a chance to talk. I convinced him he was being overzealous with his changes. I also admitted that I lied about being shot at."

Zennia gasped. "What? You never lie! And about something as important as your life being in danger?"

Millie didn't meet Zennia's gaze. "I'm certainly not proud of what I did, but I was too scared that life at Evergreen was going to change. I wasn't thinking clearly. But after discussing things, I've realized Ryan's simply a young man with too much ambition and too little life experience." She lifted her chin, and her eyes gleamed. "Together, though, we can do great things for the commune."

Pearl let out a sniffle. "Does that mean there won't be as much fighting?"

"Yes," Millie said. "Our diverging paths have almost come together as one."

Two more police officers came through the gate, and Zennia eyed them. "I believe I'll get out of everyone's way. I'm doing no good here."

"I'll come with you," Pearl said. "I need a cup of tea."

"And Ryan and I have much more to discuss," Millie said.

The women headed for the exit, but stopped when they reached Ryan. Jason broke away from the detective and walked over. A small but excited smile played on his lips.

"Do you have news?" I asked.

"A sheriff's deputy spotted Frank hitchhiking on

the highway," Jason said, "possibly trying to get back to the commune. As soon as the officer confronted him, Frank gave himself up. They're transporting him to the county jail right now."

I let out my breath. "I'm glad. I knew he couldn't run forever, but I didn't like the idea of him still being out there."

"He's in custody. He can't hurt anyone else." Jason pulled me in for a hug and rested his chin on my head. I closed my eyes and felt my worries slip away.

After a moment, I stepped back. "Man, I was so sure Ryan killed Birch. Even when I found out about Olive's husband and her job loss, I went right back to Ryan as my main suspect."

"With good reason. He had a strong motive," Jason said.

"Still, I should have noticed how odd it was that Zennia's neighbor didn't see anyone enter or leave the cul-de-sac after Frank left. Now I realize that's because Frank was the one who killed Birch. There was no one else." I looked back at the van. The police were inspecting it with flashlights, and I tried to imagine how Frank had felt as he drove away from Zennia's that morning.

"At least the truth's out," Jason said, breaking into my thoughts.

"And things are getting better for everyone, other than Frank of course. Olive has a new job, and even Ryan and Millie have patched up their differences. It's as close to a happy ending as we can hope for."

"Well, there's still one big question hanging over you and me," Jason said.

I searched my brain for a clue as to what he was talking about. "What's that?"

He cleared his throat. "When you told me what happened with Frank, and even when you got chased through the woods a few nights ago, well . . ." Jason reached in his pocket and paused.

"Well, what?" I asked, still at a loss.

"I've been carrying this thing around all week. I wanted to do everything right, you know?"

"Carrying what around?" What on earth was he talking about?

"I even thought about hiring a skywriter, or getting my buddy who plays the violin to serenade us. But after what happened tonight, I realize I don't care about any of that. I only care about you."

I stared at Jason as he lowered himself to one knee. A jolt went through me as I understood what he was about to do. I almost felt more scared than when Frank trapped Pearl and me by the van. Was I ready for this?

He fumbled in his pocket and cleared his throat again. "Dana, I love you, and I want to spend the rest of my life with you." He pulled out a velvet jewelry case and popped it open. A large marquis-shaped diamond sparkled in the light of the parking lot lamps. "Will you marry me?"

The world seemed to slow down as I readied my answer. Over Jason's shoulder, I could see Zennia standing nearby, a huge grin spreading across her face. Then I focused my gaze on Jason and his warm, green eyes.

"Yes," I said. "Absolutely, positively, yes."

Tips and Recipes from the O'Connell Organic Farm and Spa

Thanks for spending time with us at the O'Connell Organic Farm and Spa. Before you go, here are a few recipes and tips to take with you. Come back soon!

Tofu Stir-Fry

Now that I've actually cooked tofu, I have no idea why I never liked to eat it before. This recipe is a snap to make, and you can use whatever vegetables you have on hand, not just the ones listed in the recipe.

To make the stir-fry, in a medium-size bowl, stir together two tablespoons of soy sauce, two tablespoons of white wine vinegar, and an eighth of a teaspoon of red pepper chili flakes (more if you like your meal spicy!). Cut one package of firm tofu into one-inch cubes, add to the ingredients in the bowl, and toss to coat. Let that marinate for ten minutes. In a wok over medium heat, add two tablespoons of sesame oil. When the oil is hot, add the tofu, discarding the marinade, and cook for two to three minutes. Add half a cup of quartered white button mushrooms, half a sliced yellow pepper, three sliced green onions, and two cups of broccoli florets. Stir everything together, and then add two tablespoons of low-sodium soy sauce and three tablespoons of oyster sauce to the skillet. Cook for another five minutes or until the vegetables are done to your liking. The stir-fry serves four and is delicious over rice.

Flavored Water

Esther here to talk about water. I always try to drink my eight glasses a day, but sometimes plain water needs a little pep. I like to add fresh fruit or herbs for flavor. I put everything in a piece of cheesecloth, or even a tea ball, if the fruit is small enough, so that the seeds or bits of fruit don't get in the way. Then I let the fruit sit in the water for ten minutes or longer to really get a lot of flavor. One of my favorite tricks is to use frozen pineapple tidbits or other frozen fruit to keep the water cold without adding ice. Cucumber slices are another great choice, and I sometimes even add a few mint leaves. Just about anything will work!

Herb and Lemon Soap

Not only is it fun to make soap, but for people like Ashlee and me, who are on a budget, it's a great option for gifts. Gretchen showed me how, and it couldn't be easier. First, pick up a package of glycerin soap from a craft store. Using a microwavable bowl, heat a few blocks in the microwave in thirty-second intervals, stirring occasionally, until completely melted. Mince one teaspoon of thyme or rosemary and one teaspoon of lemon peel (you can also use other herbs and mix-ins), and thoroughly stir both into the melted glycerin until it is a nice light yellow. Make sure not to add too much of the herbs or peel, because the soap will become crumbly. Pour the mixture into any small plastic container that has been lightly oiled. I used little shallow food containers that Mom gave me a while back, but you can also use shallow yogurt containers, or cute molds that they sell at craft stores. After a minute, gently stir the soap in case the herbs and peel have settled to the bottom. Let the soap rest for an hour and then freeze it for another hour before popping it out of the container. Voilà! Beautiful soap! Be sure to use it within a few months.

Lemon Curd

It's Esther here, giving you my favorite lemon curd recipe. First, take a vegetable peeler and remove the zest of three lemons, making sure not to get any white pith in the mix. Put the zest in a blender or food processor with a cup of sugar (more if you like things on the sweeter side) and pulse it together until the zest is all minced up. Then cream one stick (eight tablespoons) of butter that's been sitting out at room temperature, and mix in the lemon and sugar mixture. Once everything is nice and creamy, add four eggs, one at a time. Squeeze in the juice from those three lemons (watch the seeds!), and mix everything together.

Pour the concoction into a small saucepan and warm on low heat, making sure to stir constantly, until the curd starts to thicken. This usually takes ten minutes, but can sometimes take longer. Once the curd thickens, remove it from the heat. It will keep thickening as it cools. You can store any left-overs in the refrigerator, but considering how good this stuff is, you may not have any!

GREAT BOOKS, GREAT SAVINGS!

When You Visit Our Website:
www.kensingtonbooks.com
You Can Save Money Off The Retail Price
Of Any Book You Purchase!

- All Your Favorite Kensington Authors
- New Releases & Timeless Classics
- Overnight Shipping Available
- eBooks Available For Many Titles
- All Major Credit Cards Accepted

Visit Us Today To Start Saving!
www.kensingtonbooks.com

All Orders Are Subject To Availability.
Shipping and Handling Charges Apply.
Offers and Prices Subject To Change Without Notice.